THE FLOWERS OF EVIL

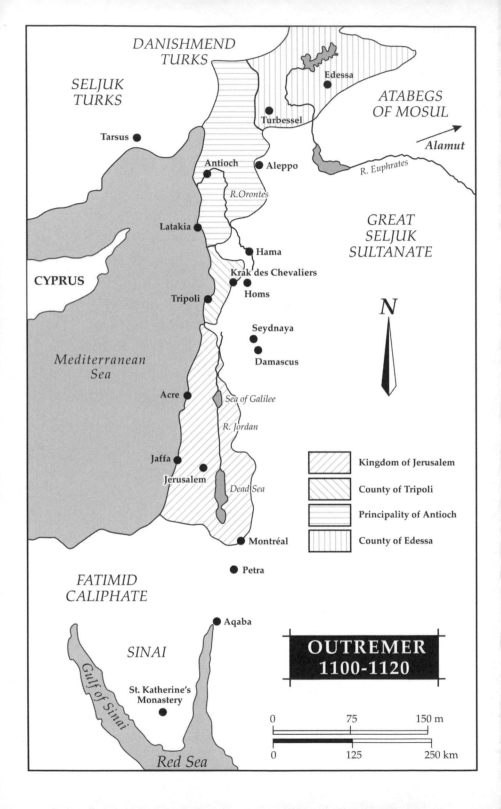

THE

FLOWERS OF EVIL

An Entertainment

by

Simon Acland

Being the Sequel to a story by the same writer, entitled
THE WASTE LAND

Charlwood Books

Charlwood Books
42 Charlwood Road
London SW15 1PW

www.charlwoodbooks.com

Published by Charlwood Books 2011
Copyright © Simon Acland 2011
Distributed by Gardners Books, 1 Whittle Drive, Eastbourne,
East Sussex, BN23 6QH

Simon Acland has asserted the moral right to be identified as the author
of this work in accordance with the Copyright, Designs and
Patents Act 1988.

All the characters in this novel are fictitious or are historical figures
whose words and actions are fictitious. Any other resemblance to actual
persons, living or dead, is entirely coincidental.

A CIP catalogue record for this book is available from the British Library

ISBN-978-0-9561472-1-9

Typeset in Caslon by Amolibros
This book production has been managed by Amolibros
Printed and bound by TJ International Ltd, Padstow, Cornwall, UK

ABOUT THE AUTHOR

Simon Acland spent over twenty years as a venture capitalist. When his company was sold in 2007 he took the opportunity to turn to writing. His interest in the myths and legends surrounding the Holy Grail stems from studying twelfth and thirteenth century French grail romances at university.

The Flowers of Evil is his second novel and is the sequel to *The Waste Land*.

Simon has also written a non-fiction book about venture capital, entitled *Angels, Dragons and Vultures - how to tame your investors...and not lose your company*.

You can find more information about *The Flowers of Evil* on the website www.simonacland.com.

ACKNOWLEDGEMENTS

Thank you to John Vernon Lord for his permission to use his splendid illustration on the cover, to Dennis Hall for his design advice, to Richard Unthank for his maps, and to Jane Tatam for making this publication a reality.

For J.E.I.

What other writers said about *The Waste Land*

Catherine Bailey "An intriguing tale…"

Douglas Hurd "The Waste Land will be thoroughly enjoyed by anyone with a taste for rollicking adventure laced with a subtle dose of literary learning."

Stanley Johnson "Sex, violence and more than a dash of romance: Simon Acland's gripping First Crusade mystery thriller rivals the Da Vinci Code for interest and suspense."

Giles MacDonogh "I found it utterly gripping."

Juliette Mead "Simon Acland's debut novel is a potent cocktail: take one part First Crusade historical romance, one part modern academic satire - and add three jiggers of coming-of-age, Grail-questing, spur-winning Knight's tale. A rollicking, galloping read from a highly individual story teller."

Tim Waterstone "Highly original and a most enjoyable read."

Reviews of *The Waste Land*

Randomjottings "It is exciting and thrilling and Simon Acland is steeped in this period of history and really knows his stuff. Hugely enjoyable, engrossing and engaging from start to finish. I loved this book and it will be going on my list of Best Reads of 2010."

Pursewarden "To produce a good piece of historical fiction requires a delicate balancing act between credible period colour and going gloriously over the top. In *The Waste Land*, Simon Acland pulls this off brilliantly."

Brothers Judd "This first instalment is terrific and we eagerly await the follow-up."

Historical Novel Review "Whether in the depiction of Hugh's loneliness at Cluny, or the gory battle scenes of the First Crusade, Mr. Acland excels at showing Hugh's development. Each scene and location is remarkably detailed, and the historical figures are equally fascinating."

Historical Novels.info "A witty grail quest thriller with a difference... Hidden in the guise of stirring adventure is a clever play on the paradox of duality. Hugh is a man of both peace and war, intellect and action, and his quest is a metaphor for the psychological and spiritual journey of the individual. The Crusade's bloody slaughter in the name of the Prince of Peace and its bitchily squabbling Greek chorus of academics together form a tragicomedy with links closer than we realize: in the past lies the present. *The Waste Land* is legendary entertainment indeed."

DRAMATIS PERSONAE

~~Although the nature of every person in this book is imaginary,~~
the following characters are based on actual historical figures:

Hasan-i Sabbah (c. 1058-1124), founder of the Assassins, known as the Old Man of the Mountain

Mohammed (dates unknown), his son

Godfrey de Bouillon (c. 1058-1100), Duke of Lower Lorraine from 1087, Advocatus Sancti Sepulchri from 1100

Baldwin de Boulogne (c. 1059-1118), younger brother of Godfrey, Count of Edessa from 1098, King of Jerusalem from 1100

Nizam al-Mulk (1018-1092), Seljuk vizier, murdered by the Assassins

Baldwin of le Bourg (died 1131), second Count of Edessa 1100-1118, second King of Jerusalem 1118-1131

Ridwan (died 1113) Emir of Aleppo from 1095, protector of the Assassins

Abu Tahir al-Sa'igh (dates unknown), known as the Goldsmith, leader of the Assassins in Aleppo

Bohemond of Taranto (c. 1058-1111) son of Robert Guiscard, Duke of Apulia and Calabria, from 1099 Prince of Antioch

Raymond de Saint Gilles (c. 1041-1105), from 1094 Count of Toulouse, Duke of Narbonne and Margrave of Provence, from 1104 Count of Tripoli and Tortosa

Hugh de Payns, (died 1136), founder of the Knights Templar

Count Hugh de Champagne (1077-1126), patron of Hugh de Payns

Godfrey de Saint Omer, Payn de Montdidier, Andre de Montbard, Geoffrey Bissot, Archambaud de Saint Amand, Knights Templar

Warmund de Piquigny (died 1128), Archbishop Patriarch of Jerusalem from 1119

Chrétien de Troyes, (c. 1120-c. 1180), poet

Bernard of Clairvaux (1090-1153), Cistercian monk, Founder and Abbot of Clairvaux from 1115, canonised 1174

SAINT LAZARUS' COLLEGE

'Hypocrite lecteur, - mon semblable, - mon frère!'

"Hypocrites! That's what they are, those readers of ours! Just hypocrites!" The Best-Selling Author smirked. "If they were honest they'd admit all they want is action and excitement. Violence, maybe a bit of sex. Something easy to read, basically pretty unchallenging. But then they don't want to be caught reading a low-brow piece of pulp fiction either. So the layer of pseudo-literary sophistication that you all sneaked into *The Waste Land* actually seems to have increased the book's popularity. If I'd cottoned on to that trick in my earlier books perhaps I wouldn't be in your clutches now."

He bestowed a smile on the dons circled around him, their glasses of dry sherry clutched tightly in their thin fingers. His benevolent expression was awkwardly at odds with the edge to his words.

'These people are my friends now,' he thought. 'I'd never have believed it. I am even beginning to talk like them. Pseudo-literary sophistication indeed!'

"So thanks to you, Master, we've got the title for our sequel."

The Best-Selling Author wondered, not for the first time, whether he should start addressing the formidable head of Saint Lazarus' College by his Christian name rather than his title. He nodded at him to cover his embarrassment and hurried on.

"*The Flowers of Evil.* Very nice – I did not understand the

1

joke at first, but thank you, Professor, for enlightening me."

The Professor of English graciously inclined his silvery head, which also had the benefit of hiding his expression of scorn at the so-called writer's ignorance of the obvious connection between Baudelaire and T. S. Eliot.

"But the plot is rather more problematic. We've got some beginnings in that document that our murderous friend had started to translate. But with him locked up, and his poor old tutor hopefully in a better place, we need someone who can decipher the rest of it."

The Professor of English winced at the sloppy use of the word 'hopefully' – how could one write books and fail to understand the correct application of an adverb? In the pause, the Classics Fellow drew himself up to his full height.

"I would be more than happy to have a go at it. I am sure that with all my experience of ancient texts I could manage an accurate rendering of the medieval French. Anyway, from the quick look I have had at the document, more and more of it is in Latin as it goes on. It is almost as if the longer poor Hugh was away from his homeland, the less and less familiar he became with his native vernacular, and the more he fell back on the *lingua franca* of the age."

The Chaplain scowled, his rubbery lips forming a sulky pout.

"If you ask me, we should have done with it. As you know, I feel utterly ashamed of my connection with a college which has served up such blasphemous tripe as *The Waste Land*. Frankly I have even been considering my position here."

The Master's eyes narrowed behind their spectacles. This insubordination was becoming too much. Having a Church of England Chaplain was out of date anyway. A multi-faith appointment would be so much more appropriate to a college that he was trying to drag against its will into the twenty-first century – whilst having to skip the twentieth along the way pretty much completely. He'd modernised the security service in Whitehall. He'd achieve the same here. And appointing a multi-faith counsellor – yes, that was the right title – would give him credibility with the two left-wing members of the House of Lords Appointments Committee who were the ones least keen on his elevation to the peerage. Or so word had it.

"Sebastian," he snapped, "we have discussed this before. None of you would have positions here were it not for *The Waste Land's* success. It is only thanks to the royalties we have received that the College has staved off bankruptcy. And our finances still remain precarious. We must capitalise on our success. A sequel is essential."

His eyes swivelled towards the Best-Selling Author and the Classics Fellow. The encouragement his half smile intended to project towards these two unlikely collaborators was undone by the alarming distortion of his bifocal lenses.

"Go to it, my friends. *Ite, laborate*, as they say."

"Is there anything that I can do to help, Master?"

The newest member of the Senior Common Room rubbed his hands together nervously. With a thoroughly modern crew cut and a pale off-the-peg High Street suit, the Computer Sciences Tutor looked out of place beneath the classical stucco mouldings of the SCR. He felt a long way from home in the ancient rooms overlooking the front quad, whose previous tenant had taught Modern Languages. At first he had been pleasantly surprised to be allocated such prime lodgings in college. He had thanked his new colleagues fulsomely when they had first met at High Table, and had attributed their embarrassed looks to charitable modesty. This naivety showed plainly that he was better suited to understanding the bits and bytes of his absolute discipline than the uncertain complexities of human nature. Before the tragic death by fire of the Modern Language Tutor in those rooms, any of the other dons would have given up sherry for a year to occupy them. They had been made still more desirable by the insurance-funded refurbishment and redecoration that had masked with clean paint the smell of smoke from thousands of the former occupant's cigarettes and the flames that had killed him. But none of the other dons, knowing how the tragedy had occurred, could overcome their superstitious aversion to taking those rooms.

"Thank you so much for your kind offer." The Master sounded almost enthusiastic towards his new protégé. "But no, I think your talents are best spent teaching your undergraduates and publishing some articles to establish our college's reputation at the forefront of modern learning. Of course, if our novelist has any more problems with his IT infrastructure he will come to you for assistance."

The Best-Selling Author did his best to look amused. He was actually rather proud of the skilful use he made of technology to ease his workload and to accelerate his creative flow.

"One thing that is clear from my brief appraisal," said the Classics Fellow, "is that the documents we now have to deal with are more fragmentary – or should I say more episodic – than the period of Hugh's story covering the First Crusade. The unity of place earlier in the story certainly left a great deal to be desired, with all Hugh's travels from Cluny to Constantinople and Antioch, then back to Cluny again and on to Jerusalem and Alamut. But at least the unities of action and time were observed to some extent. In this second piece we appear to have fragments of action dispersed over a far longer period. I may need to call on my esteemed colleague from the history faculty to help me to relate the different episodes to reality."

The History Don did not really know what the Classics Fellow was banging on about; but he was not going to admit that in front of his colleagues. So he smiled knowingly and murmured, "Of course. With pleasure."

And then the gong sounded for dinner, and they all trooped to the hall to take their stations around High Table.

CHAPTER ONE

SPLEEN

Hugues de Verdon etois,
Maintenant sez pas qui je semme.
Je sez ben que je cueille que je semme.
J'ai cueilli tous les malheurs que je peust;
Que m'importe maintenant que je semme?
J'ai plus de souvenirs que si j'avois mil ans.

Hugh de Verdon was my name;
Now I know not who I am.
I well know that I reap what I sow.
I have reaped every possible misfortune;
What does it matter to me now what I sow?
I have more memories than if I had lived a thousand years

❋

Here am I, alone in a poisoned prison, without hope, without belief,
broken, beaten, betrayed. Anger gushes from me like water from
a ceaseless spring.

My teacher - how you lied to me, how you taught me a
groundless faith! The truth you tried to hide from me - even
burning what you would not share. Did you truly believe? Or did
you teach what you knew to be false and destroy what you knew
to be true?

You called yourself a man of God! How can you be anything but false when the god you claim to worship is false himself? Falsehood feeds on falsehood.

My God, my God, why have You forsaken me? What a falsehood indeed!

And you, you vile assassin. You caught me in your twisted plots. For the use you have made of me I will have my vengeance.

But you on whom I wish most to be avenged, you whom I loved more than I believed possible, you for whom I suffered torments and for whom I shattered my beliefs – you are beyond my reach for ever.

And as for me, what do they mean – those two small words 'for ever'? I understand, I almost sympathise with the fiend who tried often and killed me once.

✳

I do not know how long it took me to surface from my madness. And when I did, I remembered clearly what had happened, and I wanted to sink back again. Blanche was dead. Our child was dead. My faith and my belief in Blanche were dead. My love was dead. My god was dead – if death is possible for something that has never truly existed except in the mind.

From the narrow window of my cell I could see the sharp snow-covered mountains slashing up in frozen anger at the heavens. Their example I would follow, but first I had to join them outside my prison walls.

Then I moved away from the window slit towards the door and jerked to a halt, half falling forward to the floor. My fall showed me the fetters around my ankles. I saw that a stout chain trailed behind and fixed them to the wall above the couch that served me as bed. I raised heavily the hands that I had put out to break my fall and found my wrists fastened by matching cuffs. My wrists and ankles were worn and bloody, as if in my madness I had pulled over and over against the hard steel, punishing my unfeeling flesh for its inability to tear free.

I moved back and sat on my bed. I would have patience. Patience was something I would have to learn. My garments were torn and my hair was matted. The stench in the room did not come only from the squalid slop pail in the corner. I saw that much of the floor was covered in filth – excrement, presumably mine, rotten fragments of food and shattered crockery.

I waited.

Some time later bolts behind the door grated back. Slowly it opened a few inches and I heard a voice speaking a language that I could understand.

"It seems the lunatic is quiet today. But be careful. He may be waiting. Don't go too far in. Allah, how it stinks in there."

Now a turbaned head came cautiously round the door.

"So crazy infidel! Out of breath today? Or have you just learnt some manners at last? There is your food."

An arm joined the head and lobbed two pieces of flat bread towards me. They mingled with the filth on the floor.

"No water today. Learn not to smash the jugs we give you – then maybe you shall have some more."

I found myself speaking back in the guard's own tongue. My throat felt rough, my voice lower than it should have been, as if it had been overused to scream and shout.

"I am calm now. Take me to your master."

"Insolent dog." The guard laughed and took his face away behind the door. I ignored the bread lying in my filth, hungry though I was. I arranged my chains and lay down on the bed, and waited.

The rays of the dying sun bled through the slit of my window. Then, through the same hole, darkness emptied into the room. I kept my eyes open, more comfortable with the dark than with whatever I might see in my head, easier awake than in my dreams, and waited.

Daylight drifted into the room and dissipated the darkness. Later, a knife of sunlight thrust in, and I stood to allow its warmth to pierce my body. Then it moved out of the range of my chain. Now that I had stopped pulling at my shackles, the wounds that I had made by tearing them into my flesh were healing fast. My wrist and ankles itched crazily, as if ants were moving under my skin. I had had to become used to that sensation every time I was hurt, ever since my first visit to Alamut. The potion brewed by Hasan-i Sabbah in the gold grail dish to the witch Medea's recipe had given my body extraordinary power to heal itself and even to thwart death.

I sighed, trying to ignore the itching, and sat back down on my bed, and waited.

Again the bolts of my door grated back and it opened a little wider than before. The guard's head came round the door, and then the rest of his body. He carried a lance fashioned from white wood, and shook it threateningly. "Stay back. Stay there. Today we bring you better food, and water. But if you move before we tell you, we will take it away."

Another guard came behind with platter and jug, and stretched to place them where I could just reach from the edge of the arc allowed me by my shackles.

"Take me to your master. Please. And please let me clean this place up. See, I am calm now. I would wash so that I can pray."

The guards looked at each other, impressed now by this piety, as I had known they would be. But they said nothing and backed through the door, which they closed and bolted.

I reached out for what they had left. To my surprise I enjoyed the taste of the flatbread and spiced houmus paste, and the purple grapes that I had eaten there before, in what now seemed a previous life. Then I lay back down on my bed, and waited.

Another night passed and the sun's blade bisected my room once more. Later, I heard the grating of bolts again and the door swung wide. My white-speared guard entered, circumspect still but no longer afraid, and Mohammed followed. Mohammed had once been my friend.

"Pwah." He wrinkled his hawkish nose in disgust. "What a mess you have made, Hugh. We must get you cleaned up. Bring him some water. Warm. And some soap. I know you like our soap!" He smiled.

I had told Mohammed once that on my first visit to Alamut I had tasted the soap left for me in that cell, never having seen such a thing in my homeland before, and thinking it a sweetmeat.

"Go. Bolt the door behind you. He will not harm me. Hugh, it is good to see you more yourself again."

I looked levelly at the man whose life I had saved. He felt my unspoken question.

"No, Hugh, I did not know. I spoke the truth when I told you outside Jerusalem that I had not been back here."

"You knew your father, though. You knew his plans. You must have known the nature of the pleasures of paradise he showed to his *da'is*. My God, perhaps you tasted that paradise yourself."

I felt a dangerous spark inside me. It threatened to reignite my anger. Mohammed saw it too and spoke with heavy haste.

"Yes, I know my father. I know he uses drugs and trickery dressed up as magic to transport his *da'is* to paradise. I know that once they have tasted his paradise they are drugged again and wake up in the real world. Their hardships here are at such odds with the pleasures there that they cannot wait to return. So they welcome death, even seek it out. Perhaps I should have guessed that Blanche was one of the attractions of paradise. Perhaps you could have known that Blanche was told to show you the same favours as the *da'is* in paradise."

I shifted angrily again – how dared he suggest that our love had been false? Maybe he was right but I would hear it from nobody. Mohammed hurried on.

"False paradise and death are not what my father intends for me. After all, I am the only son left to him. He is suspicious and unforgiving but I think he still felt some sorrow when my brother's innocence came too late to light. It must have hurt him to have ordered needlessly the execution of his first-born son. Poor Ustad Hussein."

Mohammed sighed, and looked away from me. After a pregnant pause he turned back to me.

"When he judges that I have proved myself enough, that I am faithful to him beyond all doubt, he plans for me the same initiation that you underwent. If he were younger, if his heart were stronger, I suppose he might do it for himself, but as it is I am the last chance he has for his blood-line to carry on. And you are the living proof that Medea's potion can work." Mohammed shrugged. "I saw what happened to you in Count Baldwin's camp. I am not sure I want it. Part of me does of course, but to defy death for an unnatural span…" He shrugged again. "I think I can understand why you have been sunk in madness these past months."

He started round as the door bolts grated and the guards came back.

"Enough of that before the others. Clean yourself up. I will return when I know my father's wishes. Unlock his hands."

The guards looked nervous but knew better than to disobey their master's son.

On my table they had placed a tall earthenware ewer, a shallow bowl, and a small piece of the precious soap. Alongside they had laid a white cotton robe and a woollen over-garment. I tested the water. It was warm, as Mohammed had ordered. I was suddenly eager to clear the filth from my body, to wash off my shame. But I also needed to clean the squalor of my chamber. What should I do first? If I washed and then cleaned the floor I might dirty myself again. If I cleaned the floor and then my body, the water would be cold and dirty. I shook in a spasm of anxious indecision, I who once would have given such a simple matter not a moment's thought. What had become of me? Then, exasperated by myself, I stripped the rags roughly from my body and gave myself over to the pleasure of soap and warm water.

Still naked, I placed the bowl on the floor and fell to my knees. I splashed out the used water, refilling the bowl with all the shards of crockery and solid ordure that I could reach. I used my discarded rags to wipe the rest as best I could, fastidiously keeping the filth from my skin. In future I would take Moslem cleanliness as my example, not Christian dirt. The job done as best I could, I climbed hastily off my knees, not wanting to give even the semblance of praying in case some god took it as a sign of devotion, and pulled the new garments over my head. I breathed a sigh of pleasure at the smooth clean cotton on my skin. Then, suddenly exhausted, I lay down on my bed and slept.

I had no dreams. Or so it seemed when I woke again. I felt fresh, human, stronger. I approached the window as nearly as I could. My ankle shackles still held me back, but I came close enough to breathe deeply of the cool, clear air. I stood still, and thought, and waited.

When Mohammed came back I knew what it was that I must do.

"Are you ready to see my father?"

"I am," I said. "Please do not tell him how you found me. Please."

Sympathy lay liquid in Mohammed's eyes. He turned and gestured to the guards to unlock my shackles. He led the way from my cell, two white-lanced guards behind him and two more behind me. I carefully followed through the labyrinthine passageways of Alamut, and found myself once more before that ominous door whose knocker was a bronze hand hinged at the wrist.

❋

SAINT LAZARUS' COLLEGE

The Research Assistant seethed with bitterness in his prison cell. It was comfortable enough – not much worse than his small room in the college annex, in fact, but twenty years for a murder he did not commit, eight years each for two counts of attempted murder, all to run concurrently! How could they have believed that his carefully crafted translation of Hugh de Verdon's despairing rant was a confession? That seemed to be the last piece of 'evidence' that had won over the waverers in the jury.

It would never have happened if he had been 'one of them'. Now he never would be. His academic career was over. It was not his fault that he had a face like a murderer's. His lawyer, a useless creature, probably not to be believed, but what could you expect on legal aid, said he could be out in ten if he behaved well. So behave well he would. Already he had avoided rising to the taunts of 'scarface', and when the other prisoners had been unable to get a reaction they had at last left him alone.

He'd have the last laugh though. They did not understand what they had unleashed by including the verbatim text of the Gospel of Lazarus in *The Waste Land*. Without him they would never now find the original; they probably had not even noticed that it was missing. The Society's vengeance on them would be swift and vicious. Until they had recovered the document they would be unrelenting. And the bastards thought that he was the one suffering society's vengeance. He was the only one who was safe. By the time he came out it would be over.

He broke into peals of harsh laughter. And then he suddenly stopped, wondering fearfully whether those secret tentacles might not in fact stretch even inside prison walls.

✳

CHAPTER TWO

THE BARREL OF HATE

La Vengeance éperdue aux bras rouges et forts

✳

As Mohammed swung open the door and I saw again the narrow book-lined passage that led into Hasan-i Sabbah's great oval library, I nearly lost my self-control. Mohammed looked at me with sympathy, mistaking my hesitation for the same apprehension that he showed himself. I saw that his fear of his father almost matched my hatred. Somehow this thought gave me strength. I would defeat Hasan. I raised my head and straightened my shoulders, before remembering the role I must play. By the time I entered the womb of the room, it was with bowed head and submissive demeanour.

The Old Man of the Mountain stood there, his back to us, just as I remembered him. I despised him for that habitual stance before the great arched windows, his white cloak carefully arranged to support the impression of an eagle, his turbaned head turned slightly to one side to silhouette his aquiline nose. One so careful to impress must have weaknesses. I would exploit them.

But first I had to control myself. As he turned, I found

13

myself shaking with rage and hate. I lowered my gaze. He interpreted these tremors in my favour.

"Good, good. I see you have learnt some respect. Last time we met you showed every sign of wanting to harm me. And just for a woman. After all I had done for you. You should be grateful. If I had not initiated you with Medea's magic, you would be dead – in King Baldwin's noose, if not before in the battles for Antioch or Jerusalem."

My expression must have betrayed some surprise, my eyes must have widened, for he continued, "Yes, King Baldwin, for your Duke Godfrey is dead of his exertions. He did not enjoy the fruits of his victory for long. His brother does not suffer from the same false modesty – no title of *Advocatus Sancti Sepulchri* for him – no longer does he style himself merely Count of Edessa. Now he is King of Jerusalem; he had himself crowned two months past."

I had to conceal another furious surge of hatred. Here was another reason for me to avenge myself on my second enemy. Godfrey, at least more than anyone, had been a father to me. His warmth, his zest for life, had been irresistibly appealing. It was his bear mauling, suffered through Baldwin's treachery, that had begun his decline. This new channel for my hate diverted some of my loathing of Hasan, making it easier for me to inject the right submissive tone into my address.

"My Lord." An unmistakable flash of satisfaction at my obsequy lit the Assassin's face. "My Lord, I have had much time for thought in my cell."

"My people tell me that for most of the past year you have been ranting and raving like a lunatic, not one capable of clear thought."

The past year? Could I really have been in that cell for a year? A whole year? Already Hasan had stopped me in my tracks. Then I remembered that it did not matter. For me, time had less value than for other men.

"My Lord, I had moments of lucidity in my madness. And

14

in these last few days, when my foolish frenzy left me, I have been able to see clearly. Blanche is of no import. She received her just deserts. She behaved as might be expected of a weak women, and you had every right to exploit her for your ends. I bear you no ill will for that. I know now that my love was immature, incontinent, and misplaced."

It was all I could do to hold his gaze and keep my voice steady. Fortunately I was prepared for the unfaltering stare of his disconcerting yellow-ringed eyes.

"I also know now, from my reading of the gospel you had me seek, that the god I used to worship is false. It should have come as no real surprise to me, for the wickedness and cruelty I saw perpetrated in his name from Constantinople to Jerusalem had already shaken my beliefs. I want to convert to Islam. I want to study your religion. I know something of your Nizari creed from your son."

I glanced at Mohammed. He was observing this conversation in a respectful silence which nevertheless did not cloak his surprise at my words. I turned back to his father.

"Meanwhile, as I learn, tell me what services I can perform. Perhaps I can use my pen in the service of your cause. Perhaps my knowledge of languages could be useful to you. I could copy and translate. Perhaps even the strange regenerative power I have..."

"You think I am so foolish as to trust you beyond these walls!"

"I will prove my loyalty to you by whatever means you wish. If I can serve the true cause better inside the walls of Alamut, so be it. That should be for you, my master, to decide. But maybe, at some time, you might find a use for a servant who looks and sounds like a Frank, and has no fear of death because he cannot suffer it – except only in the way that you and I know."

Hasan-i Sabbah turned back to his window, as if to conceal his expression from me, and to think without being observed.

15

From this gesture I read that my words had made an impression. It would be a long and slow process to build up his trust. But it would help that there were none he truly trusted; it might be enough to reduce his suspicion of me to the same level enjoyed by his other tools.

I exchanged glances again with Mohammed, who looked excited and smiled at me with warmth. He erased his friendly expression as his father turned back, sweeping him with a cold stare, which then fixed on me.

"Very well. You are fortunate that one of the duties laid on us is to convert infidels to the true faith. You may have a Koran. And I shall indeed give you a task. You will copy the Gospel of Lazarus; after all, we want its message promulgated far and wide. Then everyone shall know the falsehood of the Christian religion.

"Mohammed, when he is here, may help you read the Holy Book. Because the Koran is the real word of God dictated to His Prophet, unlike your so-called Bible, it would be heresy to translate it from the Arab tongue. And Mohammed will explain to you the conditions of the *Shahadah,* the testimony of faith that you will have to pronounce to convert to the true religion." An expression of grim satisfaction crossed his face. "Of course, you will have to be circumcised."

"Of course." I humbly lowered my head, wanting to show neither an expression of the triumph I felt, nor any prick of concern at this last news. Hasan continued in a fiercer tone.

"But do not think that you will be allowed to be alone with the document, or to handle it. I will not risk your destroying it, nor attempting some rash escape. You will be given writing materials and shackled to your desk. One of my men will hold the document where you can see it but not touch. Another will watch you with him while you work."

"Master, that will be a privilege for me."

Hasan scornfully nodded in a gesture of dismissal. We turned and left. My friend was in high spirits as he escorted me back towards my cell, this time walking alongside me with the two armed guards at front and back.

"Hugh, why did you not tell me? I can teach you all that you need to know. I shall be away from the castle at times, I am sure, but when I am here…"

And so my routine began.

At dawn, I woke and prayed. The next few hours were given over to the reading of the Koran. Mohammed was true to his word, and helped me to decipher its back-to-front Arab script. Then came more prayers and more reading. How like Cluny, for all that my old abbey was so far distant in geography, time and experience. Were all religions so similar, so equally false? My new faith called for six periods of prayer every day. At Cluny we had eight daily services, so I suppose at least in that I was two better off than before.

After the noontime prayer, the third of the six, the direction of the sun into my room gave its best light and I exchanged reading for writing. On the first day that I began my task as Hasan's copyist, some sheets of writing material were brought to me, presumably already prepared somewhere in the castle by another invisible scribe. I grumbled to Mohammed about them.

"Look – what is this stuff? It is not what I am used to. The surface feels rough and porous. How does your father expect me to do a worthy job for him? At least permit me to prepare my own quills and ink. Without a quill suited to my hand, without ink of the right consistency, I cannot fulfil to my satisfaction the task he demands."

Mohammed laughed. "This is what we call paper. You will find it just as easy to use as parchment. It is indeed a little porous; that is one of its advantages, for the ink will sink gently into the surface. It is easier to make than parchment and does not cost the life of a goat. This we obtain from the city of Samarkand, where they make it out of pulped wood, but they say that it first came from further east, from China. Your ink

17

you may make yourself if you wish, and I will bring you materials. But what is this quill you want? Here our scribes write with pens made from reeds."

"I am used to writing with a pen made from the wing feathers of a goose."

Mohammed laughed.

"A goose? Well! I will see what I can find."

He scurried off to fetch me my materials. When he came back later he was apologetic.

"I have found you your feathers, but I must watch you carefully while you use these tools. They think you could do some damage even with these!"

He placed a small knife on my desk, alongside an oil lamp and half a dozen goose quills. I felt shaken for a moment, recalling the wounded goose that had fallen in the snow on my last arrival at Alamut. In that happier time its red blood on the white background had reminded me of Blanche's fresh complexion. I shuddered and pulled myself together.

At my instruction, endorsed by Mohammed, one of the guards nursed flame from a tinder box and lit the oil lamp. I warmed the tip of each quill to harden it. The guard extinguished the lamp and removed it from my reach. With the knife I carefully cut across each quill in a diagonal, and then sharpened them to the right thickness, and split them. I removed the feather flights, which were carefully gathered up by one of the guards, I presumed for use on items of more aggressive intent than my pens. With a grin, I held the little knife by its blade and ceremoniously offered it back to Mohammed, who took it in silence.

"Now for the ink," I said. "What is this that you have brought?" In a mortar I saw a pile of soot and something that looked like a nugget of resin. "Do you not use oak galls, vinegar and vitriol?"

"Sometimes we do add gallnuts to this mixture of lampblack and gum arabic. But when writing on paper it is not really necessary. And the gallnuts reduce the intensity of the black colour. Here, crush the gum into the soot with a little rosewater."

I took the pestle and followed his instructions, crushing the mixture finely, and then added some more liquid.

"It is a long while since I have made ink. It seems too runny. Can you find me some material with which I can dry it as I write?" Mohammed looked puzzled. "That was what we used to do at Cluny all the time to avoid smudges."

And so I started my work copying the Gospel of Lazarus. After every line that I wrote, I carefully pressed down my piece of material, gradually building up a secret image of the text in reverse. My guards appeared impressed with the care I took.

"Only the highest quality work is good enough for my master Lord Hasan-i Sabbah," I used to say to them.

My reading of the Koran and copying of the Gospel of Lazarus continued in parallel. Almost daily, to leave him in no doubt about my enthusiasm, I asked Mohammed when I could properly pronounce my *Shahadah*. He explained the seven conditions that I would have to fulfil: knowledge, certainty, sincerity, truthfulness, love, submission and conformity. But I came to realise that my conversion would not be permitted until I had completed at least my first task as a copyist, and so I worked away as fast as I could. My gaolers had no idea that the satisfaction I showed at my rapid progress was derived as much from the unsuspected copy of the document that I was making for myself on the material that served as my blotter, as from the neatness with which I copied the Greek text.

Eventually the day came when I reached the last sentence. *'And then Jesus went back into the rocky desert and we saw him no more.'* My task was complete. Mohammed was happy for me, and took the precious document away in triumph to his father. When he returned the following morning to help with my instruction he brought the news that my conversion could now take place. I felt some inner shame before the honesty of his friendly emotion, but I calmed my conscience by thinking of the progress of my plan.

The following day I was taken from my cell for the first time since my previous visit to Hasan. The familiar formation of four guards ushered me through Alamut's passages by a route I had not followed before, and I came to a peaceful courtyard with a shallow square tiled pool at its centre. A priestly figure stood alongside, the supercilious expression on his haughty features perhaps betraying doubts about my sincerity, or maybe just showing his scorn that I was abandoning the religion in which I had been raised.

"Here you must wash," explained Mohammed. My manacles were removed, and I stood completely unfettered for the first time since my confinement began.

"Strip, and enter the pool."

The water was icy.

"Wash your right hand three times, and then the left. Make sure to rub between your fingers. Now wash your genitals, between your buttocks, and then your hands again. Cup your right hand, drink from it and rinse out your mouth, then your nose. Twice more. Now you can wash your face, three times also, and your arms. Pour water over your head and rub it into your hair. Cover the rest of your body with water and rub yourself over. It is nearly done; just your feet are left. Rub between the toes. There, now you are purified."

Shivering, I stepped out of the pool.

"You may now recite the *Shahadah*."

"*Ash-hadu anla elaha illa-Allah wa ash-hadu anna Mohammadan rasul-allah*. I bear witness that there is no god worthy of worship save Allah, and I bear witness that Mohammed is his servant and his messenger."

Then it was time for my circumcision. My cock, shrivelled by the cold water, looked a sad and reluctant victim. But I knew it had to be done. The haughty priest advanced towards me and I saw a blade glinting in his hand. He seized my prepuce, pulled it towards him, and with a sharp upwards motion sliced it off. Somehow I avoided wincing, in spite of the stinging pain, and I avoided looking down as I felt the blood dripping from the wound. The priest turned scornfully away. Sheepishly Mohammed handed me a white cloth, which I squeezed over my damaged member to stop the blood and dull the hurt. Then with Mohammed's help I struggled back into my robe, and I was marched back to my room and reshackled. For the time being at least, for all that I had become one of them, it was clear that my security would not be relaxed.

I felt a great lassitude, brought by pain and anti-climax. I collapsed onto my bed and fell immediately asleep.

I was woken by an infuriating itching at the end of my penis. It was still wrapped in the white cloth, now spotted with my blood, and I gingerly peeled it off. Nervously I inspected my mutilated member. It seemed to me that the priest had not done a very thorough job. At least half the foreskin was intact. I gently replaced the cloth and curled onto my side to go back to sleep.

I woke again as usual when the first light came through my narrow window. Again I inspected myself, and to my astonishment I found my foreskin almost whole, neatly covering the head of my penis as before. It was as if my Christian body had rebelled at this Moslem practice. I puzzled, then realised that the same magic that could heal my wounds had caused my prepuce to grow back. I would have to take care not to expose myself before my captors. They might well take my re-grown foreskin as a divine sign of the insincerity of my conversion.

My routine continued unchanged. My mornings were filled by reading the Koran, punctuated by proper prayer. For all that the Koran was claimed to be the direct word of God, I detected some of the same inconsistencies and ambiguities

21

that had troubled me in the Bible. I could see that warring Islamic factions would have no difficulty finding support for their own contradictory positions and beliefs in those confusing words. But I also found much sense in the book, and some useful guidance for leading a good and proper life.

More books were sent to me from Hasan's library. Sometimes they were brought by Mohammed; but there were times when he was absent for long periods. When he returned from these trips I was surprised by the pleasure I felt at seeing him. On one occasion, I remember, he looked pale and thin. I asked with concern whether he had been wounded. With an embarrassed shrug he avoided the question, plainly unable to talk to me about the missions he performed for his father. Soon, though, he recovered and looked healthier than ever.

Hasan must have been pleased with the speed and care with which I copied or translated his books, and perhaps encouraged also by reports from my guards and Mohammed of my devout reading and prayer, for the day came in late autumn when I received another summons.

This time, to my surprise, Mohammed and my four guards escorted me by a different route through the castle's corridors. When we emerged from a narrow spiral staircase into the crisp air I found myself on a platform behind the battlements at the high point of the walls. Hasan was there before us, with four companions whose fine robes showed them to be dignitaries of significance. The order cracked out for me to line up alongside three young men, who also were dressed in long garments of plain white. I stood with them and tried to copy on my face their expressions of humble submission. Hasan scarcely glanced at me. All his attention was focussed on his guests, and I listened closely to his words.

"You would do well not to cross me. Do not interfere in the business of Alamut, for I have a army of devoted servants who will obey every command I give them. Nobody can hide from my *da'is*. You can surround yourselves with as many guards as you like. But we are patient. We will find our way through. You know that Nizam al-Mulk paid the full price for his betrayal, and so have many since. You see, my servants have no fear of death. They are all proud believers who wish to find their place in paradise as soon as they can. At my command they will embrace death.

"I see you doubt me. Very well."

Hasan span round to face us. With my three companions, I lowered my head respectfully before the stare of his yellow-circled eyes.

"My sons, your moment of glory has come. Throw yourselves off the battlements. We will meet again in paradise. Count yourselves lucky that you precede me there."

I heard the *da'i* beside me draw a deep ecstatic sigh, almost before I understood what was being asked of us. I realised that I had no alternative. I would have to follow the example of the three *da'is* or I would fail Hasan's test and destroy for ever my chance of escaping from Alamut's walls.

As I wheeled to the right, I thought I caught a glimpse of cruel amusement on Hasan's face, and a flash of horror on Mohammed's. Then I filed towards the battlement, trying not to think what I was about to do.

The first *da'i* climbed up between the crenellations, cried joyfully "*Allahu Akbar!*" and dived into the void. What seemed to me like seconds of silence followed, then a thud. There was no other sound, no scream, just an unearthly silence. Hasan's guests ran to the edge and looked over, aghast and amazed. The second *da'i* plunged into the abyss, and then the third. It was my turn.

"That's enough! By the beard of the Prophet, you have proved your point. Don't waste any more young lives."

That could have been my cue to turn away, but I had resolved not to flinch or falter, not to pause unless Hasan himself ordered me to do so. And I knew that no order would come.

Balanced on the top of the battlements I looked down momentarily, and saw three bodies, broken far below. With all the air that I had in my lungs, in a voice whose steadiness filled me with pride, I yelled *"Allahu Akbar!"*

And then I jumped.

✳

SAINT LAZARUS' COLLEGE

Animosity thickened the air in the Senior Common Room.

"Why did you have to make me kill off Godfrey even before he had appeared in the book?" The Best Selling Author was grumbling bitterly. "He was by far the most sympathetic character in *The Waste Land*."

"Facts are facts," stated the History Don baldly. "Godfrey de Bouillon died in 1100, worn out by his exertions, and broken by the wounds he had received. Your readers are not idiots; they will know. If you want him to feature, use a flashback, or something like that."

"I know why you are so upset to lose Godfrey!"

The Professor of English's loud exclamation and the unseemly giggles that followed drew the attention of everyone in the room.

"You see yourself as the Duke. You had based his personality on yourself, or on what you would like to be. All that tousled leonine hair stuff, and his insatiable sexual appetite! That is just how you see yourself." He collapsed into helpless laughter.

"Come on, Stephen," growled the Master, "there is no need to be gratuitously offensive."

The History Don had not finished. "Frankly, it is quite bad enough that you continue to twist the personality of Godfrey's brother Baldwin. I can see that he is going to be used as a hate figure again just to drive the plot forward. Surely Hasan-i Sabbah is enough? At least there are no real historical records to show that he was anything other than a vicious fanatic. All the documentary evidence of what he was really like must have been destroyed when the Mongols seized Alamut and razed it in 1256, destroying his library in the process."

"At the moment I honestly do not know where the plot is going to lead," complained the Best-Selling Author. "At least when I was writing the first book I had our murderous friend's complete translation to work with. The outline story was there, and all I had to do was fill in the details. Now I feel just as uninspired and short of ideas as I did before I started on *The Waste Land*. I just wish you would get a move on and finish translating the rest of Hugh's manuscript."

This last comment was directed at the Classics Fellow, who shifted uneasily, especially when the Master's bifocals swung in his direction.

"I am doing it as fast as I can. I do have some other duties here, you know. I have a lot of undergraduates to teach."

Everyone knew that this statement was not strictly accurate, because the College's last intake of students wanting to study Greats had dwindled to just four.

"It takes me quite a bit of time to decipher the bits of medieval French in Hugh's manuscript. And his Latin is not at all easy either. You want me to get it right, don't you?"

The Professor of English had recovered his composure enough to rejoin the debate. "And if you want sympathetic characters to replace Godfrey, well, Hugh himself is not such a bad chap."

"I can tell you that in the next chapter, based on the bits Lawrence has translated so far, you are about to see a pretty unattractive side of his character."

"Well, what about Mohammed? His personality is shaping up quite nicely."

The Chaplain had so far managed to distance himself from the conversation, but now he could restrain himself no longer. He spluttered with indignation, spittle flecking his rubbery lips, his smooth face puce.

"We don't want any more good Moslems, thank you very much. It is simply disgraceful as it is that Hugh has given up Christianity and converted to Islam. Unacceptable."

'Right, that's it,' thought the Master to himself, 'Sebastian will have to go.'

CHAPTER THREE

THE TASTE OF OBLIVION

Résigne-toi, mon coeur; dors ton sommeil de brute.

�֍

Terror and exhilaration fought each other inside me as I hurtled through the air. The journey from the battlements crowning the walls of Alamut down to the cruel rocks clawing their feet can scarcely have taken me more than a few seconds, but it was crowded with memories. Pictures of my father and brothers flashed by – their broken bodies urgently making me want to reverse my fall and giving my terror its victory over exhilaration – then my mother swooning at Cluny, the Abbot's sorrowful expression when my profane reading was discovered, and again when I deserted him for Godfrey. Then I saw Godfrey and the serving maid, myself and Blanche, Blanche, and Blanche. But they were only memories. I had just enough time to feel disappointment that no insight into the secrets of the universe had come to me. Then I twisted to the side, for something told me that would be the best way to take the impact. A lightning flash of unbearably intense pain closed my consciousness.

Then it seemed my eyes were open. Surely I was in a garden of great beauty? The rilling of running water and heavenly tunes of sweet birdsong filled the air all around. Elegant trees waved feathery branches towards me. Could this be paradise? I smelt the sweet scent of jasmine and other flowers too exotic to distinguish. But as I tried to breathe in those smells acute pain stabbed my lungs – surely in paradise there was no place for pain. Then darkness closed around me. I seemed to be entering a long dark tunnel, going up, going up. My consciousness faded once more.

More overwhelming pain was my next sensation, so all-consuming that there was no room in my being for anything else. The sound of groaning reached me from a long way off, and as I forced my eyes open I became dimly aware that this plaintive noise came from my own throat. Around me I could just make out the outline of my cell. I was alive. I suppose I had known that I would be. But I could not move. I was helpless. Mohammed's face shifted in and out of clear view above me.

"Do not try to move," he whispered. "You were like a rag doll. Your bones were broken in so many places that we have splinted all your limbs and lashed you to a board. Remember how you used your lance like that when you rescued me?" He tried a smile but it refused to shine through the horror I read in his face at my state.

I closed my eyes again and gave myself over to the familiar torment of the itching throughout my body. Had I not been tied down I do not know what harm I might have done, for the sensation was more irritating than I had ever felt before. Now, though, I tried to welcome it because I knew that it meant that my body was miraculously mending itself. The greater the itching, the worse the injuries that were healing. I really must be in a bad way! I began to laugh at the thought, but the pain in my body when my chest moved was too much and I passed out again.

"I hope your father does not ask me to do that again," I said to Mohammed when I next woke up. "It is one thing to crash on to the rocks and wake up in paradise, and quite another to find oneself itching in agony in a hell on earth." Then I tried to put an expression of puzzled devotion on to my poor face. "How will I ever find my way to paradise if I am indestructible?"

Mohammed's look of sympathy told me that he at least had no doubts about my sincerity, or the purity of my conversion.

I soon discovered that his more sceptical father had also gained some reassurance from the obedience of my jump, when, some weeks after I was fully mended, they led me once more into his malevolent presence.

"I have a task for you outside these walls," Hasan said to me. I could have danced around his library. I could tell that he was observing me even more carefully than usual, and I tried to mimic the devout excitement that a *da'i* would show at such news. Eagerly I went down on my knees, making as if to clasp his hand.

"Thank you, Master. I am happy to serve the cause in whatever way you tell me. But to have gained your trust, your belief, is a special honour indeed."

He gestured me haughtily to my feet. "You are a little hasty. I only send you because it is a Frank that I need killed. None of my *da'is* will be able to get close enough to do the deed. I have no alternative. And do not think that I will send you by yourself. You will go with Mohammed and others and you will be carefully watched.

"I want you to kill Baldwin, so-called Count of Edessa. I want him dead."

I could hardly contain my excitement. To be sent to kill the one man that I hated as much as Hasan was an extraordinary piece of good fortune. Habit forced a prayer of thanks into my head before I stopped it with a feeling of self-disgust.

"Count Baldwin continues to be a thorn in the side of my ally, Emir Ridwan of Aleppo. Good Ridwan gives shelter to my *da'is* and I would pay him back for his help. And killing such a senior Frank will announce to the others that we Assassins are a force to be reckoned with. My spies tell me that Baldwin will be at his stronghold of Turbessel one month from now. You will be able to gain entry without suspicion and strike him down."

"It will be an honour, Master."

There was little time to spare if we were to reach our goal in time. My old garments and weapons were brought to me, and once more I donned the heavy mail coat which so much sweat and exertion had moulded to my shape. Underneath, around my left thigh, I had already wound like a bandage the material that bore my reverse copy of the Lazarus Gospel. I stroked the fine Venetian embroidery on the scabbard of the sword given to me a lifetime ago by Duke Godfrey, and strapped it to my side. So my external aspect was once more a Crusader knight's. None would suspect how different I now was inside.

At first the road to Turbessel led the way of my first journey with Mohammed. Then he had guided me to the path of Atabeg Kerbogha's army as it marched on Antioch. Then I had been driven by love, desperate to find the Gospel of Lazarus for the old man and thus secure my Blanche's release. Now I was driven by hate, by my desire for revenge. I would strike down Baldwin, and I would strike at Hasan through Mohammed. At the right time I would cut him down too, depriving Hasan of his heir. Perhaps then I would return to Alamut and find some way to inflict the same fate on the father as on the son. But for a while I would leave him to suffer, to contemplate the failure of the ambitions nursed by every powerful father to found a lasting dynasty.

And after all, I would say to myself, when Mohammed smiled at me with affection and pointed out something of interest on our journey, I had saved his life once. Thanks to me he had enjoyed five years that would not otherwise have been his. His life was now mine by right to take away. Nevertheless, I lay awake at night, tossing with a discomfort which was not caused just by the hardness of the ground.

The mornings were the most difficult. Mohammed's custom when he woke with the sunrise was to offer me water to wash the sleep from my face. We would then stand together to let the first rays drink the water from our skin. Mohammed would always say, "You see, now he has taken our offering, he will be kind to us at the cruel hour of noon." Then, with the three *da'is* who completed our company, we prostrated ourselves for our morning prayers.

When we reached the River Euphrates, instead of veering southwest as I had to follow Kerbogha's host to Antioch, we turned towards the north. Most of the countryside through which we had passed from Alamut was rough and hilly; now we were in a flat plain with clumps of nodding grass, and often wildflowers. One type in particular caught my eye, its diaphanous petals pure white except for pink bruises at their base. Blanche's complexion again. They sprouted from a fat round seed head, and I saw clearly, on the heads which had lost their petals, a raised six-armed star.

"What is that flower, my friend? It looks good enough to eat."

Mohammed laughed, and leant down from his saddle to pluck one.

"This is called the poppy. Too good to eat, some would say. We use it as a medicine to overcome pain – it can help you to sleep and forget. It is called *hashhash*. It is one of the herbs that my father uses…" He glanced pointedly at our three companions. "But too much is dangerous. Soon you cannot live without it."

He took his dagger and cut round the edge of the seed head. A thick white sap oozed out.

"Too much of that and your will is soon not your own." He touched his finger to the sap and gingerly placed a drop

31

on the end of his tongue. He grimaced and tossed the flower away.

The stronghold of Turbessel sat on a rock rising from this fertile plain. In the clear early summer air we could see it from a good distance, and we stopped in a small clump of trees for the night and to make our plan.

"It is an old trick, I know," I suggested. "But it always works. Our three comrades will be prisoners, and you will be my servant. I will just ride to the gate, and say that I am bringing three brigands for punishment. I will ask to be admitted into Baldwin's presence to pay him homage and to offer him my services. Then, before I can be recognised, I will finish him. You will cut our comrades' bonds, and they will bring out their concealed weapons. With surprise on our side we should be able to make our escape, or if not, to lay down our lives at a high price for the cause and enter paradise."

I looked hard at Mohammed. "Your father will be most anxious to have you back safe and sound."

Mohammed smiled with confidence. "Yes, I know that he is. But I am sure your plan will work. It is the right thing to do."

'Perhaps my work will be done for me by one of Baldwin's men,' I thought to myself.

I could understand more easily how the three *da'is* with us, fanatics all, seeing the gates of paradise opening before them, welcomed the danger inherent in my plan. But Mohammed's own faith and consequent lack of fear must be deeper than I had thought.

Certainly his sleep appeared untroubled, whereas I tossed and turned all night. Well before dawn I gave up my attempts to sleep. When Mohammed woke with the sun, he found me standing at the edge of camp watching the horizon redden.

"What is the matter, my brother?" He clapped a friendly arm around my shoulders. "Don't worry about our plan. I will be fine. Yes, it is true – you are as good as a brother to me.

You, once an infidel, are my closest companion. And Ustad Hussain was too much the elder to be very close to me. My father was mistaken, wrong to put him to death for a crime that he did not commit, but he was not good, not always kind to me, the younger. And now all my father's hopes rest on me."

He looked earnest for a moment, as if he was about to say something serious, but then his smile flashed again. "Well, we will have many more adventures together."

To make our fiction more convincing, I spilt the blood of a hare that we had snared onto the three *da'is'* robes, also tearing them and rolling them in the dirt, to make it plain that they had not capitulated without a fight. I tore a strip of material from one, bloodied it and tied it round one of the *da'i's* heads as a rough bandage.

"There, they look just the part."

Mohammed smiled, cheerful as always, but the three others remained dour. The long daggers favoured by the Assassins were strapped hidden beneath their robes. One we lashed face down over the saddle of his horse, as if he were unconscious or unable to hold himself upright. As for the other two, we tied their hands behind their backs, and lashed their legs together under the bellies of their horses. I remembered that this was how I had been treated on my first encounter with these men, and I felt grim satisfaction for I knew from my own experience the pain that they would suffer later when the time came to dismount, as the sensation poured back to their numbed limbs.

The three *da'is'* horses were roped together, and I took the leading rein of the first. Mohammed brought up the rear, leading the two packhorses. In this order we approached steadily the walls of Turbessel. The fortress was well sited, perched on its sharp hill that thrust from the flat plain like a large pustule on skin. The way led up a small incline to the main gate. I anticipated a stern challenge, expecting the garrison to be alert in this violent border land. But no challenge came, so I shouted up to the square tower above the gate, first in my native tongue and then in Latin.

"Is anyone there to open the gate? I have prisoners here – three bandits that made the mistake of falling on my servant and me. Let me enter so that I can hand them over for justice."

After a pause, two grinning heads appeared over the battlement.

"Welcome, welcome," one of them said in my own tongue. "What a day you have chosen for your visit! Our Count is here." I felt a surge of excitement at this confirmation of the accuracy of Hasan's information.

"And he has brought our pay with him," exclaimed the other in a thick voice which announced that some of his wages at least had already been spent on drink. This was more than I could have hoped for. A drunken garrison would greatly increase my chances of escape.

The heads disappeared and I thought for a moment that their inebriated owners had toppled over backwards. But after a short delay I heard the sounds of bolts being drawn back behind the gate. It swung wide and one of the guards took the head of my horse, which shied at his guttural laughter.

"Have you heard the story? Thirty thousand bezants for a beard! Count Baldwin told his father-in-law that he had sworn to shave his beard if he could not raise enough to pay us – his loyal troops! You know the horror these Armenians have of clean-shaven faces. Daddy could not face the humiliation of having an unmanly pervert married to his daughter. So he coughed up enough to cover our back pay! How's that for a deal?"

"Here, celebrate with us." His companion thrust a leather bottle at me. I took a cautious swig, but nevertheless nearly choked on the rough wine inside. I had not tasted alcohol since the siege of Jerusalem, and it recalled poor Godfrey again, who had offered it to me that fateful morning to boost my courage. Well, soon I would have avenged him.

"Whew, that's strong stuff, thank you!" I passed the bottle back.

"No, no, keep it, there is plenty more where that came from."

Not wanting to be outdone in hospitality, his companion also handed me his bottle. "Here you go, here's another one to keep you going. You've a bit of catching up to do!" His guffaw merged into a belch, and to avoid seeming churlish I thanked them both and hung the bottles over the pommel of my saddle.

"Now where can I find the Count? I must present my respects. We rode together from Bouillon, and fought side by side at Dorylaeum and Tarsus."

This news parted the curtain of their drunkenness for a moment. They looked at me with renewed respect.

"You'll find him in the great hall, Sir."

We rode a few yards further into the court, to a place where there was a post to tether our horses. Mohammed and I put on a great show of untying our prisoners and heaving them down from their horses. As they squirmed in the pain that I had expected them to feel on dismounting, I unsheathed my sword, menaced them, and urged them forward into the great hall.

The gloom of the high room was pierced by light from half a dozen narrow windows. It took my eyes a second or two to adjust to the flickering illumination from torches fixed to the walls, and from the fire lit in the centre, for the thickness of the stone kept the room chilly even in that season. Here too a rowdy celebration was underway. One or two heads turned in our direction, but otherwise our entrance attracted little attention. My naked sword caused no alarm, for it was easily explained by my captives.

"Where is the Count?" I enquired of a knight by the doorway who seemed more alert than some of his fellows. "I have some presents for him." He gestured over towards the fire, and I noted a tall figure wearing a purple cloak over his mail, his back turned towards us. I moved towards him, pushing my pretend prisoners in front.

I had planned this moment through many restless nights. I could not strike Baldwin down from behind, not just out of compunction for a cowardly act, but because I wanted him to recognise me in the moments before he died. I wanted to see the fear in his eyes.

So I called out as I approached. "My Lord Baldwin! I have something for you! After our last meeting, I don't suppose you expected to see me again…"

The Count started to turn to see what this commotion was behind him and I began to raise my sword in an unmistakable gesture of aggression. I was about to speak my name, to make sure he knew at whose hand he was about to perish, and to shout "For Godfrey!" But the words dried on my lips.

The untrimmed beard was rough and sandy, not neat and black. The eyes were blue, friendly, not cold, hard and dark. "You are not Count Baldwin!" I mouthed. The blue eyes quickly lost their warmth as they took in my raised sword and the insult in these words.

"What do you mean? I am Baldwin of le Bourg, the second Count of Edessa to bear that proud name. Who in Hell's name are you? What is the meaning of this outrage?"

I could not strike this stranger down in cold blood. Anyway, the opportunity had passed, for the knights closest by quickly formed up, drawing their swords to protect him.

"Stop them. Stop them! They came here for murder!"

Out of the corner of my eye I saw the three *da'is* struggling to slip their bonds and reach their daggers. Mohammed had drawn his own weapon. As I parried the first blows, I saw that one of the *da'is* had been too slow. He was flat on the ground and the blood staining the false bandage round his head was now his own.

"Make for the door," I bellowed. Had it not been for the

Franks' drink-dulled reactions, we would have been done for. As it was, we were halfway to our goal before the mass of soldiery in the hall had half realised what was happening. My blood now heated by the need to defend myself, I battered my way past three men and reached the heavy door. Behind me I sensed more than saw Mohammed and the two surviving *da'is*. As I wrenched the door wide and rushed through, I turned and saw one of them fall to a sword thrust which passed clean through his unarmoured torso. The last pushed his master's son through the door, and as he did so, his eyes blazed at me with hate. Then he turned to block the exit and to buy Mohammed as long as possible for his escape. With just a long Assassin's dagger it would not be long before he discovered the cruel fraud of his paradise.

I did not dare to look at Mohammed, but grabbed his arm and urged him towards our horses. I was quickly in my saddle and saw in relief that the drunken guards had not closed the main gates. Confused by the hubbub coming from the great hall, thinking perhaps that some drunken squabble had broken out between friends, they stood by the gates with three or four comrades.

As we hurtled towards them, they sprang into action as fast as their fuddled brains would allow, grabbing up their pikes from the loose pile against the wall. One threatened me, but a swing of my blade severed the shaft, and then I burst through the gate like the stopper from a new bottle. Behind me, I heard an awful cry, and I knew that Mohammed had been hurt. My emotions were suddenly confused. Was that not the fate I had desired for my enemy's son? But it was concern for my friend that made me turn in my saddle, and relief when I saw him still riding behind me, hunched forward over his horse's neck.

I spurred my steed southwards as fast as he would go, and Mohammed's galloped behind me, his rider swaying but somehow staying in the saddle. It was several minutes before any pursuers emerged from the gates behind us, and an hour before they gave up the chase, apparently satisfied that three out of five of our party had perished, or at least realistic about the speed of our horses and our head start. I slackened my pace to give my mount a breather, and turned towards a wadi in the hills ahead. I hoped to find some water there. Evening began to fall, and we reached a thicket of pink-flowered oleanders beside a shallow pool fed by a trickle from the hills.

I pulled up, dismounted and led my exhausted mount to drink, and then turned my attention to my groaning companion. As I helped him down from his horse I felt that the whole front of his garment was soaked with blood. His face was white under the dust that covered it. I could not meet his eyes.

"Why...why didn't you kill him?" Mohammed murmured in my ear.

"It was not the Baldwin I thought," I muttered, "I expected my enemy Baldwin of Boulogne. Nobody had told me that it was a second Baldwin that I was to kill. By the time I had overcome my surprise, it was too late. I am sorry."

As I murmured my embarrassment, I had laid Mohammed out on his back, and now tore open his robe to inspect his wound. The hole in his belly was twice the breadth of my hand. The pike had thrust deep into his guts and then been twisted out by the speed of his gallop, tearing the gash brutally wider. Blood mixed with the oozing contents of his intestine. I tried to hide my horrified reaction but the stench made me gag.

"I am sorry, my friend, I will make you as comfortable as I can...but that is all I can do."

The shadow of a smile crossed Mohammed's face. "Don't worry about me. You see, like you, I have been initiated. You remember when you thought that I was away from Alamut? Well, then I was just convalescing. Oh, but Allah...the pain. Do something to help me."

Stunned, I bandaged the wound as tightly as I could. Baldwin's guard had failed to do my work for me. I knew how to complete my task of vengeance. I would have to strike off his head as he lay there helpless. That was the only way to bring his life to its end. But I knew just as well that I could do no such thing. Confused, I walked away in the twilight to the end of the valley to contemplate what I should now do.

The last rays of the dying sun caught a group of pretty wildflowers. They waved gently in the breeze, as if they were calling to me. I remembered what Mohammed had told me about the power of these poppies. If you asked me now, all these years later, whether I plucked those seed-heads because I wished to ease my friend's pain, or because of the pernicious effect about which he had told me, I could not honestly say.

I returned to Mohammed's prostrate form. He was groaning as much as ever. Why did unconsciousness not take him? I cursed. Wondering how to feed him the poppy juice, I caught sight of the leather bottles hanging from my horse's saddle. I fetched them, and let the juice from the seed-heads dribble into one. I shook it hard, and then bent down and held it to Mohammed's lips, lifting his head as gently as I could. He moaned at the effort and the movement, but a minute or so later he sighed deeply, and passed into merciful sleep.

❋

SAINT LAZARUS' COLLEGE

At times of crisis like this, the Chaplain always found that a good long walk helped to clear his head. What better way could there be of sorting out the right way forward than communing with God's creation? He really had to find a graceful exit from the College. The trouble was that his association with the awful heresies in *The Waste Land* had probably already spoilt his chances of a living. Not that there were many decent ones to be had these days anyway. At his time of life he could hardly be expected to take on one of those dreadful inner city parishes where the demand for pastoral care was simply overwhelming. Acting as a social worker for the underclass was not why he had taken Holy Orders.

If only the Master could be persuaded to dismiss him. Then he would get some decent compensation. He might even be able to extract a payment for wrongful dismissal, or at least get a few thousand as a *quid pro quo* for not going to court. The Master was so obsessed with avoiding any publicity which might possibly upset the politically correct brigade. And wrongful dismissal, even of an Anglican chaplain, would not play well with those bleeding hearts who cared about employment rights. The Master seemed to be unaware that the Fellows all realised that this preoccupation with appearances was just about securing his peerage! Why, when he was not present, his bee in his bonnet about getting into the Upper House was the favourite topic of conversation in the Senior Common Room!

Wrapped in his bitterly unchristian reverie, the Chaplain had paid little attention to the direction he had taken. He was rudely brought back to reality when a long thin missile whistled through the bushes to his right, alarmingly close to him. My God! He must have strayed too near to the field habitually used by the archery club. Normally, when they were practising, they put a warning sign out on the path. Perhaps he had been so deep in his thoughts that he had walked straight past it. Still, they would be firing from a long way off and the chances were pretty remote of a spent arrow hitting him, or doing much harm even if it did.

So it was without great panic that the Chaplain turned to return the way he had come. As he did so, something thumped into his left shoulder with such force that he was thrown off his feet. Oh God, that hurt! Using his right hand, he pushed himself up to his knees. He looked with amazement at the vicious point of an arrow protruding just under his left collar bone.

Appropriately, he was still on his knees when three more smashed into his upper body in rapid succession. He toppled forward, stone dead, into a spreading pool of his own blood.

✳

CHAPTER FOUR

THE ASSASSIN'S WINE

L'horrible soif qui me déchire…

✳

Mohammed woke next morning, seeming refreshed and in less pain. He was able to smile properly.

"I now understand what you meant by the itching. I want to tear off my bandages and scratch at my wound, however much it might hurt. But thank you. That draught of wine you gave me last night worked wonders. I had not tasted it before. I wonder why it is forbidden to us when it works so well? It must be permitted as a medicine. Is any more left?"

I fetched the bottle and dribbled some down his throat. He swallowed greedily.

"Ah, that's better. I think I will sleep some more."

I climbed the hill above the wadi to keep watch over the plain towards Turbessel. I stayed there most of the morning until I had satisfied myself that no pursuit was coming from that direction. Perhaps Count Baldwin's men were nervous about straying too far south towards Aleppo and encountering Sultan Ridwan's soldiers. Or perhaps they were still drunk.

When I came back down the hill Mohammed was awake and seemed to want to talk.

"I don't think my father would have sent me with you unless he had initiated me first. My death would spoil his plans. But it was strange, wasn't it? That great golden dish – I don't know how to describe it – do you have a word for such a thing in your language?"

"We would call such a dish a *graal*, a grail," I said.

"And the strange smell of the herbs. The enormous pressure inside your veins as the liquid rushes to replace your blood... See, I now have the same scars as you."

He pointed weakly to his wrists and ankles. I tried to smile back at him. "Well, you have now got another great scar on your belly to go with the one made by the grail lance in your side."

"Remember I called you my brother when we were travelling? You looked surprised. But you see now we really are brothers, brothers of the same blood." His warm smile filled me with anguish.

"I am sorry that I did not tell you before. My father forbad me in the sternest terms. But now that you can see me healing with your own eyes, there is no point in pretending any more. My father..." Mohammed's face stretched with concern. "What will we tell him? He does not like to hear of failure. For me, the plans he has mean that he cannot do me any lasting harm. You see, he wants to show me to the world as the true Imam, the Mahdi, by publicly martyring me, and having me restore myself to life. Then all the world will have to vouch that the Nizari faith is true. The heretical Caliph in Baghdad will fall. The power of Alamut will stretch across the globe. The ambitions of my father's life will be fulfilled.

"But for you... He has come to think of you as a useful instrument, but your failure to kill Count Baldwin will raise doubts again in his mind. I understand that it was an accident – we should have been clearer about the identity of the man you were to kill – but my father is less forgiving. I fear for your safety should you ever be in his power again at Alamut."

The expression of solemnity brought by this concern for me was driven away again by his smile.

"Is there any of that wine left? If I go back to sleep I will be rid of this dreadful itching. And besides, the pain is still quite bad."

When I had doped Mohammed I went back up the hill to my lonely seat. I watched there in a state of gloom, until my mood was matched by the gathering dark.

So Hasan was after all planning to use the secret of the grail in the way that I had feared. I cast my mind back again to our first meeting. I remembered that he had told me how he hoped to establish his Shi'a beliefs as the indisputable faith of Islam by accomplishing the reincarnation of the Imam. When I had travelled back to Alamut with the Lazarus Gospel, so naively believing myself Blanche's saviour, I had suspected Hasan's purpose. Now poor Mohammed had confirmed these plans. I also knew the character of the man well enough to see clearly that Hasan's desire was driven as much by the worldly ambition to found a great dynasty of his own as by any sincere religious belief. That ambition I could still thwart; and as for the religion, what concern was it of mine which empty belief foolish men chose to follow?

When I came down from the hill, sullen and bitter, to feed Mohammed his tincture, he mistook my expression for worry about what we should do next.

"Sleep," I ordered crossly in response to his question. "We'll talk about what to do next in the morning."

I passed another restless night and was awake before dawn. I had to shake Mohammed hard to wake him. Normally he was the first to rise. My irritation bubbled over at his sleepy smile.

"Such dreams," he murmured, "so full of warmth and colour. Couldn't you have left me there a little longer? I want to sleep! To sleep instead of to wake! It so cold here – and look, everything is still dark and grey."

Behind him though, I saw the monochrome pre-dawn light turning to brilliant colour as the sun cut the horizon and poured fire across the plain. Normally that sight would have filled us both with exhilaration. Now I longed for the shelter of the dark as much as Mohammed wanted to return to his dreams.

I fetched some water from the stream in my hands and held it out to him before it had all trickled between my fingers. "Here. For the sun," I said gruffly.

The cold liquid seemed to wash away some of Mohammed's torpor. We looked at each other, wondering who would speak first.

"So," he said quietly at last, "what do we do now?"

I shrugged and looked away towards the horizon. "We won't have another chance at Count Baldwin. Not for a while at least. They will be on their guard. We will just have to acknowledge that we have failed, for the time being anyway. Maybe if we wait until they have relaxed again…"

"But where will we go now?" The nervous anxiety in his face filled me with pity. "We cannot return to Alamut, not until we have done what we were told."

"Aleppo is not very far. We could hide there, and forge our plan to strike again."

I had a ready supply of poppy heads, but there was little more than a dribble of wine left in one of the bottles, and I needed to replenish it if Mohammed was to have his drink. Somewhere in the city I would surely find a sinful Moslem who could provide forbidden alcohol. Maybe the same thought was in Mohammed's mind, for he brightened at my suggestion.

"Yes, perhaps we could hide in Aleppo and take stock." He fell silent for a moment. "But we would have to be very careful. My father has friends there. We would need to avoid the Goldsmith."

"The Goldsmith?"

"Yes. His name is Abu Tahir al-Sa'igh. He is said to be an

enormously fat man. And my father always says that the delicacy of the jewellery he makes is nothing compared to the intricacy of the plots he lays. Why do you want to buy my fine filigree? To wind about the eagle's nest."

I looked sharply at Mohammed, thinking that the drug had completely addled his brain. He smiled at me weakly.

"That is his password. He is the leader of our sect in Syria, and the good friend of Emir Ridwan. He will not be pleased that we have failed in our task to kill his protector's enemy. Ah, I ache this morning. Is there any of your wine left?"

I needed Mohammed awake for the ride, so I would only allow him a sip of what little liquid remained. This, together with my reassurance that I would replenish our supply in Aleppo, chased the concern from his expression and replaced it with a glow of well-being. I knew that it would most likely only be temporary, and that once the effect of the draught had worn off he would be fretful and anxious again well before we reached our destination.

We came out of the hills about noon, and soon could see the walls of Aleppo in the far distance through the haze. The sun was throwing our shadows long to our left by the time we neared the Bab al-Nasr, the northern gate. I remarked to Mohammed on the impressive sight of the square minaret behind the walls, and beyond, the great dome of the mound topped by the grey walls of the citadel. He was now too edgy to respond, and I had to speak sharply to him in case he gave us away.

"Pull yourself together, for Allah's sake. There is nothing to tell us apart from ordinary travellers, but if you look guilty like that they will stop us. Then they will discover the Crusader mail under my cloak, and then, for all that I look and sound as much like an Arab as you do, we will be in trouble."

Poor Mohammed made a visible effort of will to pull himself together, and in the event we aroused no suspicion. However, it was clear that he could not last for much longer

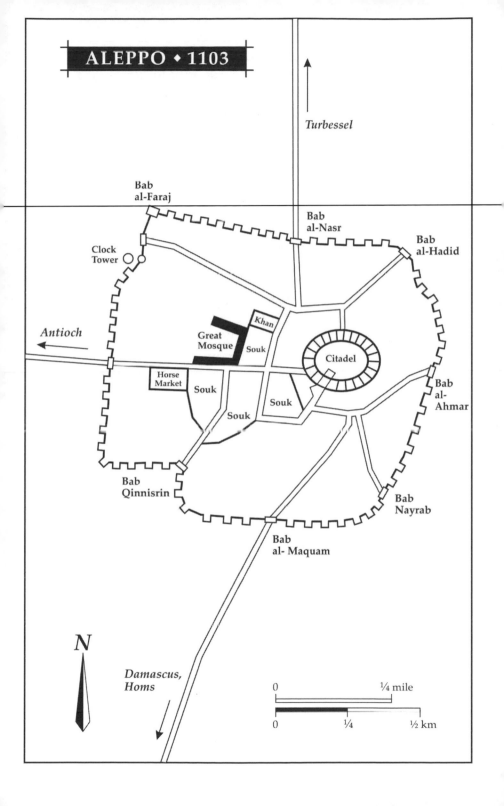

ALEPPO ◆ 1103

Turbessel

Bab al-Faraj

Bab al-Nasr

Bab al-Hadid

Clock Tower

Antioch

Great Mosque

Khan

Souk

Citadel

Horse Market

Souk

Souk

Souk

Bab al-Ahmar

Bab Qinnisrin

Bab Nayrab

Bab al- Maquam

N

Damascus, Homs

0   ¼ mile

0   ¼   ½ km

without a draught of poppy juice, and I could scarcely give it to him to drink in the street, so I decided to stop at the first place that advertised lodgings. We turned off the main thoroughfare, and quickly found ourselves in the narrow alleys of a poor quarter of town. A lantern, as yet unlit, advertised some sort of hostelry. We turned into a yard behind and dismounted. Mohammed slid from the back of his horse like an old man. No servant appeared, so I left Mohammed holding the horses and entered.

Nobody was in the shabby room. The walls were lined by low divans, littered at random with stained cushions. I called for attention and was surprised when a woman of middle age appeared down some narrow stairs. She wore no veil and her headdress allowed her elaborate braided coiffure to show.

"My companion and I need a room for the night. And somewhere to stable our horses."

"For the night? Two young men? I am sure we can accommodate you. Horses are less our thing," she laughed with a coquettishness which ill suited her age, "but there are stalls at the back if you will tend to them yourselves. And I'll need payment in advance. Two for the whole night – that will be a silver dinar each."

I nearly balked at such a steep price but then I thought of Mohammed's state. We could find cheaper lodgings on the morrow. I went back out to deal with the horses.

Our mounts showed what they thought of their poor quarters on the far side of the courtyard by resisting my efforts to lead them into the tiny stalls. I had some sympathy with them, for the stench of manure was overwhelming. Mohammed was overcome by apathy and gave little help, so by the time I had fed and watered the horses I was in a thoroughly bad temper. All they got that night in return for carrying us so well was a perfunctory rub down.

Then, with Mohammed traipsing behind me, I returned to the main building carrying our Persian-style carpet saddle bags. I paid the woman from Mohammed's purse, and then lent forward to say in an undertone, "Can you bring us some wine? He needs it."

I was disconcerted by her wink.

"Of course! It always helps, doesn't it!"

Our room was not much bigger than our horse's accommodation, with only a narrow gap between two divans. But at least it smelt a little sweeter – a slightly sickly aroma in which thought I detected rosewater and some sort of incense. I pulled off my over-garment in order to shed my mail coat. Having done so with relief I pulled the cotton robe back on. I no longer bothered to check the bandage around my thigh – it was so much part of me that I would have noticed if it had not been there as much as if I had lost a limb.

Some cold meat was brought by the woman – and more importantly a flagon of wine. I emptied half of it into one of the leather bottles and then turned my back to Mohammed as I bled in the juice from one of my remaining poppy heads. The rest of the undoctored alcohol I thought I had earned myself. I took several deep gulps and after a few minutes I felt my humour improving. After his drink, Mohammed lay peacefully soporific on his bed.

I was settling down myself when a quiet tap came on the door. Before I could answer, it opened, and two girls came in wearing colourful gauzy robes. They each attempted a modest smile which clashed incongruously with their diaphanous costumes. Both had faces that would have been pretty if they had been less made up, and eager, laughing, dark-rimmed eyes. But I have to confess than my gaze did not linger there for long. I now realised the nature of the establishment we had found.

Mohammed had propped himself up on his elbows and was smiling inanely through his stupor. I felt my member stirring. It had not been used properly with a woman since Blanche. The wine had relaxed me. Why should we not have our money's worth? Anything else would be strange behaviour and might cause suspicion.

I patted the divan beside me and the nearest girl sat down. With one hand she stroked my cheek, and with the other she took mine and placed it on her breast through the filmy material.

"You are a pretty one, not fat and ugly like most of them," she said. "I am Abla. Who are you?"

From the corner of my eye I could see that Mohammed was getting similar treatment.

She saw me look towards her friend and pouted. "Do I not please you enough? Do you prefer Hayfa?"

"You please me more than enough," I smiled. "Feel." Then, with a lurch, I remembered my regrown foreskin. Wouldn't that betray me for what I was? Mightn't it scare the girl, make her think that I was unclean, or at least cause her to gossip to her madam? I could not let her see it.

To cover my confusion, I pulled her closer and slipped my hands underneath the thin silk that covered her. She giggled, avoided my lips and nibbled my ear lobe. "You are eager," she said. "Have you been on the road a long time?"

Her warm curvaceous body, polished like copper, excited me. I was eager. I felt ready to burst. I moved her to one side. "Kneel up," I commanded. She giggled again. "If that's how you want it," she said.

I lifted up her silky robes and ran the tips of my fingers between her legs, causing another little laugh. In the Moslem style she was hairless. 'She is only my second woman,' I thought. 'How like Blanche and yet how different!' Then I lifted up my own garment and entered her. With a sigh that I took to be pleasure she pushed her buttocks back against my thrust.

On the other bed, Abla's friend Hayfa was having to work harder with Mohammed. She had pulled up his clothes and hers, and was straddling him. She leant forward, whispering

50

to him. "Don't be shy. You can do it." I felt my own excitement mounting at the sight of her bare buttocks moving over my friend. I gripped my girl harder and pushed into her. As I came, she had the good manners to make noises of pleasure of her own. When I had finished she straightened out her knees and I lay flat on top of her, my guilty member still hidden away inside.

I must have slept. Loud grunts of pleasure were coming from a neighbouring room, and I supposed that was what had woken me. As I listened, I began to become aroused again. I felt Abla awake beside me, and I looked over towards Mohammed's bed. He was sound asleep, and from the ecstatic expression on his face I knew that he was drugged deep in his colourful dreamland. In the lacework of light cast by the pierced metal lantern, I saw Hayfa's kohl-rimmed eyes dark and liquid. I beckoned her over.

Abla pouted. "Did I not please you?" I caught her arm before she could handle my hooded cock.

"You did please me. You pleased me well. You would entertain the universe in bed. But we cannot leave out your friend."

Both girls giggled as I motioned the new one between us and turned her on her side with her back towards me. She was slighter than Abla, her buttocks flatter, and when I entered her I found she was tighter too, in spite of the slipperiness inside. Mohammed had obviously managed something.

This time I wanted to make it last longer, and I moved slowly back and forth, rubbing my full length in and out. Then I saw the girls, now face to face, fondling each other and kissing gently. I could contain myself no longer. I speeded my thrusts, groaned and came in another rush.

I woke when the light filtered through the window, fractured by a delicate lattice that matched in stone the metal lantern of the night before. The girls had gone. I sat up on the edge of my divan, and stretched, feeling relaxed and pleased with myself after my debauch. Then I saw that Mohammed's saddle-bags hung untidily open, and with rising dismay I leant forward and felt around inside. His leather purse had gone. We had been robbed and now had no money.

Urgently I shook him awake. Once again, it took a long time to drag him back into the real world. His eyes opened a crack, saw me and closed again. "Leave me in peace," he murmured.

"Come on Mohammed, they've stolen your money. We've been robbed."

His heavy eyelids parted again. "Well, it was not worth it," he said. "I expected my first time with a woman to be more exciting than that. I prefer your wine. Perhaps that was what unmanned me." Then alarm opened his eyes wide. "If my father finds out he will say I have defiled myself." He clasped my arm nervously. "You won't tell him, will you?" He started shaking and suddenly looked as if he was going to burst into tears. The only way I could calm him down was to give him his bottle to finish, and when he had settled back down on his bed I dressed, donning my mail under the loose cloak once more, and went downstairs.

The madam was nowhere to be seen. The state of the shabby room betrayed the night of debauchery that had just passed there. The soiled cushions were now strewn across the floor. A pool of wine announced that not all the customers of the establishment were good Moslems, and the sharp smell of the spilt liquid merged with the sweetly acrid fumes of some burnt herb.

Two burly individuals emerged from the back. They matched like brothers, bear-like with black hair covering the bulk of their faces, and an awkward rolling gait. Their arms were almost as thick as legs and I thought they might be more comfortable walking on all fours. The only vaguely clean things about them were their matching white embroidered skull caps.

"Still here, then, are you?" one of them rumbled. "If you stay much longer, we'll charge you extra."

"You can't charge us extra. We've been robbed."

They moved towards me. "Are you accusing our girls?"

"Go get your stuff, and your feeble friend, and get out," his brother growled. "And what are you, anyway? Little Abla tells me that you are no decent Moslem. Your filthy cock's uncut. How do you think she feels about having that thing inside her? She deserves extra money for the shame of it. Pig eater. Get out."

I had my sword strapped under my robe, and I knew that I could have cut them both down. For a moment my rage told me to do it. Then reason gained the upper hand. It could be dangerous to draw still more attention to ourselves. I dropped my gaze, trying to give them the impression that they scared me, and pushed round them to go upstairs to collect what remained of our belongings.

❋

SAINT LAZARUS' COLLEGE

The Master had decided in the end that the vacancy left by the Chaplain's terrible accident should be filled by a geographer. A strong shortlist had been quickly assembled – it was pleasing to see what a powerful magnet a Fellowship at Saint Lazarus' still could be. All the candidates had the requisite experience in developing world countries and their emerging economies. That definitely gave the right political tone, and should also bring some funds into the College by attracting as undergraduates the scions of the ruling families of those sorry places. In return for bending the rules and allowing them in, significant donations would be made, of course.

And now the panel was interviewing the last of the three final candidates. The Master thought that he had got his man. He looked to his right and left at the History Don and the Classics Fellow, now the two most senior members of the Senior Common Room, and thought that he saw approval on their pasty faces. Not that it really mattered. He would take the decision, but it would be helpful not to have to steamroller his choice through.

This chap had certainly been impressive on the impact of global warming in the Sahel. Now that was a topical subject, high profile and of interest to politicians of all parties. He had a long shelf of publications to his credit, academically sound, but tending towards the populist. That was exactly what was wanted these days. And he was clearly on intimate terms with several of the leaders in the region. There was a lot of money in Nigeria, and they always had plenty of sons to educate at the best British universities – before they went back home again to exploit with crude brutality their corrupt domestic political systems. The Master stifled a snort of disgust.

Now both the panel and the candidate had relaxed. The

difficult questions had been answered. The panel's elbows were off the table, the candidate's knees were no longer pressed together underneath. Both sides exhaled and leant easily against the backs of their chairs. The tone now was almost of drawing-room small talk.

"So where exactly did you go in the Easter vacation, then?" That enquiry was typical of the History Don, who fancied himself as a traveller. He would probably soon launch off into a long story about his own last exotic holiday.

"This time I went to Syria, actually. On my mother's side I am a distant cousin of the Assad family. So I was well looked after."

The Master felt his lips pursing involuntarily. Yes, he supposed there was something of a sharp Semitic look about the man. Still, those contacts could be useful too.

"Really? That must have been fascinating."

"Yes, yes, it was a great trip. The desert scenery is spectacular. As good as anything I have seen in Africa. And those Crusader strongholds... But I must say, I was most impressed by the cities. Damascus, and especially Aleppo. There are some fine buildings there; the Great Mosque, which now incorporates the old Cathedral of Saint Helena, although I believe that the two faiths were practised there cheek by jowl until 1124 or 1125 when the rulers finally got fed up with the Crusaders' excesses in Outremer. Then there is the citadel, with those eleventh century walls looking as if they had been built on the back of a giant tortoise, and the arched bridge over its moat zigzagging impregnably up. The *souk* is quite amazing; unchanged in many places from the same era. And they were so civilised – in the Souk Al-Mandil – the handkerchief *souk* – there are still some public latrines that they think date from the late eleventh century. Think how basic Europe was at that time!"

"Yes, yes, quite," murmured the Master.

✳

CHAPTER FIVE

THE HAPPY CORPSE

Je veux creuser moi-même une fosse profonde

✳

"What will we do for money?"

For the third time I explained to Mohammed that we would have to sell the horses. His querulous questioning was beginning to get on my nerves. In fact his general state was an irritation to me. As we led our horses through the narrow streets towards the centre of Aleppo, looking out for lodgings that were cheap and discreet, he kept glancing over his shoulder, and then pulled at my sleeve.

"Hugh, I am sure we are being followed. I am sure there is someone behind us."

I shook his hand off impatiently.

"Of course there is someone behind us. The whole bloody street is full of people. Who would be following us? Nobody knows we are here. Calm down – you just need another drink."

"The Goldsmith knows."

"How can the Goldsmith know? He cannot have had any word from your father. And even your father does not know we are here. Why are you so frightened of this Goldsmith?"

Mohammed sulked for a little and then started again.

"The Goldsmith knows. Word will have reached him about our failed attack on Count Baldwin. He will have sent word to my father. He will have had his instructions back. He will be looking for us."

"It took us over a month to get here, stupid. No messenger could have reached Alamut yet, let alone come back again with instructions."

Mohammed stopped, and as the horse he was leading came to a halt, so did mine. He raised his voice.

"You are the stupid one, not me. We don't use people to carry our messages. We use pigeons. My father's fastest birds can travel from Alamut to Aleppo in little over a day. Sometimes they are taken by falcons, but mostly, in two days, maybe three, my father can know everything, and have sent back orders to the Goldsmith."

We were blocking most of the narrow street now, and the obstruction we were causing, together with Mohammed's angry voice, began to attract unwelcome attention. I froze there, looking at him with horror, and then pulled myself together.

"All right, I'm sorry. I didn't know. But why didn't you tell me before? Come on, quickly, let's get out of sight."

I dragged my reluctant horse down a narrow alleyway to the right, Mohammed's frightened words echoing behind me in the narrow space.

"Not too close to the *souk*, remember, please. That is where he is based."

As luck would have it, the alley opened into a small yard, one side of which was lined by lodgings that could be rented cheaply by the poorer sort of traveller. The ferrety little individual in charge of the *khan* was busy, bustling here and there, but friendly enough. When I said that we had business in Aleppo that I expected to keep us there for more than a few days, and that my friend was not feeling very well, he allocated us some reasonably private space screened off by a carpet hanging at the back of one of the rooms. He became less friendly when I told him that I could not pay the rent in advance until I had sold our horses. Mohammed looked shifty, which I put down to him not being used to finding himself in such straitened circumstances.

"Please just point me where to go to get the best price for the animals," I said. "They are fine creatures and when I sell them we will have enough money to pay you for months."

He appeared to share my assessment of our mounts' quality, because his manner warmed up again.

"Go back the way you came in – it's the only way out of here anyway – and turn to the right. Pass in front of the Great Mosque – that is what everyone calls it, although its real name is al-Zaqariye, after the father of John the Baptist."

The mention of John the Baptist must have made me look pensive – certainly his role in the Lazarus Gospel reminded me of the document I wore wound round my thigh – for the little man paused in his instructions.

"Yes, they say that John the Baptist's head itself is buried there. Anyway, go past another couple of hundred paces and you will see a horse market on the left. It's as good a place as any. I've a cousin there, by the name of Hashim al-Baqir. If you say I sent you, and that you are lodging in my *khan*, he'll give you a fair price. After all, some of the money will be going into your pocket and straight out again into mine. Keeping it in the family!" He laughed.

I settled the peevish Mohammed with our saddlebags and few belongings behind the carpet screen. It was not a bad spot; a window in the back wall gave some light but did not let in a draught because it was covered with a thin piece of parchment.

"You know that John the Baptist was one of the first of our fraternity, or at least that's what it said in the Gospel of Lazarus." I hoped to draw Mohammed out of himself, or liven him up a bit.

"Well, I don't know what sort of an omen it is then, finding his severed head here," he said gloomily.

I was glad to get away from him. His pitiful state irritated me; but worse was my guilt at knowing that I was its architect. But at least in my enjoyment of the hubbub in the street outside I temporarily forgot my troubles. The Aleppans were busy people, scurrying here and there on unknown errands. To the right of the road down which I led my horses I saw bright stalls in front of the low arches which announced the entrances to the *souk*. We had accidentally found lodgings quite close to the place that Mohammed feared. I could see the citadel towering over the *souk* in the distance behind, and I could now see that the great rock on which its walls were set was shaped just like the shell of a tortoise. That must have been why this place in the middle of the plain had been chosen for the city. Anyway, Sultan Ridwan had a strong fortress for himself.

The square tower of the Great Mosque's minaret was even more formidable close to than seen from a distance over the walls, but the building beside it surprised me more. It was unmistakably a Christian church, or rather a cathedral, fronted by columns of pink stone whose capitals were so finely carved that it looked as if the acanthus leaves were blowing in the wind. Ridwan must be a ruler of great tolerance, I thought to myself, to allow the two warring faiths to worship side by side in his city, and I presumed that it was this same openness of mind that caused him to give the Shi'ite Assassins his protection. Opposite the Great Mosque I saw the gold- and silversmiths' *souk*, where, I assumed, the man so feared by Mohammed carried on his business.

I found our landlord's cousin Hashim in the horse market easily enough. Like many of his breed, he had clear eyes in a deeply tanned face, and the vigorous physique of a true countryman. I could see too that he knew his trade well. He felt each of my animals over with real affection, and they stood still for him. At one point, when he was inspecting their teeth, he looked at me sharply and asked where the horses came from. I span him a tale about how we had travelled from Marrat al-Numan, remembering the name of the unfortunate town where Count Raymond's crusading Provençals had committed their unchristian atrocities, cooking alive and eating old people and children without mercy. He appeared satisfied.

I started by asking thirty silver dinars for the pair, and although our bargaining took longer than I would have liked, I was pleased when I walked away with two dozen of the coins jingling in a purse. I would have been satisfied with twenty, and he had thrown the purse in as a final sweetener when I had threatened to go elsewhere to conclude the sale. Then I hurried back to Mohammed, to make our plans.

I found him sitting against his saddlebags, with his knees up, clutching a bottle. When I pushed round the carpet that separated off our space, he jerked to his feet and attacked me with his fists. I was so surprised that I took his pummeling for a few moments, before I grabbed his arms and wrestled him down. The drug and his wound had weakened him and I was now much the stronger.

"You bastard. You traitor. I thought you were my friend. Why did you do it to me?" He dissolved into tears of self-pity.

"What do you mean? Where did you get that wine?"

"I was desperate for some. I still had a few small coins hidden in the pouch under my cloak. So I slipped out to buy some for myself. I drank, and then drank some more, but it did not do what I needed. I could not understand why. And then I looked in your saddlebag, and I found those." He pointed a shaking hand at three poppy heads, that he had trampled and were now bleeding their white sap into the ground. "I told you what that poison could do. And you just used it against me. I now understand why I feel so feeble and helpless. I thought you were my friend."

I was now also almost in tears. "You are my friend, you are my only friend. At first I gave you the poppy juice to relieve your pain. When you were wounded. Remember? Then I thought I could use it to get my revenge on your father, to turn you away from him, and to foil his plans. You see? I meant you no harm."

The wounded look in his eyes hurt me worse than any blow. He turned his head away.

Then he looked back, because at that moment a loud commotion erupted outside. I peered over our carpet, and by the entrance to the little courtyard I saw the man to whom I had sold our horses gesticulating at his little cousin. Our landlord pointed over in our direction. Behind him stood four fierce looking individuals in the same mould as the horse dealer. And there was also a grossly fat man in a smooth dove grey robe. Flabby jowls bulged around his neck, wedging his head in position. The beard around his lips was thin, as if the skin underneath had stretched and moved the hairs apart. Folds of flesh forced his arms outward away from his body.

"Allah preserve us," whispered Mohammed, who was now standing beside me, "it is the Goldsmith."

"Quickly, out through the window."

I tore the brittle parchment aside, and saw that we were even closer to the *souk* than I had thought. Our window was the height of two men from the ground, and stalls lapped the bottom of the wall beneath it. I pushed Mohammed head first through the narrow opening and jumped after him. We fell into a pile of material and scattered bolts of cloth in all directions. I ignored the curses of the stallholder and pulled Mohammed to his feet.

"Quick, we have a head start. The fat man at least will have to go round. He won't fit through the window."

I darted off, dragging Mohammed behind me. Colours of every shade flashed past, and then we were through the textile market and running past the carcasses of eviscerated lambs, their innards piled neatly beside the bodies which they had once filled. Mohammed careered into a table heaped with glistening kidneys, which slithered everywhere, provoking furious cries of protest from the butcher. In this covered part of the *souk* the spaces between the stalls were too narrow for us to run side by side. I had to let go of Mohammed. Whether because of the lack of the poppy juice that he depended on, or just because of the wine he had drunk in his quest for oblivion, he staggered and began to fall behind.

"Come on, faster," I yelled back at him. "Remember that these ones know how to kill us. The Goldsmith must know our secret."

The *souk* was a warren. None of the paths ran straight. I tried to keep my sense of direction. Then the way widened and to my relief I found myself in a more open space. I could go faster. But my relief turned to despair when I saw that there was no issue, no way out. In front of me was a high wall, with alcoves underneath on which flapped ill-fitting doors of the sort that you might see on a stable. I heard footsteps pounding behind – Mohammed's, I hoped, but also surely our pursuers. I ran into one of the alcoves, and pulled the door shut behind me. To my amazement I found myself in a latrine. What on earth was such a thing doing here in the middle of a market?

I had no choice. Ignoring the stench, I lowered myself into the hole. I descended nearly the full length of my body until my boot squelched on something solid. My eyes were almost level with the ground, and as I looked out through the gap beneath the door, Mohammed burst into the yard.

He too looked at the wall in front of him. "Hugh, Hugh, where are you? Where have you gone?"

I could not answer, because at that moment our pursuers hurtled into the courtyard. With fierce satisfaction they seized Mohammed by his arms and forced him down onto his knees in the dust. The horse trader Hashim, panting angrily from the chase, walked round in front of him.

"Where is your friend, you filthy traitor?" Mohammed shook his head and received a savage kick in his midriff. He grunted, and retched, a thin stream of pinkish vomit dribbling out of his mouth. As he raised his head again, his eyes met mine peering out from under the latrine door.

"I could not keep up with him. He runs too fast."

The horse dealer's boot crashed into his belly again. I knew that it must have struck Mohammed on his scarcely healed wound.

"I did not see which way he went. I didn't."

This denial prompted another vicious blow. For a moment he could not speak for the pain. As he struggled for breath his eyes met mine again.

"I thought he came in here but he must have gone a different way."

The horse dealer glanced peremptorily at two of his companions, and jerked his head. In response to his unspoken command they ran out the way they had come.

As soon as they had disappeared, the Goldsmith arrived in the yard. He was puffing hard and his face was oily with sweat. The bulging front of his dove-coloured robe was stained by an accidental encounter with some meat stall, but his thick grey hair, brushed straight back from his bland round forehead, was undisturbed. Why, I wondered, do they fear this grotesque figure so much? Why did they all show him such careful respect? And then I saw his eyes, as hard and greedy as diamonds, and I understood.

"We have the traitor," the horse dealer quickly said. "My men are after the other one. They will get him."

"They better had," fluted the Goldsmith in a soft, musical voice. "But let's deal with this one first." The horse dealer moved to one side and Abu Tahir's fat bulk took his place. His voice was chilling, the sweetness of its tone so much at odds with the harsh words it spoke.

"Mohammed, Mohammed-i-Hasan-i-Sabbah. Drinking

wine and fornicating. You are a despicable traitor. O
Mohammed. How unworthy of that sacred name. For either
of your crimes there is only one penalty. You have failed your
father. He has passed sentence on you. He tells me to tell you
that are no son of his. You have failed him. He does not know
you. He has forgotten you already. Before he wiped you from
his mind he gave me precise instructions about how he wished
you to meet your end."

From somewhere under his voluminous robe my friend's
executioner pulled a dagger. Contradictory like everything
about this creature, the elegance of the weapon denied its
brutal purpose, gold and silver inlay gleaming at the base of
its curved blade and on the hilt in his pudgy short-fingered
hand.

The horse dealer now stood behind Mohammed, twisted
his hand into his hair and pulled back his head. As he did so,
my eyes met my friend's one last time. His expression was
proud and fearless, even happy, and with it he offered me no
blame. Then the inlaid knife flashed with unexpected speed
and opened his throat to the white bone. I heard his breath
gurgling through his blood, trying to make a scream, but
emerging scarcely louder than the Goldsmith's quiet
exclamation, "Ah, my robe is ruined" as the spurt stained it
crimson – crimson with the liquid that made Mohammed my
blood-brother.

I knew Mohammed was not yet dead. But I was too slow
and perhaps too afraid to climb from my hiding place. The
horse dealer pulled the body backwards so that the Goldsmith
could kneel on it and work the blade of his knife through the
vertebrae. Then I knew it was over. The head was severed,
separate from its torso. The horse trader lifted it up and as
the hair unwound it slowly turned, fixing me with a glassy
Gorgon's stare. As cold and empty as if I had myself been
turned to stone, I sank silently from my hiding place into the
culvert below. A trickle of filthy waste water ran at its bottom.

Seeing light glimmering in the distance I bent double and followed it, feeling worth less than the sewage that kept me company.

I found that the drain debouched in the moat around the citadel's turtle rock. I stayed in the shelter of that sewer, changing one uncomfortable position for another. I knelt, I squatted, I stood folded in half, waiting for the welcome veil of night, ordure flowing between my legs and staining my boots. I tried to think only of the old man, standing in his distant tower, his ringed eyes ranging over his mountains, seeking me out with his will. I tried to think of the hatred that must even now be consuming him, his plans destroyed, his heir dead. I thought that he must now feel towards me exactly the way I felt towards him. But I could not forget Mohammed, and what I had done. To my fury, the tears that flowed on my cheeks began to extinguish my hatred.

✳

"If you keep killing off your best characters at this pace," the Professor of English grumbled, "you will have to create a whole new *dramatis personae* by the second part of the book. Don't you realise how hard it is to bring new people to life? You should not be so profligate. I know that readers of your type of literature (if one can call it that) expect a fair amount of bloodshed, but don't you think you are going a bit far?"

The Best-Selling Author scowled in return. "Basically I am following the plot I have been given. This is what happens in Hugh's manuscript, if Lawrence's translation is to be believed. I don't have much choice in the matter."

"Or maybe you are planning a bit more resurrection," the Professor of English continued. "Dear, oh dear." His unfortunate giggle tittered round the room.

The History Don interjected, as usual preferring fact to fiction, "Personally, Stephen, I am a bit more concerned by our real death than the deaths in *The Flowers of Evil*. Poor Sebastian. What a silly mistake to make. And the members of the archery club – it was pretty tough for them. At least the inquest exonerated them totally. It was really not their fault."

"I know." The Professor of English got to his feet. "It was terrible. And even if I did not always see eye to eye with him, I still miss him. Our discussions at High Table already lack that extra bit of spice. Anyway, I've got a tutorial to take. If I can find my way through that dreadful mess of scaffolding by my rooms, that is."

"Come on, Stephen, you've been complaining about the state of that stone wall for ages. You can't go on moaning, now that I have found the budget to fix it. Anyway, the work won't take much longer. And talking of that, Lawrence, do get on and finish the translation, and then we could see whether we need to adjust the original plot a little. I do agree that there may be some merit in that."

The Classics Don looked a bit affronted, but knew that he could not ignore such a direct request from the Master.

When the Professor of English emerged into the quad and crossed it into the narrow passageway that led under the offending wall to his rooms, he was pleased to see that the work had in fact been completed. The scaffolding had been cleared away.

'Well, that has been done unusually quickly,' he thought to himself. 'Things are looking up.'

Unfortunately he wasn't, or he might have seen the top of the ancient wall slowly toppling towards him. He had reached the middle of the passageway when the whole thing collapsed over him, hammering him, crushing him under its stones, with a thunderous rumble which caused the remaining dons in the Senior Common Room to halt their bickering and hurry out to see what had happened.

✳

CHAPTER SIX

POSTHUMOUS REMORSE

Et le ver rongera ta peau comme un remords.

✳

At last night fell and swaddled me soothingly in its black velvet. Cautiously, like some shy nocturnal creature worming from its burrow, I nosed out of my hole, seeking holds for my toes and fingers. No swimmer, I could not risk slipping into the water. Splashing there I would attract attention, and might even ruin the ink on the precious material tied around my thigh.

It was fortunate that the builders of the moat had not bothered to dress too carefully the stones that lined its outer edge. They were rough and offered gaps between, into which I could work my fingers and toes. I scrabbled my way to the top and peered over. In the dark the few passers-by were not watching the moat. I did not have to wait long before I could jump up unseen onto level ground. I dusted myself off and walked forward.

I had one more task to complete before I shook the dust of Aleppo off my feet. Abu Tahir would not expect me to come looking for him; how could he, for earlier that day I would not have expected to go looking for him myself. My vengeance on King Baldwin could wait a little longer. First I would avenge Mohammed. I tried urgently to tell myself that the Goldsmith's death would assuage my guilt. Underneath, though, I knew that my shame would remain with me as surely as my memory of the lifeless stare of Mohammed's severed head.

If I were caught, my fate would be the same as Mohammed's. The Assassins would be out in strength, and they knew how to kill me, but I counted on them having cast their net to catch a white-robed man trying to leave the souk. The money from the sale of the horses I still carried in the purse that the accursed dealer had thrown into our bargain. How he must have laughed inside at my expense as we haggled. I hoped that I would encounter him too; he also should die. I loosened my sword in its scabbard, trying to cast myself in the role of avenging angel, but unable quite to find the hypocrisy that would have been necessary for that particular piece of self-characterisation.

In one of the narrow streets which led away from the citadel and back into the *souk* I found a poor shop which sold garments. Its wizened owner must have thought it his lucky day, for I had little appetite for bargaining, and paid a price for two robes which was higher by far than he could have hoped. In an alleyway I cast off my white garment, and struggled into the black robe I had just acquired. Over it I placed my second purchase – a lurid costume in red stripes of which I would normally have been ashamed. I pulled its hood up well over my head. A handful of charcoal from an unlit brazier served to blacken my brown beard and hair. Thus disguised, and fancying that my loud garb was already attracting some uncomplimentary glances for my poor sartorial taste from passers-by, I strode into the *souk*. A busy trade was taking place in the relative cool of the evening in the flickering pointed light of many pierced metal lanterns.

From that morning I knew how to find the sector of the

souk where precious metalwork was traded, just opposite the Great Mosque. I threaded my way in that direction. As I stood aside to allow a heavily laden donkey to pass down one of the narrow alleys, I made polite enquiry of a passer-by who had also been forced to halt for the same load.

"I come from out of town, from the north. Where might I find the store of the worshipful Abu Tahir al-Sa'igh? My cousin recommended him to me. His wives were well pleased with some gold trinkets purchased there. I would like to buy myself the same peace when I return home."

My informant smiled sympathetically and gave me the directions I wanted. I thought that I had misunderstood when I came to the place indicated and found a little fellow there who could scarcely have looked more different to Abu Tahir. Everything about him hung loose, his clothes and even his skin, as if both were far too big for his frame. Before I could move on in disappointment, like the good trader he was, he addressed me.

"Why do you want to buy my fine filigree?"

Trying not to show my surprise, I answered quickly, "To wind about the eagle's nest."

"Go into the back room," he said, with a knowing look, "that is where you will find the products most suitable for you." He rapped a quick rhythm on the heavy door behind him. When it opened, I stepped in past the tall black-robed figure who had admitted me, moving quickly enough for neither of us to see the other's face. I heard him carefully shoot the heavy bolts back again.

Facing the door, behind a table which was spread with fine gold jewellery, the Goldsmith sat, resplendent in a clean dove-grey robe which stretched smoothly over his great belly. He looked up from examining his craftsmanship. The delicate hooped earring he was holding almost disappeared between his pudgy fingers.

"Welcome, welcome, we have been expecting you," said the

even fluting voice that had pronounced poor Mohammed's death sentence.

I felt the presence of the man behind and knew I would have to finish him first. In one movement I drew my sword from under my robes and spun round. To my delight I saw that he was Hashim the horse dealer. As recognition sparked fear in his face I cut him down.

I swung back towards the Goldsmith, who was rising to his feet, his bulk toppling the table so that the jewellery scattered tinkling on to the floor. His curved dagger flashed out like lightning but grated harmlessly on the mail under my cloaks. My sword met no such obstacle as it dipped into his gross belly like a quill into red ink. At first his bland face showed little change of expression, just gentle surprise, but then, as I moved my weapon from side to side to open his guts, it bulged with agony. I filled with pleasure as his body tipped over and began to empty its lifeblood.

"The second robe you have ruined today," I said with venom, and wiped my blade on his chest before returning it to its sheath.

Avoiding the pool of blood spreading on the floor, I quickly pulled my loud striped robe off over my head. The horse dealer lay on his side by the wall, and I struggled to sit him up and to dress him in my garment. I turned his face to the floor, making sure that the hood was pulled well up so that his features could not be seen unless he was rolled over. I had luckily made my purchases well, for the black that I now wore could scarcely be told apart from his. We were of similar height and if, as I hoped, the men outside went first to tend to Abu Tahir, I should be able to make good my escape before the horse dealer's identity was discovered. So I made sure that my own face was hidden beneath my hood, heaved back the bolts on the door, leapt through and shouted, "Help, help! The man in stripes has killed the Goldsmith! I have taken the murderer's life, but the master is dying."

71

The man with loose skin jumped to his feet, and rushed into the back room, followed by two others. I slipped away and merged unobtrusively into the crowd. I was a long way off before I heard in the distance the hue and cry being raised.

How I hoped to get out of that city! But I remembered nervously how Constantinople's gates had been closed at dusk. When I reached the Bab al-Maqam, which guards the way south towards Damascus, not only was it still open, but many travellers were passing in both directions beneath its honeycomb vault. I could only guess at the reason for the custom of leaving it open after dark – the warm climate perhaps, causing many to travel and trade in the cool of the evening, or the nomadic nature of some of the people. Whatever the reason, I was grateful.

I walked blindly away from that accursed town until there were no more travellers around me and I was alone in the dark. Then I found a small knoll to one side of the road and sat there, looking back like Lot's wife. 'My soul is cracked,' I thought.

At some point I must have fallen asleep and rolled over onto my side, for that was how I found myself when the dawn woke me. In the trickle of a nearby stream I rinsed the charcoal from my beard, trying hard not to think of the words that Mohammed would have spoken to me while we looked together at the rising sun. Then I rejoined the road and started walking.

After an hour or so, I caught up with a caravan that was just getting underway. Several strings of camels were joined nose to tail by ropes. The first camel in each string bore a rider perched on the front of its hump. The others carried great bags of goods. Most of the Arabs who accompanied the caravan walked beside their animals, giving the heavily laden animals the occasional prod or word of encouragement. The supercilious creatures paid no attention, just swaying forward at their own unchanging pace.

I easily identified the master of the caravan from the orders he was shouting. He broke off as I approached and looked at me carefully. His eyes were set close together and deeply buried in sockets that were wrinkle-ringed from their perpetual battle against the glare of the desert sun.

"I am travelling to Damascus," I explained. "I go to join a cousin there who is in the carpet business. I can pay well for my food and I can fight if we meet bandits. May I join your party?"

"It is a rule of the desert never to refuse company to a lone travelling stranger. You will do your share of the work and pay me three dinars when we reach Damascus. Pwah, but you smell like a *Franj*." He wrinkled his nose with distaste. I shifted uneasily at the uncomfortable accuracy of this insult, but then remembered that I probably still smelt of the latrine drain.

"Do me a favour and wash when we next reach water. You are fortunate that we have a consignment of Aleppan soap in the caravan. You will pay extra for that, for it fetches a high price in Damascus, where they do not have the secret of how we make the laurel and olive oil set hard together."

I thought we would have to travel a long way before I would be able to satisfy the caravan master's request. The landscape south of Aleppo stretched flat and dry as far as I could see. As it crunched under my feet it brought back to me the horrors of my march across Asia Minor after the battle of Dorylaeum. Then we had been ill-prepared. The wells and cisterns along the way had been poisoned or broken by our retreating enemies. Most importantly, though, we had horses and mules but no camels. I had never travelled with these extraordinary animals before; now I began to understand why the Arabs revered them so. After a couple of days, I no longer disputed their right to the superior expression with which they looked down their noses at the two-legged creatures who claimed to be their masters. Their stamina and endurance were extraordinary. My lacerated spirit was soothed a little by their regular rolling gait, the rhythm of which I tried to emulate. By copying them, I found that I could walk myself into a trance in which my sorrow and shame were stilled.

At the end of each day I watched with admiration as the camels followed their orders to lie down, communicated by a sharp tap of their driver's stick and then his harsh, outlandish cries. Each camel felt the soil with one foot for a soft place. Then its front legs folded in half, kneeling as if to pray, and dropped with a muffled thud and loosening of breath. Luggage or rider lurched forwards. Next the hind legs folded in the opposite direction, so that the burdens were thrown backwards again. With a third lurch the front legs were collapsed under the ungainly body. When all four limbs were stowed away the camel rocked from side to side to bury its knees in the cooler soil – or perhaps to make it more difficult for the drivers to tie the strap around the upper and lower parts of one front leg behind the knee joint to prevent it from rising again until the morning. Some of the more loquacious amongst the beasts loosed off high-pitched bellows of complaint, which were stilled when they were relieved of their loads. They then settled to chew their cud, dribbling green between their loose lips as their jaws moved from side to side.

I patted with tentative affection the hump of the animal at whose side I had trudged through the long day, and looked with interest at the soft soles of his wide splayed feet. So that is why they are able to shuffle easily even through loose sand, I thought. Then, when I looked up, I saw that something awful had happened to the camel's face. A huge pink mass had squeezed out of its mouth and in apparent distress the poor creature pushed its neck back, raising this grotesque extuberance towards the sky. I exclaimed in involuntary horror, and the caravan master, who happened to be passing by, laughed abruptly.

"Do they not have camels where you come from?"

I tried to cover my confusion. "Yes, of course, but my family were too poor to own anything save a few sheep and goats. I have not had the privilege of travelling with them before. Tell me – what is wrong with her?"

Samir – that was the name of the caravan master – laughed again. "Him – you fool. That female over there is in heat. This male is displaying for her by turning his throat inside out. If you did that for your woman she might not be very pleased, but to a camel – well, I suppose it must be handsome. In the morning I will let them mate, and then you will see a thing. Camels are the only beasts that I have seen where the female lies down for her mate. She has to help, for, you see, a camel's penis points backwards."

My eyes widened, and Samir took my surprise for disbelief. "It is true! Some say that Allah – praised be his name – made the camel last from the pieces left over from the rest of creation. The last organ of reproduction did not fit the remaining body very well. Myself, I like better the story they tell about the Holy Prophet. You see, when He was wandering in the heat of the desert the only place He could find shade was under the belly of a standing camel. He rested there, but the provider of His shade began to piss, and to avoid being soaked, the Prophet reached up and turned the camel's member round so that it pointed safely away from Him. Ever since that day, camels have pissed backwards."

He laughed again and moved on to deal with his chores.

It was a week before we reached running water – the River Orontes near the town of Hama. Its presence was announced by lush fields and orchards growing in the rich dark soil of the river valley. After the barren gravel of the desert it seemed as if some magic dust had been scattered over the land. Between deep banks, I could see vast water wheels turning, I assumed to drive the millstones that ground the produce of the fields around. But as we neared the river, I observed that the wheels were responsible for creating the crops around, not crushing their seed. Each was fitted with wooden buckets, which lifted water from the river and by an ingenious mechanism tipped the precious liquid into channels – aqueducts – which carried it to the fields.

As these wheels turned, they moaned softly. Maybe their mechanisms protested at the endless work they had been given. Maybe the wind sang in discontent through these man-made obstacles which denied it free range over the land. To me it sounded a lament for the friend that I had lost, and I began to feel raw again, the soothing work of the camels undone.

Samir was true to his word and tossed me a small piece of the precious Aleppan soap.

"There – now get rid of that smell! Wash it downriver to those *Franj* in Antioch!"

I mustered a smile. "You could give your camels a scrub too, you know. They don't smell so good when you stand downwind from them."

He laughed. "They say it is better to endure the wind of a camel than the prayers of a fish. Don't fall over in the river!"

Samir's reserve and authority had mellowed as he became accustomed to me and saw my naïve respect for his animals. Also, I worked hard and willingly. I explained away my accent and my ignorance by saying that I came from the mountains towards the north of Persia. I presumed that his courtesy did not permit him to ask me further questions about my origins or even my religion. He perhaps suspected me of being a Shi'a, but I was sure he could have no idea of what I really was.

I also provided a new pair of ears into which he could pour his stories of Damascus. Although an Aleppan by birth, he spent his life travelling and trading between the two cities and his love for the southernmost was as great as his pride in his home.

"Just wait until you smell the orchards and the jasmine flowers! If this south wind is blowing, you will smell the city well before you see it. No wonder the Prophet refused to set foot there, in case by enjoying an earthly paradise He did not

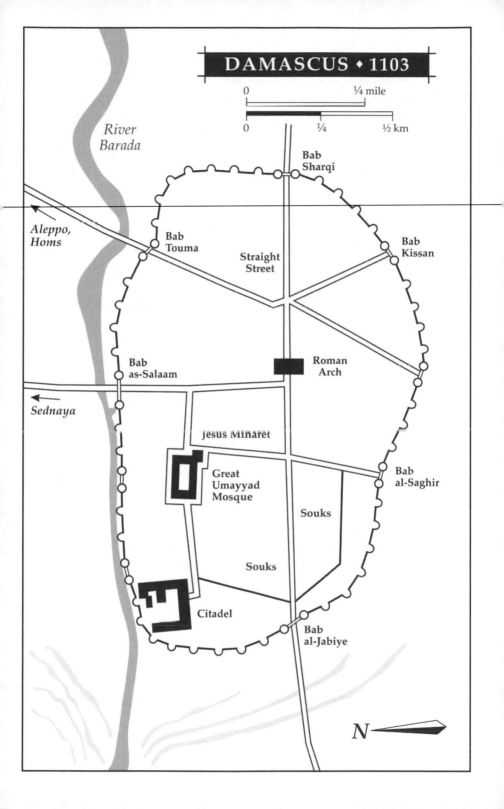

DAMASCUS · 1103

River
Barada

Bab
Sharqi

Aleppo,
Homs

Bab
Touma

Bab
Kissan

Straight
Street

Roman
Arch

Bab
as-Salaam

Sednaya

Jesus Minaret

Great
Umayyad
Mosque

Bab
al-Saghir

Souks

Souks

Citadel

Bab
al-Jabiye

N

reach the paradise of Heaven. And when we are there, and my business is done, I will show you the Great Umayyad Mosque. Until I do the *hajj* there is no holier place we can pray, at least while the Dome of the Rock is in the hands of the *Franj.*"

Samir lived up to his name, which, he liked to say, meant 'evening talking companion' in the Arab tongue. When I was listening to him I felt cleaner, as his enthusiasm washed over my guilty gloom. But once I was alone in the dark with my thoughts, the good effect of his words on my spirit faded faster even than the benefit of the Aleppan soap on my body in the heat. This road of mine to Damascus was just as painful as Saint Paul's, and marked by no sudden revelation.

The breeze was blowing in our faces as we approached the city, and as Samir had predicted my nose did sense it well before my eyes. Even the camels quickened their pace. And then we were in orchards of almond trees, and fields of orange and lemon trees, their blossoms exuding soft scent alongside their sharp-coloured fruits. The smell of jasmine was everywhere in the breeze and in places sweetened the air so much that it almost cloyed. Then I could see the River Barada rushing in front of the walls, a moving moat pouring down from the melting snows of the mountains to the west. The beauty of the place was a cruel contrast to the ugliness in my heart.

I played my part helping to unload the caravan, and, having completed my work, paid my three dinars for the privilege. Then Samir offered to keep his promise.

"Come, my friend, before you go to find your cousin, come and pray with me in the ancient mosque."

We walked from the direction of the *souk* where we had unloaded the camels and approached the main gate to the mosque, the Bab al-Barid. I saw at once that this was a structure to rival any that I had met on my travels, perhaps more ancient in parts than Haghia Sophia which had in turn outdone the church at my old abbey of Cluny. I saw not one, but three minarets.

Then we were through the gate, and confronted a wall of polished marble, topped by mesmerising mosaics in green and gold. In wonder I followed Samir into the graceful courtyard, where more mosaics above a marble wall at least twice my height pictured the beauties of Damascus or maybe paradise itself. In my misanthropy it seemed a paradise indeed because after the Arab style no people were pictured there to spoil the graceful buildings and trees, or the fruit and sinuous vegetation. In the middle of the courtyard stood an elegant ablution fountain, and at either end structures raised on ancient columns of Roman style.

Samir gestured dismissively to the left. "Over there is where the Shi'as pray. That is where they took the head of Hussein ibn-Ali after the battle of Kerbala. We'll go into the prayer hall with the decent Sunni."

The many columns of the hall grew like a forest between a crowd of peaceful worshippers, some bowing, some prostrate on the floor, a sea of believers in constant motion as they made their obeisance, rose, and moved away to be replaced by others.

When Samir had finished, he stood. I copied him and we moved towards the door back into the street. On the way he pointed to a domed structure in green glass.

"You see before you the tomb of John the Baptist. There lies his severed head."

I looked at him in surprise, feeling a surge of sadness at the unwelcome memory it brought of Mohammed. "I was told that lay in Aleppo."

Samir laughed. "That is what Emir Ridwan would have everyone believe in his rivalry with his brother Duqaq. He would claim every glory from Damascus. But even I, an Aleppan by birth, must recognise the justice of Damascus' claim to John's head."

I thought to myself sadly that they had all lost their heads

– John the Baptist, Lazarus – after all I had seen his skull in Marseille – and Mohammed. Doubtless sometime I would follow and then none like me would be left.

We passed through the side gate into the street beyond and Samir pointed up at the square minaret.

"That one is called the Tower of Jesus. From there he will descend from the city of the dead on the day of judgement to fight the evil one."

I turned to look at Samir, feeling surprise once again at the reverence attached by Moslems to the man worshipped by their Christian enemies as the Son of God. Then, as we parted in the street and I bade a confused farewell to Samir, it dawned on me what I had to do.

❋

SAINT LAZARUS' COLLEGE

The Classics Fellow felt a weight lifting off his shoulders on several counts. Then it occurred to him what an unfortunate choice of metaphor that was. Imagine how Stephen must have felt, having the life crushed out of him under the weight of all those stones. Oh well, what had happened, had happened, and one could not afford to be too sentimental in this life.

Anyway, he felt lightened – no, that was not a good image either – relieved, that was better. He felt relieved to have got that translation finished at last. That should get the Master off his back – oh dear, there was the same image again. And it had to be said that it was an extraordinary story. Hard to believe, but presumably true, although Mark would probably deny that. Why were historians always so sanctimonious?

And he was also relieved to have been invited to the Gridiron Club for dinner. That would get him away from the sepulchral atmosphere of High Table, where there were fewer and fewer people to talk to. And he had such happy memories of the Grid from his own time as an undergraduate. Such a jolly, unpretentious place. The right class of chap. He would be able to have just a little bit too much to drink without having to suffer the Master's disapproving looks.

The Grid lived up to all his expectations. The good honest fare had not changed much since his own day. Nice steaks, simply grilled, with *maitre d'hotel* butter and plenty of mustard. Fantastic *pommes frites*. A steady supply of decent claret. He swirled the purple liquid round his glass – ah yes, the wine dark sea indeed! – and took another large mouthful. Perhaps he should go a bit easy. With affectionate condescension he listened to his host ribbing his other two guests. It was so nice to see a few undergraduates still wearing tweed jackets. He had known that the dear old Grid would remain a bastion of sartorial decency.

What was that noise, rising above the hubbub of Christchurch voices? How annoying, the fire alarm. Probably just a practice, though. Or maybe not. Everyone seemed to be taking it pretty seriously – they were getting up and moving towards the exits. Oh God, flames were bursting out of the kitchen. Come on then.

Even in his inebriated state, the Classics Don was surprised how difficult he found it to get up from his chair. What was going on? Every time he stood up he was pulled back down again. He looked under his chair, beginning to panic, and saw that somebody had tied the laces of his half-brogues together. And not just together, but round the legs of his chair too. In normal circumstances it would have been a harmless undergraduate prank, and as the only don in the club he was fair game.

Oh Lord, he was not just the only don in the club – he was the only living soul left in there. He fumbled under his seat, desperately trying to pull the knots apart. But whoever had tied them had done a good job. He felt himself becoming faint with the effort. It was not good to have his head down between his knees after a large meal and all that wine. If he could just get out of there he'd promise to give it up for a month.

But it was too late. He succumbed to the smoke, and his smooth face crunched down onto the floor. The chair, still tied to his feet, spilled over on top of him. Then the flames started to lick lasciviously at his unconscious body.

✳

CHAPTER SEVEN

THE DREAM OF A CURIOUS MAN

La toile était levée et j'attendais encore

✳

I stood in the street outside the Great Ummayad Mosque and thought of severed heads. There in the mosque, so they said, lay John the Baptist's. The skull of Lazarus I had seen with my own eyes in the Church of Saint Victor by the quayside in Marseilles. Then my poor friend Mohammed – that was the freshest, most horrifying memory, of course. Hussein ibn-Ali, revered by the Shi'a, well, he was not an initiate, anyway as far as I knew, and so was no concern of mine.

But I did know of one initiate who remained. Surely the most important of all. Nowhere on my travels had I seen or heard tell of his head. Jesus might still be alive. Of all the initiates that I knew of, perhaps he was still entire. I remembered his wisdom, expressed not just in the proper writings of Matthew, Mark, Luke and John, but also in the forbidden Gospel of Lazarus. If I could find Jesus, perhaps he could teach me and help me to understand. Perhaps he could soothe me and bestow forgiveness.

I stood there utterly alone in that unfamiliar city, my only few possessions about my person, but now I felt strangely calm.

I had a purpose again. I had to find Jesus. I had to learn from him how to lead my life. Then I might find peace.

In the hope of some guidance, some inspiration, I turned back into the ancient mosque. It was a mistake. As soon as I stepped inside I saw the man with loose skin, the Goldsmith's assistant from Aleppo. He was emerging from the Shi'a end of the place of worship. I melted back into the shadows by the door as he hurried past into the street. Had his eyes flicked over me? Had I seen recognition there? I could not be sure. I could not risk the Assassins finding me in Damascus. Forgetting my intention to pray or at least reflect, I too hurried back through the door. I looked left and right and left again and flushed with relief when I saw his head bobbing up and down in the crowd. I followed a careful distance behind.

Samir had talked much about the unfraternal rivalry between the brothers Ridwan and Duqaq and their fiefs of Aleppo and Damascus. Indeed such was his conversation that you might have taken him for some great diplomatist, not a mere soap trading caravan driver. From our evening talks about the politics of the region I could deduce that if Aleppo welcomed the Assassins and gave them shelter, Damascus was likely to be bitterly hostile to their kind. So I could hope that the man with loose skin might be in Damascus secretly and alone, or at least that he might not have access to the same resources that the late Goldsmith had enjoyed in Aleppo. I was fairly sure that he could not have followed me directly when I had escaped from the northern city, but perhaps he had scouted for me to the south on the assumption that I was most likely to flee in that direction. Or perhaps some different business of the Assassins brought him to Damascus. When I had arrived at the Goldsmith's shop in Aleppo, they could only have asked me for the password because they had been expecting someone. It had been my good fortune to be mistaken for this mysterious agent. Otherwise I would have been unable to enter the Goldsmith's den and extract my vengeance for Mohammed's death.

I cursed the Goldsmith's henchman for not filling his skin. If his frame had been the right size it might have been easier for me to see him over the heads of the crowd. My own height helped, but I did not want to show myself too plainly in case he looked back. I had a nervous moment whenever he turned a corner and disappeared from view. I had to hurry to make up ground, provoking curses as I jostled idle Damascenes taking their leisure in the streets. Fortunately I always found him again.

It was getting dark when he passed through the city's northern gate into the sweetly jasmine-scented orange groves beyond the walls. Now I was forced to fall further back because otherwise he would have seen me if he had looked round. It was lucky that he was dressed in white, whilst I still wore the black robe I had adopted in Aleppo. Even in the fast darkening twilight, I could see him still shimmering ahead in the dusk, whilst the night falling kindly around me afforded me its shelter.

My ghostly prey came to a halt in a clearing between the fruit trees. I froze before its edge, because shadowy movements and quiet voices told that he had met some colleagues in the open there. I fell to my knees and wriggled awkwardly forward, my caution fighting my anxiety not to let my quarry escape.

The clearing was wide, and my enemies were gathered at its centre. I could see, and smell, some camels crouched there. A council of war began, but prosecuted in such quiet voices that I could only catch broken fragments of their conversation.

The first word that I identified, perhaps because it was mouthed with excitement, was '*Franj*'. It was repeated, more loudly, by the others in the group. I had been right to be worried. I had indeed been spotted in the mosque.

From the ebb and flow of different voices, I guessed that a debate was taking place about what they should do about me. One voice – belonging, I thought, to the man with loose skin – kept repeating the word '*Franj*'. Presumably he was arguing insistently that they should pursue me. Perhaps he was motivated by a desire to avenge his master's death. Now I heard the word '*Homs*', also repeated several times in a deeper, authoritative voice. I assumed that this must belong to the leader, perhaps to the man that the Goldsmith had been expecting. It sounded as if the majority of the group wanted to go on to Homs. That, presumably, was where their task awaited them.

Now, in frustration, the man with loose skin raised his voice again. Then the conversation ceased. I assumed that a decision had been reached. I sensed the rocking of rising camels, and breathed a sigh of relief when they moved away towards the north-east.

After an interval I heard soft-shuffling hooves coming back in my direction. I pressed myself down into the sandy earth. From the dark velvet of the night a camel emerged, moving towards me. My fear turned to excitement. The chance was too good to miss. I needed something to ride if I was to escape. This I could handle. I was sure that I could manage a camel – I had watched carefully how they did it when I had been with the caravan. And I had an opportunity to finish one of my enemies.

The tall beast was loping straight towards me on the most direct line back to Damascus. I made to pull out my sword but then thought that if I could take the rider alive I could find out what the Assassins planned. With that information I could better make my escape. Quickly feeling around in the dust I found a rock which neatly fitted my palm. As the camel neared, I rose from my place of concealment and grasped the rider by the arm. With the advantage of surprise, it was easy to topple him to the ground and before he could cry out I struck him on the head with my rock. His body went limp. In the dark I could see just enough of his form to pull up the skirts of his robe, pinning his arms to his side and obscuring his head. The rope girdle that he had worn around his middle served to truss him up firmly in a neat package.

I turned away to where the well-trained camel was standing, a seemingly uncaring witness of my tussle with its master. In good humour, I mimicked its supercilious expression through the dark, grasped its reins and ordered it down. Then I struggled with the Assassin's supine body. The unconscious dead weight of the Goldsmith's assistant was greater than I had expected. No sooner had I wrestled my prisoner over the camel's hump and secured him, than the animal lurched to its feet, as it was trained to do once it was loaded. Breathing heavily and cursing, I ordered it back to its knees and clambered onto its saddle myself. I was ready for the jolt forward, back, and forward again. When it was on its feet I pulled its head to the north. To go north-east was to follow the band of my enemies. South led back to Damascus. Due east there was only desert and wilderness. High mountains closed off the west and the coast, although that was where I really wanted to go for there I stood the best chance of finding Baldwin and completing my diet of revenge. Then I could start my search for Jesus and peace.

I urged the camel forward and it loped on steadily, tirelessly, through the night. I stayed as close as I could to the hills on my left, but I could not climb far into them for to do so would take me away from camel country, and I feared damaging those splayed feet on sharp rocks.

Behind me I heard occasional stifled groans from my prisoner. When the first light of dawn touched the horizon to my right I decided to halt, to check that the Assassin was still breathing, and to see what I could find out. My camel required no persuasion to stop after our long nocturnal journey, but it was with some difficulty that I persuaded it to sit down.

I slithered awkwardly off the saddle, my muscles stiff because they were unaccustomed to the strange rocking motion of this ship of the desert. Then I unstrapped my packaged prisoner and slid him to the ground.

I rolled him onto his back and pulled down the robe. I cried out aloud with surprise and stepped back. Instead of the face of the man with loose skin, Samir was looking angrily up at me. A dried trickle of blood ran from under his hairline where I had cracked his head with my stone.

"How can this be? Why are you here? How can you be one of them? You are a Sunni."

The face that I had known before as friendly was now contorted with hate. The close set desert eyes fixed me with loathing from the depth of their wrinkled sockets.

"And I know what you are now," he spat. "Heathen bastard. Corrupter of my master's son. You might as well have killed him yourself." I felt myself flinch. "I knew there was something strange about you. I had my suspicions and so kept you close by me. You had no such suspicion of me, you fool – I followed successfully the ploy of *taqqiya*, dissembling my real beliefs to further the true cause. Go on, finish me, send me to paradise. The others will come back and find you. And if they do not survive killing the traitor Emir of Homs, there will be many others behind them."

My hand moved to the hilt of my sword, and I pulled it from its sheath. But somehow I could not bring myself to use it on him. Until shortly before I had thought of him with affection. Samir had shown me kindness. In a panic of indecision I stood there. Should I ride to warn the Emir? How was it that he had attracted Hasan-i Sabbah's ire? Any enemy of Hasan's should be a friend of mine.

Samir's gaze did not falter. He thought that paradise beckoned. I knew I should finish him. But I could not bring myself to skewer him where he lay helpless. My squeamishness filled me with self-disgust. I could not hold his gaze and I looked over to the dawn now spilling rapidly into the eastern sky.

When I looked back I saw that I had been wrong. Deep in the wells of Samir's eyes there glistened fear and uncertainty. This man was not quite sure what would happen to him after death. His faith was not absolute.

"Have you ever been to Alamut?" I demanded. If there was any chance that he was one of those who had used Blanche I would slaughter him without hesitation – and, I told myself, slowly too.

"I know how to find it but I have never had that honour," he replied, tersely. Now he saw my hesitation and his doubtful expression turned to a sneer.

"I am going to spare you," I said slowly. "I will leave you here."

This statement of mercy sparked real fear. "No, no, please. I have seen what happens to men who are left tied in the wilderness. The birds come, the vultures. They wait until their victim is weak from thirst. Then, first, they go for the eyes, before he is even dead. Please do not do that to me. Make a clean end of it. Please."

I was ten years old again. The image of my brothers' broken bodies and their crow-pecked eyes hovered in front of me. I remembered the slimy feeling when I had dipped my fingers into their empty sockets and I found myself clenching my left hand into a fist. Angrily I pushed my sword back into its scabbard. Then I grabbed Samir roughly under the armpits and dragged him back to the camel. The animal turned its head to watch with some alarm as I wrestled my prisoner's heavy body back over the saddle and tied it face down again. Well-trained, the camel lurched to its feet as soon as it felt its burden secure. With weary resignation I resolved to walk alongside and took its rein.

The light now revealed some sort of track that led gently upwards into the foothills. I followed this path, half-hoping that I might find some sort of settlement near which I could dump Samir with a clear conscience. When I saw in the distance a small cluster of dwellings I found myself mouthing from habit a brief prayer of thanks that my act of mercy had been rewarded, before breaking off in irritation and the knowledge that there was nothing behind this good fortune except chance coincidence.

As we came closer, I saw to my surprise that the dwellings clustered around an ancient building that was unmistakably a church. I did not want to get entangled giving complicated explanations to the villagers, so I pulled my long-suffering camel to a halt and ordered it back to its knees. For a second time I unstrapped Samir and dumped him unceremoniously to the ground.

"There are people up there. Christians by the look of it," I said gruffly. "You can crawl up the hill and throw yourself on their charity. Maybe, if they treat you kindly, it will teach you to be a little less uncompromising in your beliefs."

I did not dare look Samir full in the face for fear of catching his inevitable expression of scorn at my weakness. Quickly I climbed onto the camel. In response it rocked upwards. As I pulled its head round I glanced back quickly and thought that I glimpsed surprise and grateful relief on Samir's face.

✳

SAINT LAZARUS' COLLEGE

The small interview room at Oxford prison was uncomfortably crowded. Buried in the guts of the cell block, it had no windows. The air smelt stale and foetid. The thickness of the atmosphere was at once cause and effect of the tension there.

"Well, you sent a message asking us to come." The Master's voice was harder than usual, betraying his revulsion for the poor creature before him. "You had better tell us what it is about."

The Oxford Detective never enjoyed confronting criminals that he had put away. He valued his own decency, and this seemed too much like gloating. He wished the Master would be a little more gentle. And it was hard not to feel some sympathy for the wretch. With that twisted face and the livid scar it was hardly surprising that he had turned to crime.

The Best-Selling Author gazed determinedly at the floor. He avoided viewing the grimace which passed for the Research Assistant's smile, but he noticed his two companions stiffen and looked up.

"You think you are so clever. But actually you are pig ignorant. Morons." The harsh nasal voice paused as the Research Assistant waited for his insult to sink in.

"Now look here." The Master bristled. "If you are going to talk to me like that we will just leave immediately."

"I wouldn't, if I were you. If you want to live, at least."

Now the Research Assistant had their attention. The room was absolutely silent.

"How the coroner can record three deaths by misadventure in the same Senior Common Room beggars belief."

The Oxford Detective shuffled his feet. He too knew that the three deaths could not be pure coincidence.

"The only death which was accidental was the one that you threw me in this slammer for. How many times do I have to

91

tell you that I did not kill the bastard? I'll not deny trying to bash you over the head, Master, but I just wanted the key to your safe so I could retrieve the manuscript. But my supervisor was just drunk and smoking in bed – what do you expect? He was definitely an accident waiting to happen.

"But these last three – all I know is what I have read in the paper – but I can see the pattern. Sebastian, Stephen, Lawrence. Shot by arrows, crushed by a stone wall, burnt to death in the Gridiron Club. The Gridiron Club. Don't you see?"

The Research Assistant glared angrily at the blank faces in front of him.

"It is how each of them was martyred. Saint Sebastian was shot full of arrows. You must remember those Renaissance paintings. He was a young man so it was the perfect opportunity for all those gay painters to be paid for portraying a naked male torso. Saint Stephen was stoned. And Saint Lawrence was burnt to death – on a gridiron, for Christ's sake."

Fear and alarm had now registered on the row of faces.

"What is your first name Barty short for?"

This question was targeted with some aggression at the Master.

"That is what my close friends call me. It's short for Bartholomew."

The Research Assistant barked with laughter.

"Saint Bartholomew was flayed alive." The Master looked as if he had suddenly swallowed whole a very large unripe plum.

Then, puzzled, the Research Assistant looked at the Best-Selling Author.

"But I have not been able to work out Buster Wallace."

The Best-Selling Author now looked even more awkward than the Master.

"Well, that's just my *nom-de-plume*, you see. Justin Hufferington-Smythe did not sound quite right for the part of the market I address. And probably would not fit on the spine of the book." He tried to regain his *sang froid* with a self-deprecating smile.

"Ah, Saint Justin, yes. Scourged and then beheaded."

"Don't worry, gents." The Oxford Detective felt that it was high time to intervene. "We'll get you round-the-clock police protection. Twenty-four seven." He now looked sternly at the Research Assistant. "That's all very interesting. I can see that you can make some sort of pattern out of all that. But who is doing it? And what is the motive?"

The Research Assistant sighed with exasperation. "Have the Templars appeared in the story yet?"

"The Templars? No. I have been waiting a long time for them," replied the Master with surprise. "They are rather an enthusiasm of mine, to be honest, and I know that they always sell books. But Mark insists that they cannot be brought in yet because they were not founded until 1119."

The Research Assistant sneered, further twisting his ruined face. "Your factual friend in the history department would also say that they were destroyed in 1307. Philippe le Bel crushed them – with a bit of help from Pope Clement – and had the Grand Master Jacques de Molay burned at the stake. The Inquisition tortured all the knights and forced them to recant – if they did not die on the rack first. They had got too rich and too powerful. Some say that they amassed their wealth because they possessed some secret that the Church could not contemplate becoming public. They were blackmailers.

"But do you really think that all the legends about them continuing in secret after the 1307 disaster can be untrue? Dan Brown called them the Priory of Sion in the *Da Vinci Code*. He probably got that name from Baigent and Leigh's *Holy Blood and Holy Grail*. Maybe Brown is right. Or maybe they were absorbed into the Knights of Malta. Or some obscure lodge of freemasons. Whatever they are called, their sworn purpose is just as it always was; to protect the secret contained in the Lazarus Gospel so that they can benefit from it. They will not stop until they have recovered the manuscript and prevented the publication of your new book. *The Waste Land* can just about be shrugged off as fiction. Anyway, they could not have stopped it being published – they did not know what was in it. But now they will take their revenge. And anyone can see that you set *The Waste Land* up for a sequel. The sequel might be more damaging to them. And this time they can stop it.

"And just ask yourselves about the name of your college. And why Chrétien de Troyes died before he completed the *Roman de Perceval*. At least in prison one has time to think about these things."

The Research Assistant's audience sat open-mouthed, aghast. An unspoken question hung between them in the stale air.

"I'm called Darren. There is no Saint Darren. And I'm here. So I reckon I am safe."

His harsh laughter was still echoing round the room after the last of his visitors had filed disconsolately out.

❉

CHAPTER EIGHT

THE DANCING SERPENT

Je crois boire un vin de Bohème,
Amer et vainqueur

✳

When I left Seydnaya – much later I was to find out that such was the name of the place near which I had left Samir – I followed the track back down from the foothills for a short way and then struck out towards the north-east. I knew from my journey down to Damascus that Homs was roughly halfway between that city and Aleppo. I supposed that was why it was such a bone of contention between the rival brothers Duqaq and Ridwan. I could guess from what Samir had told me that the assassination of its emir was intended to deliver it into Aleppan hands. I also knew that Homs sat in a strategic position, dominating the mouth of the valley that led to the coast. With Samir I had skirted past it – perhaps he had not wanted to show his face in the city whose ruler his comrades planned to kill – but I remembered the proud situation of its citadel on a rocky outcrop in the middle of an otherwise flat plain. When I had done what I could to frustrate the Assassins' plans I would turn down that valley towards the coast.

The Assassins could not know that I was on their tail, but I remembered the haste with which they had left the grove where I had happened upon them. I assumed that they would be riding as hard as they could, and I knew that I had already lost time in my detour with Samir. So I pushed my poor camel forward as fast as he would go. The foothills through which I passed were pleasant, scattered with groves of almond trees. Over to the east stretched the desert, flat, hostile and unvarying. As the sun rose higher, it seemed that the heat was already greater than it had been on my southward journey. I took to resting my camel through the middle of the day and setting off again in the late afternoon when it was cooler. Another advantage of riding through the night was that I was able to move unseen by other travellers.

Once more I had cause to praise my mount's stamina. Had I been riding a horse, my journey might have been more comfortable, but I could not have hoped to cover so much ground. My camel loped steadily forward. It made little complaint save when I stirred it from its afternoon rest. It seemed to be almost indifferent to whether or not it ate or drank. After the second day the plain opened out to my left and the mountains fell away, and I knew that I must be nearing Homs. But I also knew that I had not come up with my quarry. Unless they had avoided the main route they must still be ahead of me.

And so, indeed, it turned out. On the third day, instead of pausing when the sun began to rise high, I cantered on through the shimmering haze rising hot from the plain. On the horizon a pimple broke the flatness, and grew fast into the citadel of Homs perched on its rock.

Some dwellings of mud were scattered at the feet of the citadel's walls, interspersed by black tents. I heard the wailing of women from inside. I paused my camel to inquire what this meant of a small boy tending a herd of goats, almost knowing the answer before I received it.

"Three men with daggers stabbed our emir as he left the mosque this morning." His shrugged indifference showed that he thought little change would be brought to his poor life by this great event. Then bloodthirsty enthusiasm entered his tone and his dark eyes widened, "My father says that all three of them were hacked into small pieces by the emir's guard."

I rode on to the gate. It was closed. In response to my shouts for admittance a surly guard appeared on the rampart above.

"The gates stay closed by order of the Queen," he bellowed down at me. "None may leave, nor enter, save with her express permission. Away with you!"

He must have detected hesitation in my demeanour. "Now! Or I'll encourage you on your way with a few arrows."

There was nothing for me in Homs. I had arrived too late to frustrate Hasan's plans, and his fanatical agents had received the reward that they sought. I had less to fear now. Samir was the only remaining Assassin who could identify me. With a feeling of some relief, I pulled my long-suffering camel away to the west. Soon we reached the River Orontes, and there, at last, my camel was able to drink his fill.

We rested, and then set off again in the early afternoon, splashing with ease through the ford across the river, whose waters I could see were now well below their spring high point. In return for starting earlier than usual, I allowed the camel to amble at his own stately pace.

My thoughts now turned to finding Baldwin. I would deal with him and then my revenge would be done. It must make sense to head south towards Jerusalem. I did not expect to find Baldwin in his capital, for, knowing the restless ambition of the man, he would be at some frontier of his kingdom, extending it into his unfortunate neighbours' territory, or violently protecting it from their incursions. But Jerusalem at least would make a good starting point.

The slow rocking of the camel after my hard three day ride,

and my pleasant musings on revenge, lulled me into a soporific state. The sun was low ahead of me, not yet touching the horizon, but shining straight into my eyes. My heavy lids narrowed against it and needed little encouragement to close completely. I think perhaps I fell asleep in my saddle. In any case, my next memory was a rude awakening in a heap on the ground with a lance at my chest. A voice seemed to be shouting at me in a language that I had not heard for so long that I could scarcely understand it.

"Answer when you are challenged, you Arab dog. You will die for your impudence."

I shook the sleep and shock out of my head. Slowly I answered in my own tongue, for that, I realised, was the tongue in which I had been addressed.

"Wait, wait. I am one of you. Sir Hugh de Verdon is my name. I am a veteran of the battles for Antioch and Jerusalem. I was of the late Duke Godfrey's household."

The lance point leaning through my Arab dress against my mail twitched, communicating the surprise and disbelief of my questioner.

"Let me up; I will show you."

Hesitantly the lance was withdrawn a short distance, allowing me to stand. I lifted my Arab garment to show my mail underneath. Squinting up against the sun at the silhouette of the knight and his two companions above me, I said, "Take me quickly to your commander. I have important news from Homs."

"Homs? What has happened in Homs? It is from there that we fear an army to lift our siege of Qalat al-Hosn. The damned castle commands this whole valley. Count Raymond held it once four summers ago and he wants it back."

"Count Raymond? Count Raymond of Toulouse is your leader?"

"Raymond Saint Gilles, Count of Toulouse, indeed, and now Count of Tortosa too after our great victory outside Tripoli."

For a moment I had thought that I might have fallen in with Baldwin's men again, and I felt a surge of relief that I would not once more become his prisoner. That emotion was followed by some little disappointment that my encounter with him would be delayed.

"He is a brave soldier and a great leader of men. Without him we would never have survived Antioch," I lied, remembering the self-important Prince who had lain on his sick bed while Bohemond of Taranto had led us to victory. Then he had quarrelled petulantly about the ownership of the city. I remembered also how he had allowed his men to run amok in Marrat al-Numan, and wondered if my interrogator was one of those Provencals who had gorged himself on the flesh of babies in that benighted town. I felt my anger rising but forced it down and injected as much eagerness into my tone as I could manage.

"I was with the noble Count in the cathedral at Antioch when Peter Bartholomew uncovered the Holy Lance!"

"All right then, you had better come with us. Get back on your camel. But don't try anything. Our horses can easily outrun you and I'll not be so gentle a second time."

I don't know which was weariest, my camel or me, as I ordered the animal to his knees. Once I had climbed on, burdened by me and the water he had taken in, he struggled to straighten his front legs in the last step of his jerky upwards dance and flopped back to the ground. But then my curses and blows stirred him to try again and we were up. We were both tired enough to allow the knight to take the reins and to suffer without protest the ignominy of being led.

The sun had now almost touched the horizon in front of us. My guides – or my captors – were clearly anxious to reach their camp before darkness fell. The rays of the setting sun poured up the wide valley, reddening the faces of the three men around me.

"Look!" said the one riding on my right. He pointed

upward and I saw there a great castle outlined against the burnished sky. From its flat-topped rock it commanded the valley, and as if in admiration the sun lapped its walls with colour. "When we have taken it we will build there the strongest fortification the world has ever seen!"

'That may take a little while, given how strong it looks already,' I judged but managed enough discretion to keep my thought to myself. Thereafter we rode in silence, and it was not long before we reached the camp. I saw at once that my unspoken judgement about their siege could not be faulted. At the siege of Jerusalem Raymond had been able to call on some five thousand men, perhaps a third of the total Crusader strength, after hundreds of his men, disgruntled with his arrogant style, had leached away to our contingent under Duke Godfrey. But now, in this little camp, he cannot have commanded even one twentieth of that number. Was this all that remained of the great army which had set off in its tens of thousands from Provence just a handful of years before? Perhaps Baldwin's strength had been equally reduced. If so, reaching the King and executing my task of revenge might be easier than I feared.

I was taken straight to Count Raymond's tent. His grand manner was unchanged, as if he still had thousands at his beck and call. His single eye scanned me with as much arrogance as ever. But his hair had lost all pretence at blackness, and was now bleached a pale gray by age and Outremer's sun.

"Ni! What have you brought me here?"

Hearing the Count's nasal accent again, I had to struggle to keep a discourteous smile from my lips. I bowed deeply, which had the benefit of hiding my face until I had composed it with appropriate respect.

"My Lord Count, I had the honour to make your acquaintance in Antioch. There is no reason for you to remember, but Sir Hugh de Verdon is my name."

To my surprise Raymond hauled himself painfully to his

feet. I had not expected such a courteous greeting. I noted fleetingly that he suffered from a severe limp, but then my attention was drawn by the look of apoplectic rage on his face.

"Ni! So you are one of treacherous Tancred's creatures, are you? You have a nerve appearing here before me after the way he treated me." He turned towards one of the knights who had brought me in but I interjected quickly before he could give his order.

"No, my Lord, I was never with Tancred. I was Duke Godfrey's secretary. I was in Duke Godfrey's retinue during the siege and battle of Antioch. I took part in the great battle that saw off Atabeg Kerbogha."

"Duke Godfrey, ni? He did me few favours, but at least he did not trick me and throw me in one of his prisons." Raymond's anger seemed to threaten to get the better of him again.

"Threw you in prison, my Lord? I had not heard of such scandalous behaviour." I injected as much outrage and surprise into my voice as I could muster. "I have been held a prisoner myself for a long while, in a Saracen prison to the east of here. So I had not heard of your captivity at Norman hands. And I am here with important news for you from Homs. The Emir has this very morning been murdered. His city is in a state of panic and from what I know will shortly become a pawn in the game between Ridwan's Aleppo and Duqaq's Damascus. Both may have armies far larger than yours, but they are divided and will be at each other's throats. I hope that you may turn this news to your advantage."

Raymond brightened. "Ni, this could indeed be useful news. I beat them outside Tripoli when I had my faithful three hundred against thousands of theirs! Call my council!"

Then, as he dismissed me and turned away he spoke to a knight whom I took to be his quartermaster, "Get this man whatever he needs!"

I was ushered out of the tent with greater respect than had

been shown to me on the way in. I immediately requested two horses for the morrow, and the equipment that I lacked – most of all, a shield and a lance. I explained that my duty was to rejoin King Baldwin, my former master's brother – with caution lest Baldwin too had done something to upset the irascible Provençal. However, it transpired that Count Raymond now grudgingly acknowledged Baldwin's position as the King of Jerusalem, so that here I was on safer ground. What is more, I learnt that Baldwin had last been heard of heading to besiege the port of Acre.

So when the next morning Raymond's sadly small band of men received their orders to raise their siege of Qalat al-Hosn, such as it had been, to strike camp and to march in battle order towards Homs, I seized the opportunity to head in the opposite direction with my new supplies. Once again I seemed fully a Crusader knight. But my Arab garments, which had served me so well, nestled safely in my saddle bag. Who could tell when I might need them again?

My plan was simple. I would move towards the coast, avoiding human habitations. Once close to the sea I would turn south and follow it down towards Acre. There I would make further enquiries about Baldwin's movements. Then I would find him, surprise him – for he thought me dead – and take my revenge. Afterwards, almost like Hasan's *da'is*, I scarcely cared what happened. Or at least I could not see that far ahead. Except that, if I did survive, I would search for Jesus.

In the foothills of the mountain ranges that ran along the coast I could find grazing for my horses, and streams to water them. I planned to eat and drink when I could but was not too concerned, for although hunger and thirst would discomfort me, Hasan had freed me of any absolute need for such sustenance to survive. I thought that the dangerous animals that made the mountains their home – lions, bears, jackals, perhaps leopards – would stay well away from me. If they did dare to come too close at night my horses would be good sentries and would alert me if I slept.

As I rode I thought often of Baldwin, stoking my hatred. Around my neck I felt the burning noose to which he had subjected me at our last encounter, choking the wind out of me, if not the life. I remembered the pain and the humiliation of the kicking I had taken from him and his henchmen. Then I recalled the attempts he had made on my old master's life. I had thwarted the first attack with poison on Godfrey – and later killed the dark Armenian Bagrat who had tried to administer that venomous draught. I shivered at the memory of the barbaric thrill I had felt when I wrenched my blade through Bagrat's stomach, killing a man for the first time. But I had been unable to protect Godfrey when Baldwin's sabotage to his saddle had dropped him at the mercy of the bear he was hunting. Godfrey had survived, indeed recovered, but the awful wound in his loins had taken its toll and stripped him of his vigour. How Godfrey would have enjoyed the game here in the hills through which I now rode! I smiled at my memory of his zest for life. It was Baldwin's fault that his capacity for enjoyment had come to a premature end. So Godfrey had slept with his brother's wife. That was Baldwin's fault for being a cold lover. Then, with sudden insight, I wondered if Baldwin had preferred Bagrat. I had always thought that his wife Godehilde had died from their poison. And the poor Pecheneg prisoners tortured outside the walls of Constantinople, the Norman Crusaders left heartlessly to their fate before the closed gates of Tarsus, the women and children in that little village in Armenia...yes, Baldwin deserved to die.

Nursing these bitter thoughts, I passed into a stand of extraordinary trees. Red branches waved at me with dark green feathery fans of leaf. Their smell swirled in the air and filled my nostrils. I could not have joined my arms around their rough flaking trunks. I stopped, amazed, to gaze at such magnificence. Breathing deep, I sucked in the crispness which cleaned away my caustic thoughts. The ground around was carpeted in rich brown fragments of bark and fallen foliage, which exuded the same resinous aroma under the pressure of my horses' hooves. These trees, I realised, must be the famous cedars of Lebanon, spoken of with such love in the Song of Solomon. Under each spread a pool of deep shade. But as every one stood a respectful distance apart from the other, light filtered down between, allowing grass and other plants to grow. I rode deep into this magical forest before stopping to sleep under the canopy of the greatest tree I could find. There, I rested for a while on my back, my eyes wide, watching its branches brandish their leaves blackly against the clear starry sky.

Dawn broke and with regret I rode on. As I came closer to the forest edge I found clearings where many of these great trees had been felled. Had they been destined for Solomon's palanquin, I wondered, or intended as the beams of his temple? Perhaps those were worthy purposes for timber such as this, or even as the coffin of some princess. But I feared lest they had been fashioned instead by the wicked hands of man into the weapons that helped to fill coffins.

Much further on in my journey, many days later, those trees were still in my mind, when the painful realities of war were brought back to me again. As usual, the flight of vultures and other carrion birds gave their warning from afar. I came into what had once been a village. It was full of the bitter odour of the times. Heaps of ash, some still ominously smoking, showed where small houses had once been. In places a few crude stone walls still stood. At my approach blood-soaked birds lazily lifted their well-fed weight from their meals to flap a little further off and settle down again on another corpse. I also startled two small children, doubtless orphans made by this massacre, who scurried off to cower in another ruin. I realised that in my mail I must look like their attackers. I dismounted and approached them slowly, as one would a scared animal. They were too tired, or too hungry, or too hopeless, to run further.

"Who did this?" I asked in Arabic as gently as my anger allowed. They looked surprised to hear me address them in their own language. One was too afraid to answer, the other, the smaller, too afraid not to.

"The King. The King of Jerusalem," she muttered blankly. "My father shouted that, before…"

"And which way did they go?" I said quickly.

She just jerked her head to the south.

I wondered how the children had survived; from the state of the bodies I judged that the attack must have taken place at least three days before, and the corpses would have brought jackals and perhaps even larger predators, lion and leopard.

"Do you want to come with me? You cannot stay here."

The two pitiful little creatures exchanged glances. They were scared of me, but more scared still of whatever they had seen at night in this place of death.

"Yes," said the small one, the girl, in a voice so quiet that I could scarcely hear. So I lifted them both onto my spare horse. I knew nothing of children and was surprised by how light they were. As food, all I had were a few wild berries, which I offered to them. They guzzled them greedily and washed down the poor meal with the dregs of water from my leather bottle. Then I led them on carefully at a gentle pace. I hoped to come to another, happier place of habitation, to be able to leave them there in someone's care.

Acre I knew must lie to the west, through the hills now on my right. I needed to find out whether it had fallen, or if it was still besieged. Then I could work out the lie of the land and make my plan for confronting Baldwin. So I turned down the first valley that looked as if it led in that direction. The way soon narrowed into a defile, stony underfoot and almost completely blocked in places by boulders. I thought that I had made a mistake and I was about to turn back, when a menacing group of ragged men grew from the ground in front of me like Cadmus's army. I was about to pull my mount's head round and ride back the way I had come for all I was worth, when I remembered the children. And then I looked round and saw that another group of men had appeared from the rocks behind me. Several had bows, drawn back and arrows notched.

"Be careful of the children," I shouted in the Arab tongue. "Hold your fire."

"What is this?" growled a black-bearded man in front of me. His head was wound round with a filthy grey turban, but I now saw that his robe was a little less ragged than his companions'. From this, the curved sword strapped at his side, and his air of authority, I took him as the leader of this motley band. "A *Franj* who speaks our tongue? But no surprise that he uses it to give us orders." One or two of those nearby gave a grim laugh at this sally.

"Why are you here? And why do you have those children? Are they yours?"

Again, this raised a weak laugh. The bandit captain seemed proud of his wit.

"I found them in the ruined village back there. I could not abandon them to the lions and jackals, so I brought them with me, hoping to find a safer place to leave them."

"Most likely he was going to eat them. These *Franj* eat children if they can't get anything else." This unhelpful comment came from an unsmiling older man, in whose prematurely white beard and blank palsied face I read some unspeakable loss. From his place beside the captain he shook his spear at me aggressively. It was makeshift but looked sharp enough. "Let's not waste any more time."

"He has not answered my other question," objected the captain. "And I like his face – he looks honest – I can always tell an honest man." Again the brigands laughed, with the exception of the man beside the captain, whose expression remained slack and empty. "Why are you here?"

"I am here to kill the King." It was my turn to provoke laughter among the gang. "King Baldwin is my sworn enemy. He has blood on his hands for which I will make him pay." The laughter had turned to sullen disbelief. I saw that I was losing them and the circle around me tightened.

"Wait. Ask the children what to do with me. Ask them how I treated them."

"Ask the children?" The captain roared with laughter again. "You would have us ask the children? Should I put them in charge?"

"He gave us some food," piped a small voice from behind me. "And the water left in his bottle."

The boy spoke for the first time. "He did not hurt us."

"Very well," said the captain. "It seems your act of kindness has bought you some time. Take off your sword, dismount, and come with us."

Reluctantly I unstrapped my sword. The Venetian embroidery on the long leather scabbard was worn in places, battered and stained since the day when Godfrey had given it to me and made me a knight. That – its moment of gift – was perhaps the happiest memory that it evoked. Its violent actions since brought forth more ambivalent feelings. But it was my most precious possession, and I quailed to see it held by the slack-faced man, presumably the gang's lieutenant. He caressed the sheath with greedy hands, pulling the sword halfway out to examine the blade, but still with no expression on his pale flaccid face.

For a while we tracked the bottom of the defile. In places it opened out, before closing in again. I thought it a fine place for an ambush. Then, in single file, we turned sharply to the left up the hillside on what might have been a path made by deer or by goats. Looking back I saw that two of the band were taking great care to eliminate all trace of our passage, concealing any marks made by the hooves of my horses, and sweeping from side to side with a pair of tree branches.

The track followed round the side of the hill, rising all the time. From below, it seemed to reach a dead end and peter out, but as we came closer I saw that it passed into a fold in the hillside that was masked from view by a thicket of rough shrubs. Then, behind, loomed the mouth of a cave. Inside, a wide space opened into the pale limestone. It smelt dry. The earth floor was clean, and well swept. The few belongings that I could see in the cave – some weapons, and items of bedding – were neatly laid out. A small cooking fire burned in one corner, giving flames but little smoke. Plainly the wood had been carefully chosen for its dryness. Two men looked up from it as we entered. The leader of this rough band deserved respect for the order he had instilled.

My horses were hobbled near the entrance and watered. I was pleased to see that someone had thought to cut them some fodder on the way up. My pleasure faded, though, when the debate began again about my fate.

The man who had taken possession of my sword spoke again to his leader. Perhaps he thought that his ownership of my weapon would be more secure if I were done away with. The passion in his voice was at odds with the absence of emotion in his ruined face. The others listened to him carefully, seriously, but without the affection that they showed at their leader's humour. I imagined the white-bearded man killing, suffering and causing pain, fighting with ferocity but with no expression on his face, and I shivered slightly.

"We must finish him. We swore never to allow an infidel into this place. He will betray us and you will regret it – all for some sentimentality over the way he has treated a pair of children."

I took a pace forward, and halted at the angry looks which were turned my way.

"You are wrong to call me infidel. I am as good a Moslem as you. *Ash-hadu anla elaha illa-Allah wa ash-hadu anna Mohammadan rasul-allah.* I bear witness that there is no god worthy of worship save Allah, and I bear witness that

108

Mohammed is his servant and his messenger. If you wish, I will recite to you from the Koran. With which *sura* shall I start?"

A sardonic smile played across the lips of the leader. I could read nothing from the blank face of my enemy but imagined him seething inside with anger. I was preparing myself for his next argument when a scout rushed into the cave. All attention turned to him.

"A body of mounted *Franj* have camped at the mouth to our valley. I counted knights five times the fingers on my hand. Their leader is a tall man on a black horse, with a beard as black as his horse and a face as pale as your beard." He pointed at the man who wanted my death. "But the shape of his beard is not like yours." He turned back to the leader. "It is small, trimmed neat along the jaw and over the upper lip."

"That must be Baldwin." I spoke with rising excitement. "What banners did they carry?"

The look-out must have thought me some strange new recruit to the band. Anyway, he responded to the authority in my voice.

"I saw one with three red circles on a gold field…"

"Boulogne…"

"…and one white with a gold crown over a red cross…"

"…the Kingdom of Jerusalem. Without a doubt it's Baldwin."

I turned to the bandit leader. "Have you ever fought knights like this before? I know this man, and I know how he fights. He will not rest until he has eliminated every last one of you. Or until he is dead. I will kill him for you, and I will show you how to drive his men away."

"We will do what we have always done. We will post our archers above the valley, and pick them off as they ride up. That is how we have always kept at bay the men of the Emir of Acre." I could see nothing in white beard's expressionless face, but thought I detected uncertainty in this last sentence of his.

109

"You fool. These knights wear mail that is too strong to be pierced. Look."

I grabbed an arrow from a quiver stacked against the cave wall behind me. The circle around me backed away, expecting me to do them some harm. But I slammed it into my own chest as hard as I could.

"You see?"

For a moment I thought I had gone too far. My opponent began to slide his – my – sword from its scabbard. Then the commander stepped forward and placed his hand on his lieutenant's sword arm.

"Wait. Let's hear what our guest has to say. Remember the proper rules of hospitality." His troop laughed and the tension eased.

"Well, first, if you use archers, you must aim for the horses. But many of those are armoured too. And they are great strong beasts – you can stick them with many arrows and still they will not fall. Hot oil would be best, if you had it, but rocks will serve. You need to lure them into your valley, to a place which is narrow enough to throw rocks down on them. Their armour is then little protection. But unless you kill their leader – Baldwin – they will fight hard. Even if you force their retreat, they will come back in greater force – again and again until they achieve their end. So I will take Baldwin on hand to hand and kill him. But I will need my weapons."

I looked hard at the palsy-faced man. The leader was serious for a moment, and thoughtful.

"I like your plan with the rocks, and it will be done. But how can you be so sure that you can kill this king of yours?"

"Because…because he thinks I am dead," I answered with heavy earnest. "Four years ago he hanged me. He watched me swing by my neck for hours. He will think I have come back from beyond the grave to claim him. He will be terrified. That will give me advantage enough."

"But how…" Then the bandit commander shrugged and

grinned as he saw several of his men surreptitiously making the sign against the evil eye.

"He's no ghost. He's solid enough. Look." He punched me on the shoulder. "Ouch. Hard too."

This time, though, his humour had no effect. His lieutenant blankly refused to relinquish my sword. Some of the band – especially those who had made the sign against the evil eye – supported him. Others were for giving me my chance. All did agree that men should be posted along the top of the valley with a plentiful supply of rocks, and at least this part of my plan was prepared. But I was in despair when they tied my arms and legs tightly for the night and secured me to a large boulder near the entrance to the cave. Most then disappeared through an archway at the rear, which I assumed led into an adjoining cave, or into some inner sanctum where they slept. Perhaps they kept their women in there. At least I was close to my horses. We looked at each other and I tried to imagine their sympathy. Then I closed my eyes in an attempt to sleep.

I must have succeeded, because the next thing that I remember was a soft voice, and a hand nudging me. "Wake up, wake up." It was the boy. "Here." He had my sword. His small fingers made easy work of my knots. I ruffled his hair. "Thank you."

Then, just as I was about to rise to my feet, another figure entered the room. The bandit commander's expression was stern. The boy turned, tensed and ready to run. I made to slide my weapon from its sheath.

Then the black beard cracked open in its habitual smile. "Ah. So you have it already! You young fellow – you are a man after my own heart, but you had me worried for a moment when I could not find the sword in there. Now go," he ordered me, "wait at the far end of the open space beyond the defile. We'll lead your Baldwin in there, and then, good luck." Reading correctly the expression of concern on my face, he said, "Don't worry about that. After all, ghosts cannot be held by ropes! The boy will not get into trouble. And the two guards outside are my trusted men. But when you are done I think you should ride on. Disappear back into the spirit world! May Allah be with you."

As quietly as I could I slung my saddle over the back of the larger of my two horses. I placed my lance in its sling and hung my shield from the pommel.

"I can only take one," I said to the boy. "That other, he is for you." Surprise and then delight turned his expression from solemnity to joy. For a moment he looked his real age, not old and weighed down by all his sorrows. "Thank you and good luck," I said to him, feeling warm and ready to face Baldwin.

That warmth ebbed away quickly in the cold hour before dawn as I waited behind a boulder out of sight at the end of the little valley. I stomped up and down, shivering, as much from nerves as from the cold, for at this time of year even in the deep valleys of the hills the temperature did not fall too far. My horse hung his head unhappily, picking up my nervous mood, and sorry to be separated from his companion of several weeks. The sun caught the top of the gorge, and my attention, and picked out a small group of mountain goats perched precariously on a ledge far too narrow for a man. Was I on such a ledge, and about to fall into oblivion? Then they moved, jumping onwards with incongruous but surefooted grace.

They had heard movement further down the valley. Soon I could hear noise too – harsh shouts, falling stones, and the sliding of iron clad hooves on rock. Up one side of the valley I could see the brigands' decoys scrambling, sending stones and dust showering down. A missile flashed up the hillside – a crossbow bolt – and then another. This second struck its mark, and slowly its target began to lose purchase and slip backwards down the slope. I could see the bolt lodged in his buttock as he scrabbled to arrest his fall. A cheer rose from throats unseen in the valley beyond. I looked away and climbed slowly into my saddle, and waited.

The intruders' noise became louder. I was counting on Baldwin being at the front of his small contingent. Cowardice had never been one of his faults. I hoped that kinghood had not been accompanied by caution. I wanted him – I needed him – to see me. I judged now by the echo of the hooves that they were through the defile. I imagined that they were fanning out from single file to form up and make their plan for following the brigands cautiously up the slope.

I edged my horse from my place of concealment. My end of the valley was still in shadow. There, fifty paces ahead of me, stood a body of men, mounted and clothed in similar style to me – mail, surcoats, some more heavily armoured with helmets enclosing part of their face, and greaves on their legs. Then I lost their detail. All my attention bore on the man at their centre – on a fine black stallion, his surcoat black with a gold crown and red cross, a helmet of highly polished steel with a narrow nose guard reaching down to his cruel thinly moustached mouth. On the rim of his helmet rested a gold circlet announcing that this was indeed the King of Jerusalem.

I stopped on the edge of the shadows. My lance was upright in my right hand. My shield still hung from my saddle. One or two of the more alert knights pointed towards me. My tense excitement seemed to speed the passage of time so that they seemed to me to be moving their limbs as slowly as old men. I nudged my mount forward. The rays of the rising sun now caught my head. I felt its warmth and light like a halo. With my left hand I pulled back my mail cowl and shook out my hair. Now I took up my shield and bellowed as loud as I could.

"Baldwin. Black Baldwin. I, Hugh de Verdon, am returned to avenge my death at your hands. I strike this blow for myself and for my master Godfrey and for all those unfortunates whom you have hurried so unjustly from this world into the next."

My lance was now set. My horse had continued to walk forward so that Baldwin was now only twenty strides away.

I could clearly see his horror, and his pale face seemed to turn paler still. My senses were extraordinarily acute, sharpened by suspense. I heard every word he spoke.

"No. It is not possible. I saw you swing for two hours, maybe three. How can one who was dead be alive once more? It is like the Moses legend – the man we heard of down south in the city of rock! No!"

Now I set spurs to my horse. It leapt forward. A frenzied war cry broke from my throat. Baldwin's haughty expression crumpled into terror. He wrenched his mount around to gallop for the narrow exit from his valley of death. His horse was quick but my momentum was too much for him. I lanced him just above the small of his back. He threw up his arms, as if commending his soul to God or to his true master in Hell, and collapsed from his saddle, twisting the lance from my grasp. I rasped out my sword and hacked once to each side at the knights behind, but then I was in the narrow defile and riding as fast as the rocky going would allow.

I took one quick look over my shoulder. Baldwin's men had overcome some of their shock and surprise, and some were rushing into the defile after me. Then I heard great rocks thundering down from the cliffs above, and crashes and cries of consternation behind me. My bandit friends had fulfilled their part of the plan. With satisfaction I thought to myself that they would have earned themselves peace in their mountains for a good long time.

✳

SAINT LAZARUS' COLLEGE

Spirits in the Senior Common Room were low as the dons contemplated their own mortality. Tempers were frayed by fear, in spite of the security now established in the College. In the past, the Master had often been heard to complain about the excessively cloistered and otherworldly nature of the establishment over which he presided. He used to be fond of talking about how he wanted to open up the College to the real world. Now he was rather grateful that there was only one way in and out, through the gate to the front quad. It had been easy to set up a security barrier there. Nobody could come or go without passing through the porter's lodge. To its former occupants' chagrin, it was now staffed round the clock by at least two burly security guards. The undergraduates were all complaining, but so what, thought the Master. If it made it a bit more difficult for them to lead their lives of drunkenness and promiscuity, so much the better. They'd just have to do their rutting with fellow members of the College – that is why they had wanted to go co-ed, after all and do all their boozing in the student bar instead of causing trouble in the pubs of the town.

"1103."

The Master looked up angrily. It had been made very clear to all the Fellows that they were at serious risk if they strayed outside the College walls. Who was the idiot planning to take the train to London?

"1103 – these events absolutely fix the time of Hugh's story."

The Master relaxed. It was only Mark banging on about his factual obsession again. But how could he worry about dates at a time like this? Had he not taken in that his saintly namesake had been dragged to death behind a horse? The Master shuddered slightly as he wondered, not for the first time, what it felt like to be flayed.

"There is no doubt any more. And they also resolve a minor controversy. You see, the assassination of Janah ad-Daulah, the Emir of Homs, in 1103 is well-documented. It was the first time that the Assassins had struck in Syria – or the first time that it was recorded at least. And there is also reference to King Baldwin's unfortunate accident at the hands of the bandits on Mount Carmel. But it was not clear which happened first. Now we know.

"And friend Hugh will be deeply disappointed. He seems to think he has finished the King. Not a bit of it. For a while they did despair of Baldwin's life – a lance in the kidneys would be pretty nasty now, let alone in the early twelfth century. But they were tough then. Baldwin recovered. He did not die for another fifteen years – in 1118 actually. His panic must have saved him. It must have been more difficult to drive a weapon in deep if your target was moving away from you. And perhaps Hugh just got a bit too excited at the thought of fulfilling his revenge."

The Geography Fellow stared superciliously at the History Don. "The lance must have missed the kidneys themselves and just passed through the soft tissue of the back. It is simply not possible to survive a wound in the internal organs without modern surgery and antibiotics. You historians would do well to learn a little about medical reality, you know."

The History Don looked decidedly irritated to find the newest member of the Senior Common Room trespassing on his own factual territory. He was about to reel off a string of examples of long-dead soldiers who had survived such injuries. However, the Geography Fellow's inability to resist showing off his own knowledge diverted the conflict.

"I went through the Lebanese cedar forests, you know, when I was on my Middle Eastern trip last year. Not many trees are left, but having seen the few that are, I can tell you that our Hugh's description is spot on."

The Best-Selling Author guffawed loudly. He had accepted

the Master's invitation to take up lodgings in the College until all danger was past and was rather enjoying the comfortable cocoon of academia.

"Actually, that was me." His voice oozed with the smooth satisfaction of a flattered writer. "There was nothing in Hugh's manuscript about the trees. These medieval chaps don't seem to have paid much notice to natural beauty. Seem rather to take it for granted. So I have to put in a bit of lyricism of my own to make up for it – my readers expect it, you know – some nice descriptions they can chew away at with their own imaginations. And to be honest, I have not been to that part of the world myself. Its amazing how much local colour you can get from guidebooks and internet videos.

"The trouble is…" The Best-Selling Author's voice took on a confidential tone. "The trouble is, there is a complete gap in Hugh's story at this point. I suppose poor old Lawrence would have called it a *lacuna*. He deals with Baldwin – sorry, Mark, rather he thinks he has – and then loses interest. I know where he ends up, but not how he gets there. Do you think you could help me out a bit with your local knowledge?"

The Geography Fellow looked rather pleased. "I did not actually go through Israel on my trip, but I am sure I can come up with some ideas. They may not be totally authentic, but I will do my best."

✳

Chapter Nine

THE POSSESSED

Il n'est pas une fibre en tout mon corps tremblant
Qui ne crie: O mon cher Belzébuth, je t'adore!

✳

I had hoped to feel fulfilment at the completion of my vengeance. Instead I was empty, drained of all emotion. Sure now that I was not pursued, I slackened my pace. It would take no little time for Baldwin's men to regroup and extricate themselves from the brigands' ambush. Then they would have to lick their wounds and carry back their master's body. I pictured their mournful cortège but still knew no joy.

When I reached the end of the bandit valley I turned to the south. A little further on I came to a stream. My horse pulled his head towards it, reminding me that he had not been properly watered since the afternoon before. A stand of small oak trees ran down to the bank's edge, pierced here and there by the sharp dark blade of a cypress. This seemed as good a place as any to halt and to take stock. I dismounted, let my mount drink his fill, and then led him a short way into the wood. I looped his reins over a low oak branch and then sat down, resting my back against a cypress's rough trunk.

So I had taken my revenge on Baldwin. Of that much there

118

could be no question. My act had been clean, fair and just. So much better than the vengeance I had meted out to Hasan through his son. I shivered, and not because of the cool shade in which I sat. I wished that Baldwin had taken me with him. Why had he not dared to face me, so that he might have stuck me with his lance, as I did him? But that would have achieved little. And what had he meant with those last words of his? What had they been? 'It is like the Moses legend – the man we heard of down south in the city of rock!' Something of that sort. I shifted against the tree in discomfort that was spiritual more than physical.

I had fulfilled my purpose, yet now had a never-ending vista opening empty before me. Somehow I had to fill it. Finding Jesus was the only act left to me that could have any point. If anyone could teach me how to lead my life, it must be he. But how could I set about finding him? Where would I have gone in his shoes? I tried to put myself inside his head.

I pulled up my mail coat and rolled down my breeches. Carefully I unwound the gospel which was bandaged around my left thigh. To my relief, the back-to-front writing was still mostly legible, although pale in places, and sometimes smudged. When I read that gospel for the first time, trapped in that catacomb of dread under Jerusalem, it had helped me to understand Jesus. Perhaps now it could help me again.

I pored through the text, searching for clues. From time to time my horse shifted beside me, unaccustomed to his long rest. Jesus could not have gone back to the places he had frequented before his crucifixion, that much was clear. If he had appeared again, the Acts of the Apostles would have told a very different story, if they had told any story at all. Paul's Epistles would never have been penned. Peter would not have made much of a rock for the church – a church that had in fact been built on the shifting sands of falsehood. I remembered Lazarus' description of his gospel as 'the book that you fear' on the papyrus hidden in Peter's Cave Church in Antioch. How much more would those fathers of the early church have feared the actual reappearance of a Jesus who, according to them, was safely in heaven.

It was mid-afternoon when I struggled to the end of my text and read the last sentence. 'And then Jesus went back into the rocky desert and we saw him no more.' That made sense to me. If I had been Jesus, after everything that had happened, I would have wanted to shut myself away from the world, and to lead the life of a hermit. But it did not give me much of a clue about where this 'rocky desert' might be.

I wrapped the precious bandage back around my leg and clambered with great weariness into my saddle. Peter had come north, first to his homeland of Galilee, and then on to Antioch. I knew that much from my own sojourn there, as well as from my reading of the Acts of the Apostles. Jesus surely would have travelled in the opposite direction. So I rode on southwards.

Once more I travelled away from the main routes, avoiding places of habitation whenever I could. I felt an outcast, incapable of facing my fellow men. So the way I chose skirted around the Holy City a safe distance to the north, and then brought me into the valley of the River Jordan. At the first opportunity I forded the river, thinking that the eastern side would be more deserted. I wondered if I had passed the place where Jesus' baptismal initiation had taken place. The description in the Gospel of Lazarus of the arcane rite we had shared gave little clue to its location.

Then the river valley began to open out and I saw a great inland lake occupying a deep depression in front of me. Reaching it, I urged my horse down to the water's edge, thinking that he could drink his full. He shied away, and when I dismounted the smell rising from the water told me why. It stank of salt, and in places bubbles rose, bringing a black tarry substance with them to the surface.

I headed down the side of this useless brackish lake. When

I saw a small settlement ahead, I turned away east down a wadi which carried a trickle of fresh water. I stopped there for the night before rising with the sun and carrying on my way. With each step south it seemed that the temperature became greater, and the land drier and more barren. My horse began to suffer, and once again I wished for a camel in his place. I had wanted a rocky desert. Now I had certainly found one. Perhaps this was the desert into which Jesus had wandered all those years ago.

The heat pressed down on me and I had to stop before the sun rose too high. I allowed my horse to rest in what little shade the wadi afforded. He stood there, eying me reproachfully, his flanks heaving. He was too tired, too weak even to flick his tail at the flies which seemed to be the only things alive in this inhospitable place.

When the sun was lower in the sky I prepared to ride on, giving my horse the little that remained in my water skins. My own thirst was excruciating but could do me no lasting harm. The drink revived him a little, and I pressed him southwards through the sunset. The moon was nearly full, and flooded the desert with a pale, silvery light that was soft and welcome after the vicious sun. My poor horse began to stumble on the rocks underneath and I knew he could go no further. I decided to stop to give him a few hours rest. He was so exhausted that he lay down to sleep. I lay on my back, wakeful, and watched the mottled silver disc of the moon move slowly through the scattered stars.

It was still before dawn when I judged that my horse had had enough rest. I could see the faintest smudge of light on the eastern horizon and I was anxious to move on, to find water before the sun got too high. I tried to nudge my horse to his feet, gently at first, and then harder. Then I realised that the poor beast would not move again. He had died in the night.

Stiffly I gathered together what I needed. It made a small

enough bundle. I left behind the shield and the saddle that I had had from Raymond of Toulouse's grudging Provençals, and began to trudge south.

The sun rose through the sky with none of his sister's benignancy. He was angry and aggressive. His heat boiled my sense of pointlessness and impotence into the same heated emotions and sullenly, stubbornly, I drove myself forward through his furnace. Once or twice I looked back, and saw the distant spiral of black vultures marking the place where my horse's body lay. The second time I glanced towards these birds of ill omen, I saw a cloud of dust that must be raised by desert riders. As it rolled closer four riders shimmered into view through the sand and the heat.

I remembered what Mohammed had once said to me about the desert tribes who punished anyone who had the temerity to trespass upon their ancestral lands. As I turned and prepared to defend myself I laughed a bitter laugh. What did it matter anyway?

The four camels that raced towards me were the finest I had seen. They were tall, proud and rangy. The first, the tallest, was almost pure white in colour. They slowed, circled round me, and came to a halt. Their riders looked down at me. They were fierce looking men, dressed in long shirts of an indeterminate colour, with tattered cloths wrapped around their heads. Where their hair showed beneath these rudimentary headdresses it was thick and matted with sand, a contrast to their thin, wispy beards. Their leader looked down at me, his tawny eyes flecked with hostility.

"*Allahu Akbar*. Why do you wander in the desert, stranger? The birds' signal of death called us to you."

The man beside him murmured, "Perhaps he is the wanderer of whom we have heard tell."

At these words hostility turned to surprise and hope.

"Is that who you are? Are you the healer? What brings you here from the southern desert?"

My surprise was just as great as my questioner's. Before I could frame any sort of answer, he jerked his head curtly at one of his fellows, who forced his camel to its knees and indicated that I should climb up behind him. We lurched upwards and cantered on in silence – mine brought by surprise at this unexpected treatment, theirs I supposed by habit or simply a desire to keep the sand out of their mouths.

The camels and their masters, adapted to the harsh land where they made their home, rode apparently oblivious through the heat. The sun, tiring at last of its unsuccessful efforts to hinder our progress, had sunk low in the sky to the west by the time we reached a camp of black tents. It was placed by the opening to a wadi which I supposed funnelled moisture when it rained, for there remained enough scrappy vegetation here to provide sustenance for my hosts' herd of small black and brown goats. I saw also other camels hobbled but able to move far enough to graze, and made out the mud brick rim of a well. Dried droppings like walnuts pitted the surface of the sand.

"My son is ill, dying," explained the Bedouin leader. The urgency with which the rider in front of me pressed the camel to his knees told me that the child must be very sick indeed. "Show us what you can do."

I could scarcely tell my hosts – hosts or captors? – that I was not whom they thought, that they had confused me for another. It was better perhaps to do what I could to comfort the child, and, when my care failed to cure, to face the consequences. So I allowed myself to be led to the tent where he lay.

At the sight I filled with pity. The boy was perhaps six or seven years old. He squirmed on a blanket that looked as if it had been made of camel wool a long time ago. His emaciated body was covered in pustules, livid even against his dark skin. A woman squatted beside him on her haunches, swathed in a voluminous indigo cloak so that only her eyes showed. That she was his mother was confirmed by the anguish blazing from them. She waved away the flies that tried to come to drink from the moisture around the poor boy's eyes. These he opened at my approach. They were black, unnaturally large in his face, and shone with painful resignation.

What could I do? I squatted down beside him in the manner of the woman, full of impotent pity, and reached out my hand to his forehead. It felt hot, furious with fever, and hoping to sooth him I let my hand rest there. For a moment I closed my eyes, habit almost forcing me to think a prayer. My fingers and my palm began to become uncomfortably hot. My first thought was that the boy's fever was rising fast and that he could not last long. Then I realised that the heat came from me, from within. I felt some strange power surging through me into the small body lying there. Surprise opened my eyes and I saw that he had stopped twisting and turning on his blanket. His pain and resignation turned to confusion, then composure, and he sighed gently, closed his eyes and lay still.

The mother did not speak, leaving the anxious father to ask the question. "Is he dead?" Anger lurked beneath those words.

I felt suddenly drained, exhausted, as if all the life force had emptied out of me. It was as much as I could do to take my hand from the boy's forehead and rise to my feet.

"No. He sleeps. Leave him be until he wakes. And now I must rest."

I staggered out and was shown a place in the men's tent to sleep. I collapsed to the ground and was immediately unconscious.

When I woke from my deep and utterly dreamless sleep the sun had already climbed well into the sky. I knew how my patient fared as soon as I emerged through the tent flap and saw the Bedouins' expressions. In the father's face gratitude outshone awe. The others were reluctant to meet my gaze or to come too close. Both told me that whatever strange magic I had worked had driven away the boy's fever.

I asked the father if I might enter the other tent and when he assented I knocked against the flap and entered. The boy was sitting up on his camel wool rug, laughing like a six year old should. When he saw me, he stopped, alarm mixing with his joy. The eruptions over his skin were fading fast. With a smile of reassurance I reached forward to feel his forehead. It was cool to my touch.

With difficulty I concealed that I was as surprised as my hosts. Deference was now allied to their natural desert hospitality. A carpet – threadbare but the best they had – was laid out for me and I was made to sit down. From the fire they brought a sharp-spouted jug of beaten copper and poured a thick black liquid into a small pottery cup for me. It tasted bitter but refreshing. They rolled a handful of flour with water and laid the dough in the embers of the fire. When it was sealed they flipped it over, and once cooked this simple bread was passed to me with ceremony. Their silent respect gave me time to think.

So I had discovered by chance that I was able to transfer some of my regenerative power by touch, and so somehow to heal others. Could I repair wounds, I wondered, as well as cure disease? With a sharp pang I thought of what might have been if I had been at Blanche's deathbed. I dragged my mind away from the past. This wanderer of whom they had spoken the day before, this healer whose powers I apparently shared, must surely be the man I was seeking. There could be no other explanation. I now had to find him without revealing to these Bedouin that I was not he.

I had saved the boy's life, it seemed, but at the cost of condemning one of the goats to death. The grateful father pulled it bleating from his small herd, wrestled it to one side and cut its throat over a large dish. As the poor beast's innocent life blood pulsed out into it I could not help but think of the

125

grail. Quickly it was skinned, dismembered and given over to the women to cook. More coffee was poured for me, brown fruits were offered, their sweet flesh surrounding long thin stones, and the men settled down to talk.

"Well, Master." The father addressed me with the utmost respect. "We have never heard of you before travelling north of *petra*. Truly Allah answered our prayers and brought you to us. Jamal is the only son left to me. Three others have I buried."

"There are many rocks in this desert," I replied, wondering why he had used the Greek word. "By which would you bound my wanderings?"

"No, Master, Petra I mean, Petra the stone city, the city of ruins."

"Ah, Petra, of course!"

It fell into place. I now understood part of the meaning of Baldwin's last words; and perhaps too the final sentence of the Gospel of Lazarus.

"Some impulse brought me here, guided perhaps by Allah, may he be praised, in answer to your prayer. But to Petra and the south I must return."

The meal came, stewed goat piled on a mound of rice, which I feared must be this family's entire food supply for days. Respectfully they waited for me to dip first into the communal dish, before joining in, kneading balls of rice and meat in the fingers of their right hands. With ceremony my host offered me the choicest portions of goat. These included an eyeball, which I understood to be the greatest delicacy of all from the flourish with which it was extended. So I could not refuse. I fear my attempted smile of gratitude turned to a grimace as the orb gave every impression of swelling in my mouth. I forced it down whole, which provoked a violent but involuntary belch. My hosts seemed delighted, and appeared to accept that I could eat no more, however much they pressed me.

The next day I took my leave. They provided me with a fine she-camel and equipment for my journey and also pressed on me robes of their own kind, insisting that they were most comfortable for riding through the desert. They pointed me towards the route they called the 'Highway of the King', and not wanting to raise suspicion by showing ignorance I thanked them without further questions about the way. We parted with great cordiality but beneath their smiles I detected gladness that their mysterious visitor was moving on. Even the vigour with which the cured boy waved me off expressed relief.

The bizarre landscape through which I wandered now seemed to echo the strangeness I felt inside. First I rode for leagues through rocks the warm grey of old sunlight. Then, as the sun set, they turned to copper statues burning with some inward flame. After another hour's ride I came to a field of knee high grass whose soft furry heads rocked gently in the breeze, silvered by the moon. Here I stopped, thinking it good grazing for my camel. In the morning the grass was gold, not silver, and I moved on.

The wind had blown steadily but gently through the night, and now it began to get up. Sand began to stream from the dunes, and a brown wall rushed at me, closing in a blanket of stinging fragments around my camel. I pulled my headdress over my face, grateful for its protection against the rags of dirt-ridden air that now tried to clothe me. My camel shuddered to a halt, and I dismounted and turned her back and mine to the wind to shelter side by side as best we could.

The storm roared around me with hungry ferocity. We were alone in the world, my camel and I, isolated in a cloud of angry grit. I imagined the animal's supercilious expression of injustice at her treatment by the elements. I could not share her resentment because to me this punishment was what I merited. Eventually whatever force that drove the storm decided that I had been chastised enough – or just took pity on my innocent mount – for the wind dropped and with it the sand in the air.

I stood up and tried to shake the dirt out of my clothes. Then I gave up, for it had worked its way into every crevice of my body. I rode on over the mail-scaled sand, feeling that I was deservedly wearing a hair shirt.

Now the way was obscured by soft waves of windswept sand. My trust in my camel was repaid when she brought me to the paved remnants of an ancient road. Four days more I travelled, as the barren landscape changed from gold to deep grey to black, then to red and back through the colours again. I followed bald paths worn over the ages through the rock, shallow depressions through the gravel, and occasionally found again traces of antique paving. In places I skirted villages and watered my camel without interference at their wells. Once or twice I had to halt to ask directions; always they pointed me further south.

At last I entered a deep gorge whose strangely clipped cliffs were streaked and marbled in many shades of pink. The gorge narrowed and twisted, and then I came to a wall in this strange place, built of grainy stone of compressed sand, pink like the cliffs around, from which it had doubtless been hewn. That nothing hung in the space where a gate should have been told me that the city it once defended was a city no more. Here and there the cliffs to the side were pocked with holes, with occasional embellishments of columns and pediments, as if they were dwellings of some kind – but whether for the living or for the dead and their ghosts I knew not.

The canyon twisted past a building cornered with four tall pointed stones and I threaded through a great arch to enter a paved street. This thoroughfare was now lined with niches filled with statues of strange gods. From the offerings placed before them I learned that there must after all be some people here. Then, through the gorge which had narrowed and deepened so that I could scarcely see the sky over my head, I glimpsed a six-columned temple carved deep into the rock, its leafy capitals and triangular pediment weathered but just as fine as anything I had seen even in the ancient city of Constantinople. I paused, and gaped, and rode on.

The gorge now opened out and I entered a wider, flatter area that I took to be the main part of this stone city. Here buildings had once been constructed from blocks in the traditional way, all quarried from the same distinctive pink rock, but now they lay scattered in broken heaps. I rode down a street of shattered colonnades. Once it might have rivalled Antioch's main street, the similar style of whose arcades I remembered. When I had arrived there I had found a different form of desolation, for then the walls had been splashed with blood and dog-worried corpses still lay bloating in the aftermath of siege.

Here I now saw a few living people, some emerging like crabs from hiding holes in the rocks. One old man was bolder than the rest and greeted me, addressing me in the Arab tongue which suited my desert costume.

"Welcome stranger! Come with me. Allow me to provide you with a roof over your head. Mine is the only *khan* left in this sorry city that is not open to the stars. All the travellers who come to poor Petra stay with me. What would such a monopoly have been worth in our glory days! Caravan after caravan once passed this way, bearing rich cargoes of frankincense and myrrh from the south, or pitch and copper from the mines to the north. Then came the earthquake and shook down our fine buildings. That was in my grandfather's day. The temples and market we might have built again, but the great cisterns that our forefathers had crafted from the living rock were cracked and broken beyond repair. So with no water the trade went elsewhere." He waved vaguely towards the north. "Don't worry, though," he went on, imagining concern beneath my fatigue, "there is still plenty to slake your thirst and your camel's. And you will find a handful of other travellers, so if you have money you can share in the goat that I will kill for them."

In the saddlebags given to me by my grateful Bedouin I still hoarded some of the coin that I had received in Aleppo from the Assassin horse dealer. So I was able to accept this offer and take lodgings in the old man's battered caravanserai behind the arcaded street. Like the ill-fated place in Aleppo where I had briefly stayed with Mohammed, it lay close by the market – or what had once been the market. I steeled myself against my guilty memories, for in this place I thought to have my best chance of finding an answer to the riddle spoken by Baldwin before he died. The thought of Aleppo also made me fear that the Assassins' tentacles might stretch this far south, and even that the keeper of this caravanserai – or some of his guests – might be agents of theirs. Then I dismissed the thought, sure that my identity was well concealed beneath my Bedouin robes. Anyway, I liked the old man. His proud face was quite different to the ferret in Aleppo who had betrayed me to his horse trader cousin. He was welcoming but not unctuous in spite of his plain need for my custom. The thick walls of his establishment, if one could call it that, were crumbling, mostly unroofed, with gaps where stone had been carted away, presumably to be reused in other buildings.

I would have been happiest left to my solitude in the corner where I stabled my camel. But in order to share in the other travellers' talk and learn what I could, I prepared to eat in communal conviviality. Two listless wanderers were already hanging about and with twilight a couple more drifted in, on foot so that I assumed they had already stabled their mounts and had been about some business in the stone city. Trade here was perhaps not completely dead. Then, as darkness fell, the look of the place was transformed by the flickering of the cooking fire around the walls. I could almost imagine what it must have been like in the heyday of this strange place. The smell of the spitted goat reminded me that I was famished and my spirits began to rise.

The old man stopped bustling about and indicated that the goat was as ready as it ever would be. He dragged the frame of the spit away from the fire so that I and the four other guests could hack off chunks of meat. I soon found out how much sharper was my knife than my teeth, and that the goat our host had slaughtered was almost as old as the grandfather he had spoken of. I chewed the stringy meat in silence, trying to reduce it enough to swallow.

My neighbour's teeth must have been sharper than mine, or his gullet wider, for he was able to dispose of his mouthful quicker than I and began the typical talk of travellers.

"I hear the monks are building again at Saint Katherine's Monastery. A mosque, of all things there, so I am told. Who had ever heard of a mosque being built by Christian monks inside the walls of a monastery, eh? And the monastery that shelters the place of Moses' burning bush at that."

The man on my other side contradicted him.

"No, they have not started building yet. I passed that way only a week ago. But yes, I heard of their plans when I lodged there."

"Why is it so strange?" asked another. "After all, Moses was a prophet for us Moslems as well as Christians – and for Jews too, I believe. We are all people of the Book. And they say that the Prophet Himself, praised be His name, promised the monks there protection if they would house all travellers, whatever their religion. Fair enough, I say. They have often sheltered me and shown me hospitality."

"Are you sure it was the Prophet, not the hermit?" The fourth man spoke from the far side of the fire and through the flames I saw his hand moving surreptitiously in the sign of the evil eye.

"The hermit?" The first man laughed shortly. "That's just an old wives' tale. In all my trips there I have never seen him. You know what these monks are like – they'll spread any story to stoke the reputation of their foundation."

"Tell me the story," I begged. "I have not been that way before."

The sceptic looked at me sharply. "From your accent I'd say you come from the north. But you are dressed like a man of the desert. And your face – well, if I did not know better, I'd say you had a face like a Frank!"

"Come, come, we are all friends here." The man who had first spoken of the hermit interrupted. I was grateful to him for deflecting this unwelcome attention, even if his interjection was prompted by a desire to tell his story rather than any wish to protect me. He drew a deep breath, and leaned towards me conspiratorially. "Somewhere up on the mountain, the mountain of Moses, lives a hermit, they say."

His neighbour spoiled the dramatic effect of his pause. "No, surely not! A hermit you say?"

"Ah, but this is no ordinary hermit. This one has been there since the time of Moses. Some even say that he is Moses himself!"

"Then you do not know your Bible, friend." This admonition came from the man who had spoken first. "It tells us that Moses died looking over the Promised Land."

"Well, maybe he is not Moses. But he has been there for far longer than a normal man can live. Is that not true?"

This last appeal was directed at the old man in charge of the khan. He shook his head in a cautious affirmative.

"I do remember my grandfather telling such a tale. And the Bedouin have an ancient legend about a wandering healer who appears out of the desert in their hours of greatest need. But back in the days when I used to travel to Saint Katherine's I never heard the monks talking of such a person. So I'd say it is unlikely to be true."

"I'll see what I can find out when I go that way," I smiled, "and I'll come back here and tell you the real story."

I could not sleep at all that night. I tossed and turned in frustration that the dark hours passed so slowly, and before first light I packed up my things and saddled my camel. The old man came up to me, his hardened expression speaking his suspicion that I was trying to leave unnoticed without paying what I owed. I attempted to buy back his favour by offering him a coin worth a little more than my debt, but saw from the set of his face as he tested it in his teeth that I had not succeeded. Sorry, I urged my camel to its feet and set off again.

If the pilgrim path had not been clear I could still have found my way without difficulty just by heading south. The land began to slope away from me and in the distance I saw a long finger of sea. A small village sat at its tip, of fishermen to judge by the few boats drawn up on the shore and the nets spread out in the sun. I guided my camel round this habitation, turning slightly east towards higher land again. I saw no other travellers, even at the wells where I watered my mount. Herds of gazelles scattered at a safe distance away from me, and as I passed clumps of thorny scrub flocks of pink finch-like birds swarmed up, their wings thrumming through the hot air. Once I was safely past, they settled down again. They were no less suspicious of other humans than I.

After two days' ride beyond the sea, tall peaks had emerged in clarity from the horizon's violet smudge. My path led upwards towards a pass. I halted for the night by some grazing, and set off again at first light. I was through the pass before the sun was high, and in the valley below I saw an ancient monastery.

✳

SAINT LAZARUS' COLLEGE

For much of his life the Master had been based in the real world, and so was perhaps less well-suited to the cloistered existence that was now forced upon the members of the Senior Common Room for their own safety. In fact, for all his anger towards the History Don over the misunderstanding about the trip on the 11.03 to London, the Master felt a compelling urge to catch that very same train himself. As it happened, he did have an important monthly meeting in the Vauxhall Ziggurat that housed the office of the agency that he had once overseen. He was reluctant to miss it. He knew how quickly he would lose power and influence if he stopped attending these committees in his *ex officio* role. When the peerage had been secured he could forget about them, but he was not quite there yet. If he took the 11.03 he could get to his club just in time for lunch – Heavens above, he would be safe enough there. And one never knew what useful people he might bump into there. He would have a little time to kill before taking the Underground down to Vauxhall from Green Park, and there he would also be perfectly safe in the crowds.

Wearing a light raincoat, and carrying his tightly rolled umbrella, he breezed past the Porter's Lodge, nodding briskly at the security guards lurking inside.

Following orders, one of the guards immediately put a call through to the Oxford Detective.

The Master was cautious enough to get into the more crowded of the two First Class compartments on one of the little trains – manufactured in France, he always noted with irritation, from the provocative name emblazoned on the step into the carriage – that ran up and down to town. And once at Paddington, rather than trusting himself to the solitude of a taxi, he packed himself safely into an Underground train with the great unwashed.

As a result he was not in the best of tempers when he arrived at the Club, but he was immediately soothed by the faded elegance of the familiar surroundings once he had climbed the steps onto the worn flags of the hall past the porter's respectful greeting.

The cure was completed by an excellent plate of smoked eel and the first partridge that he had tasted that season. At the communal table he had joined two old friends, neither of whom were exactly without influence. He had been a little disconcerted when they had both said that they did not have enough time to go upstairs for coffee. Not wanting to give the impression that he was less busy than they, he had looked at his watch and said, "Good Heavens, is that the time?" and left with them.

Now he had almost an hour to kill before he could reasonably head south to Vauxhall. His irritation began to mount again as he marched along Piccadilly. He stopped half-heartedly in front of an oriental carpet shop and studied the faded rugs between the lurid signs announcing "Sale – 50% off". He noticed the Semitic proprietor staring hungrily at him from the dark interior, and avoided his eye, turning to continue down the street.

Suddenly he had an uncomfortable feeling that someone was following him.

In front, a banner hanging from the Royal Academy of Arts announced 'Byzantium 330-1453'. He turned under Lord Burlington's exquisite archway and took his time to cross the courtyard. He must have been mistaken. There was nobody behind him apart from a couple of foreign students the length of whose skirts beggared belief on this autumn day. 'Surely they won't be allowed in dressed like that,' he found himself thinking.

At the front desk he bought a ticket, and proceeded up the sweeping staircase. On an impulse, he rented one of the audio guides. He listened with growing impatience to the attendant's instructions, expressed haltingly in a strong French accent, and then clamped the headphones to his ears and entered the darkness of the first exhibition room. As this was one of the Royal Academy's blockbuster shows, it was packed with people and he felt safe in the crowd again.

Rather to his surprise, the Master found himself absorbed by the intricate detail of the treasures on display. He admired gold and silver metalwork, skilfully chased and pierced, and rich manuscripts illuminated in crimson, cobalt and gilt. He paused longest in front of a display case holding a mosaic of Jesus as the Man of Sorrows, painstakingly assembled from astonishingly tiny fragments of glass.

Then he was distracted by the reflection of a figure on the glass side of the display case. It was familiar. Surely it was the Oxford Detective? The Master span around, but in the gloom he only caught a glimpse of a soberly dressed person hurrying from the room. Had the Detective followed him from Oxford to keep an eye on him? If so, why had he not just come to make himself known? The Master felt a flash of irritation; he did not like being nannied like this. Then another thought occurred. Perhaps the Oxford Detective was not there to protect him. Perhaps… . After all, the police force was riddled with freemasons, and the freemasons were said to have links with the Templars.

The Master hurried into the last room of the exhibition, which was devoted to icons from the famous Monastery of Saint Katherine at Sinai. He took a cursory glance at one of the paintings, of nervous monks climbing a ladder to heaven, some being welcomed, and others being dragged down to hell by menacing black winged devils. 'A bit like getting into the Lords,' he forced himself to think, with hollow humour, trying to quiet his fear of his pursuer. Then he handed in his headphones, hurried across the courtyard, and turned right towards Green Park Tube Station. Every so often he turned to look over his shoulder, and occasionally he thought he could make out the features of the Oxford Detective bobbing in the crowd.

He threw himself down the steps, rushed through the ticket barrier, and down the escalator to the Victoria Line. He reached the platform just as a train pulled out, taking all the passengers with it. He was left alone, and steps were echoing towards him in the passage behind. He was about to turn round to confront his assailant, when with relief he saw another man emerge from the tunnel at the far end of the platform and come towards him.

He began to walk hurriedly in his direction, then slowed, hesitated, stopped. Wasn't that a gun the man was holding?

"So you are from the Templars," the Master said in resignation. The man with the gun halted in surprise a few paces away. "Aren't you going to flay me first? My name is Bartholomew, you know."

"What are you on about? Templars? Flay you? From Mossad, more like. And this is a Beretta 70."

The barrel of the gun lifted towards the Master, its black mouth seemingly enlarged by the silencer around it. It loomed as large as the Tube tunnel alongside the platform, all-encompassing. The Master heard the roar of an oncoming train and braced himself for the thud of the bullet.

At that moment the Oxford Detective hurled himself past the Master and wrestled for the gun. He tore the weapon out of the would-be assassin's hands, but the momentum of his leap carried him over backwards onto the track into the path of the oncoming train. The Mossad agent took to his heels.

When they extracted the mortal remains of Detective Sergeant Paul Peters from the undercarriage of the train they found at least that he had died quickly. The wheels had completely severed his head from his body.

❋

CHAPTER TEN

DE PROFUNDIS CLAMAVI

J'implore ta pitié, Toi, l'unique que j'aime
Du fond du gouffre obscur où mon coeur est tombé.

＊

The Monastery of Saint Katherine looked as if it had nestled forever in the Sinai desert at the foot of the mountain where Moses received the Commandments from God. From the top of the slope down which I approached, I could see a basilica and the other buildings requisite for a community of monks. As I came closer under the shadow of the thick walls, its peaceful purpose faded and it looked more like a simple desert fortress. The reliability of its water supply was attested by the cypress trees and orchards outside the walls. Once in my naïve piety I might have believed this to be the very site where Moses struck the rock and brought forth water, for there was no doubt about its presence. The track swung me through this oasis of pleasant greenery towards the main gate. Here the monastic affirmed itself once again over the military, for the gate was wide open and the two monks standing there hailed me with a welcome, not a challenge.

"Greetings, traveller, greetings. We ask not from whence you come; we give simple thanks that you have arrived. We pray that your time with us will be long and peaceful."

Almost against my will, I found myself smiling at the honest warmth of these words. They had been spoken in Greek, and I responded in the same tongue. It fell strange and unfamiliar from my lips; I had spoken little save Arabic for so long. If the two monks were surprised to hear their own language emanating from one who looked like a man of the desert, they showed no sign. Instead, with steady courtesy, they guided me towards the courtyard where I could leave my camel, and to the simple cells for pilgrim travellers beyond.

As soon as I had laid down my few belongings a mellifluous bell sounded for the noon prayer – what I would have known as Sext. Habit, courtesy, and a desire to appear no more than the honest pilgrim that I pretended to be, rushed me to the church. I took my place with the other visitors towards the back of the wide nave, beside one of the massive pillars which looked to be hewn from a single piece of granite. The perfume of incense tickled my nostrils. As the community filed in from the side, the pungent aroma was reinforced by the clouds pouring from ornate gilded thuribles carried by the two leading monks.

The soothing Greek chant echoed under the round ceiling and relaxed my limbs. I raised my head to study the rich mosaic gleaming in the round apse above the high altar. I saw that it depicted the Transfiguration of Christ. To his right sat Moses, opposite an Elijah whose brooding expression suggested that he wished it had been he, not his predecessor, who had seen the bush burning in this place. I identified Saints Peter, James and John sitting at their feet, and around them the remaining eight apostles and ten prophets. Two further men I did not know, but from the similarity of their costume to the monks' in the nave I thought them perhaps the Abbot and Prior of the monastery when the mosaic had been completed.

It all seemed so normal, so familiar. The calm brought by

the ritual broke at my realisation that this was the first time that I had knelt in a Christian house of prayer since Alamut – and indeed since well before Alamut. The last time I had even entered a church had been in Jerusalem, during the brutal sack of the city, and then I had not been there to pray. For a moment the emotions aroused by the chant, the incense and my surroundings flowed peacefully. Then they were frozen by cold, conscious thought. Smugly I said to myself that I knew rather more about Christ's real transfiguration than these monks who had sat here under this fine mosaic for half their lives. Then, ashamed of my conceit, I tried to push that thought from my mind. But in its place I found anger that they owned peace and certainty, whilst I suffered the agony of knowledge.

The midday meal followed the service, and we filed into the refectory beyond the church. With relief I found that the pilgrims ate in the same room as the monks, so that we would be governed by the same rule of silence. I would not have to find platitudes to share with my fellow visitors.

When the simple meal of rice and vegetables was done, the Cellarer sought me out. As appropriate to the one who was in charge of pilgrims' comfort and well-being, he looked a convivial soul. The monks here were not tonsured and his reddish hair flopped in a thick fringe over his forehead. His beard tapered like a fox's tail over the white surplice swelling over his stomach. He appeared to have enjoyed the constraint of silence during the meal less than I. Or at least now he appeared keen to talk.

"I had marked you down as a Moslem from your garb," he rumbled. "But your presence in church, and your command of our language, shows you are one of us. Not that we do not welcome Moslems here. Mohammed himself once sought shelter here and was welcomed. His *achtiname* - we keep the original here in the library – his proclamation – has protected our monastery ever since from the followers of Islam. But the power of their prophet's shield might be broken if we failed to welcome them as travellers. Indeed, recently we have been encouraged to begin the construction of a mosque alongside our church. It is only right and proper to provide our Arab guests with every facility to practise their religion, and in these troubled times having a mosque here will provide protection perhaps stronger than can be delivered by the power of prayer."

A look of embarrassment passed over his face, as if he felt that he had been indiscreet. I made sure to smile warmly to signal that I did not disapprove of his comment.

"Your abbot is plainly a wise and practical man."

"This advice came from the one who is wiser still than the Abbot," smiled the Cellarer.

"And who might that be?"

Now the Cellarer's smile froze. "I am sorry. I beg your pardon most humbly. I should not joke like that. I must make confession of my indiscretion. Of course there is no-one here wiser than the Abbot, save our Lord God himself."

He covered his confusion with a hasty sign of the Cross.

Again I signalled that I had taken no offence.

"Of course not. For a moment I thought that perhaps you meant one of the wise hermits who shelter, so I hear, in the caves hereabouts. On my journey here I heard a story about one, even more ancient than the others, who possesses the power of healing."

"The power of healing? There are many hermits in these holy mountains, for sure. Some are old, indeed, but I have never heard of one who could heal the sick. That would be a fine thing indeed!"

I was certain that the Cellarer was lying. Some gleam of alarm had briefly lit his expression. His speech had been hurried. Now he abruptly changed the subject.

"So do you have everything you want? For how long can we expect to enjoy the pleasure of your company here? And how should we address you?"

"My name is Lazarus," I replied.

"Well, Lazarus, may you find here what you seek. May your stay here be fulfilling." He bustled off.

For the rest of the day I participated in the Holy Offices. Throughout I hoped that somehow the nature of the name I had given might reach the hermit's ears.

The next morning, after Matins, the Cellarer sought me out again. I could tell from his shamefaced expression what he was going to say before he spoke.

"Lazarus, my friend, it pains me to bring you this news, but we cannot accommodate you here beyond tonight. We have had word of a large caravan of pilgrims one day's journey away. I have the unpleasant task of telling all the guests who have been with us that it is time for them to move on in the morning to make room for the newcomers."

I bowed my head in a gesture of resigned assent but I could not keep the shadow of a knowing sneer out of my face. How dare they turn me away? The Cellarer's affable features turned momentarily sour behind his red beard.

I spent the rest of the day participating in the monastic life and went to bed after Compline. My slumber was troubled and I was not sure whether I slept or woke when the bell announcing Nocturns sounded three hours before dawn. Fed up with my day of ceremonial lip service, I resolved instead of attending the service to climb to the top of the mountain to see the sun rise. Perhaps, like Moses, I would receive some form of inspiration there.

The general direction to the summit was clear enough, but in the dark it was hard to keep to the path. Here and there, on the steeper ascents, crude steps had been hacked into the side of the slope. Mostly, though, I stumbled over rough rock, cursing when I stubbed my toes on stones, or tripped and barked my knuckles or bruised my palms when I reached out my hands to protect my knees. Some compulsion hurried me to reach the top before dawn broke.

The mountainside had begun to reveal itself in cold shades of grey as I reached the last crest, which then softened into blue as the rising sun nudged the horizon. I forgot my aching muscles and battered hands. Lines of orange and yellow streaked the sky and began to run down over the earth below, pushing away the black shadow of night. The dark was rolled back, revealing a landscape the colour of burnt cake, and I knew why Moses had been unable to descend to the valley empty of inspiration.

"It is truly a magnificent view."

I span round. The rising sun was now warm on my back, and its light transfigured the face of the man who had spoken behind me, making it shine so brightly that I could not clearly make out his features. He seemed to be absorbing the sun's light, concentrating it, and throwing it out again. Almost I expected to see apostles, prophets, angels, cherubim. But there was just one man, and I fell to my knees.

"I come here often at this time. It sets me up for the day." He sighed. "I hear you call yourself Lazarus."

"I am sorry. I thought using the name might bring you to me. My true name is Hugh. But I do have word from Lazarus for you – an account he wrote of your days together."

His eyebrows lifted in a quizzical expression.

"Our days together? So who do you think I am?"

Awed though I was, the warm humour in his gaze forced a smile to my lips.

"I think you are the man of whom Lazarus wrote. You see, like you and Lazarus, and John before you, I too have been immersed, initiated, baptised according to the secret of the grail."

His eyebrows rose a little further. "The grail? What is the grail?"

"The dish, the great golden dish that was used to catch the blood in our ceremony."

"Ah," he said, "You have said so."

"Do the monks know who you are?" I asked. "How do you keep your presence here a secret?"

"Does any one of us know who we are?" he countered. "The monks have made me solemn promises that they will keep my presence here to themselves. They are used to hermits who wish to be away from the world. They know that I have lived here a long time, and that I have powers of healing. That power of healing I have put at their service. Now they are an unusually healthy community."

For all the solemnity that I felt, I could not resist laughing with him.

"Also, they see that after I have performed an act of healing I am drained, emptied, exhausted. If they shared me too much with others they might find themselves less healthy. And every so often I move on, stay somewhere else for a while, so that when I return none are left who remember me from before. But there is something about this place here that always draws me back."

He gazed raptly over the landscape below. Some minutes passed, for him slowly in deep thought and contemplation; for me hurried past by my amazement. I watched his expressive face changing. He looked old yet young, wise but playful, sad and then full of humour. His must be an extraordinary store of knowledge and experience and I could not wait to open it. He must have the answers I needed.

He pulled himself back to the present with a visible effort. He sighed and turned back to me.

"Forgive me. I am alone so much that I have forgotten my manners." He stepped forward and pulled me up to my feet. I quivered at his touch. "I suppose the monks have asked you to leave? Well, you had better stay with me a while. You can tell me your story."

"And you can tell me yours?" I asked hopefully.

He smiled. "First you had better get your things. We don't want to alarm our friends in the monastery, so I suggest that

144

you take your camel and ride back the way you came. Wait at the top of the pass. I will meet you there."

My face must have registered disappointment or suspicion.

"Come, come. Do you not trust me? You might have to wait a while, for four legs are faster than two, but I will be there."

Ashamed now, feeling almost as bad as Saint Peter, I stammered an awed goodbye and took off back down the hill.

For all I know, I might have flown down from Mount Sinai like some ancient saint. I have no recollection of walking back. My next conscious memory was of finding myself in front of the monastery gate, aware that I needed to compose myself before the monks. The two on duty at the gate smiled in recognition and I explained the pallor that I felt over my face by saying that the way to the top of the mountain and back was too far to go before breaking one's fast. Then I hurried straight to my cell to collect up my belongings.

Strapping my sword on under my Bedouin robe felt alien to me now, wrong. But I had no other way of carrying it. My mail coat, too, which weighed down one of my saddlebags, that seemed an unnecessary item for the life that I planned, but I could hardly leave it behind to be found in the monastery. The fox-haired Cellarer came to my cell, alerted to my return doubtless by the monks at the gate. I told him with all the innocence I could muster of the splendour of the sunrise that I had witnessed at the top of the mountain. This assuaged the sharp suspicion of his expression just enough for him to force a smile as he gave me a small bundle of provisions and wished me well on my way.

My camel was not pleased to see me, understanding that my appearance meant the end of her lazy time in Saint Katherine's stables. Finally, though, she knelt for me, and I rode out through the gate to turn north in the direction from which I had come. I tormented myself with the fear that I might not meet anyone at the top of the pass. When I got there I hobbled my camel and settled myself down to wait nervously in the dwindling patch of shade thrown by a rock.

Perhaps I dozed off, or perhaps I was still in a state of blank shock. A stone landing near me in the dust started me back to life. I looked up and filled with excitement at the sight of the figure from the mountain in the rocks above me. He beckoned me to him. I needed no further invitation. I pulled my camel to its feet and led it away from the trail.

"I don't want to risk showing myself too openly," he said. "I can do without too much attention. Already I think it is time to move on. I will take you to another cave that I use as shelter from time to time. It is further south from the monastery, in the mountain beyond Sinai."

I noticed that he carried with him a bundle even smaller than mine.

"Your beast will not be able to reach it, and anyway is too easily seen. You will have to set her loose. She will be fine, better free."

I heaved down the saddlebags and undid her reins and saddle. Her nose twitched and her jaws worked from side to side in surprise at being untrammelled. She stood still there for a few moments as we walked on, unable to believe her good fortune. When she judged that we were far enough off for her to be out of reach of punishment, she turned and ambled away.

My companion smiled when he saw me struggling under the weight of my saddlebags. "What do you have in those things? I prefer a simple life myself, without too many possessions. And you will trip over that sword of yours if you are not careful."

Hesitantly I explained that I had been a knight.

"You should write down your story when you have told it to me," he said.

I unstrapped my sword but I could not bring myself to jettison it, nor my mail. He helped me with good humour, and over my protests insisted on taking turns to carry the heaviest items.

It was almost dark by the time we reached our destination, a small dry cave high up a hillside, whose entrance was concealed from below by a fold in the rock, and from the side by a thicket of thorns.

He threw himself to the sandy ground inside. Exhausted, I followed his example. "Sleep well," he said. "We have plenty of time for talking tomorrow, and in the days after tomorrow."

❋

SAINT LAZARUS' COLLEGE

The Master slumped beside the fire in the Senior Common Room. He was pale, silent, too shocked by the events of his trip to London to make any objection to the ludicrous direction the Best-Selling Author's story was now taking. He had been reassured slightly by the news that his would-be assassin had been apprehended at Heathrow Airport. Under interrogation he had owned up to being a renegade Mossad agent with a grudge. It seemed his lover had died on a mission thwarted at the Master's behest. No connection to the other deaths in Oxford had been identified. Nor did there appear to be any link to the Templars.

But the Master could not get out of his head the manner of the Oxford Detective's death. With his own eyes he had seen him fall on to the track. He had clearly seen that nobody else had been involved. So was the fact that he had been beheaded, like his two holy namesakes, just a grisly coincidence? Or was some sort of supernatural force involved?

The Master had an awful feeling that he was losing his grip on reality.

✳

CHAPTER ELEVEN

THE SPIRITUAL DAWN

Des Cieux Spirituels l'inaccessible azur,
Pour l'homme terrassé qui rêve encore et souffre,
S'ouvre et s'enfonce avec l'attirance du gouffre.

✳

When I woke, the cave was empty. I assured my suspicious mind that he would not have brought me here just to desert me. And sure enough, as I stirred, the entrance to the cave darkened and there he was.

"Often I don't eat or drink for days, even months. I don't need it," he said. "Are you the same? But by God I get hungry. Did the monks give you anything?"

I fumbled for the bundle that the Cellarer had prepared and untied it. Greedily he reached in for a piece of flatbread, which he broke. He offered half to me and I wondered if I really saw a special twinkle in his eye.

"Here, this is yours. You don't mind sharing?"

"Heavens above, no, no, of course not."

"Come, I have a feeling that you and I will be together for some time. We must be equals – it seems we are blood brothers."

"But, Master, I want you to teach me."

"I cannot teach," he laughed lightly, "you can only learn. And I am not your master."

He gazed at me merrily while he munched his bread, his Adam's apple bobbing up and down under his beard with each swallow. I studied him closely, trying to pin down his features, his physiognomy, trying to remember every detail. But so many expressions flowed across his face. Even the colour of his hair was hard to tell – one moment it seemed brown, like mine, but the next fairer, gleaming where the sun caught it, or even white, or grey, and then dark again. I swallowed my mouthful and prepared to question him.

"No, don't ask," he laughed. "Tell. Tell me about Lazarus."

I could not have resisted his request if I had wanted to, and in response I reached under my robe for the bandage that carried the faint imprint of Lazarus' words.

"I found the gospel Lazarus wrote. It was hidden in Jerusalem, in a place called the Church of Saint Anne – built on the site of your mother's house to commemorate her."

His quizzically raised eyebrows caused me to pause, to stumble for a moment.

"I'd been told to find the gospel and to take it back as ransom for someone that I loved."

"But you were betrayed." His gentle words were more a statement than a question. "I know. It happens."

His sympathy brought my words tumbling out, rolling one over the other.

"I'd had to go all the way back to Europe, you see, to my monastery at Cluny where my journey started. I must have followed the same route as Saint Lazarus – and the Holy Virgin, and the Magdalene, so the legend says – I found Saint Lazarus' head in the church of Saint Victor in Marseille – I'm sorry – but nothing of the others save stories. Then I came back again. We took Jerusalem. I found the book and managed to escape from the catacombs. I got back to the prison where they were holding her and she was dead."

I paused and found I could not look him in the eye. I felt mine filling with tears.

"I think I went mad for a while. Anyway, when I came round, they let me copy the book for them but they did not know that I blotted it on this sheet. So here I have all Lazarus' words."

"Well! Come then! Read it to me. Read me this holy shroud of yours, your winding sheet. The rest can wait till later."

So I read. Some of the words were hard to decipher, but much I by now knew by heart:

'Others have undertaken to compile a narrative of the things which have been accomplished among us, just as they were delivered by those who from the beginning were witnesses and ministers of the word. Now, I wish to record an honest account for you, that you may know the truth about those things of which so much has been written.

'In the days of Herod a decree went out that all the people should be counted. To be counted, they returned each to their own city. So it came to pass that Joseph, who was of the royal house and lineage of David, returned to Bethlehem with his wife Mary, who was heavy with child and close to her term.

'At Bethlehem all the inns were full, for many had travelled there to be enrolled, and they took shelter in a stable. While they were there, the time came for Mary to be delivered, and she gave birth, and wrapped her baby in swaddling clothes, and laid him in a manger. And the baby, a boy child, was given the name Jesus.

'Now the royal house of David had kin in far off lands to the north, on the shores of a black sea. Three wise men travelled from those lands to pay their homage to their new kinsman, and they bore rich gifts. In that humble stable they fell down in worship and offered their treasures, a gold grail, myrrh, frankincense and other spices, and recondite recipes for their use.

'When Herod the King heard of these travellers he was troubled, and he summoned them to him to know their business. At first they would not speak, but demanded to be free to pass on their way. In a furious rage, the King brought young children before them and killed them one by one, until in pity they were forced to speak to stop the slaughter. Thus Herod learned their secrets, but when he searched for Joseph, Mary, and the child, he found them not, for they had moved on.

'The family sought refuge from Herod in lands away from Galilee, in Egypt, and later settled in Nazareth, that the words spoken by the prophet might be fulfilled: "He shall be called a Nazarene." And so the child Jesus passed to manhood in safety.

'Joseph's royal lineage gave him proud ambition. He planned to use the magic of his northern kin to restore his House of David to its rightful position. But Joseph was old and ill, and so he thought that for himself the Magi's herbs would not serve. The grail must pass to his only son.

'Joseph loved his son. He could not risk his precious blood, the last of his line. And so he asked a cousin, by the name of John, to prepare the way for Jesus. John went with Joseph to a distant place in the wilderness of Judaea to be baptised and immersed in the sacred mysteries.

'John emerged from this trial a man of strength and vigour, and soon his voice was carrying loud throughout the land: "Repent, for the kingdom of heaven is at hand." Of him spoke the prophet Isaiah when he said "The voice of one crying in the wilderness: Prepare the way of the Lord, make his path straight."

'Then Jesus came from Galilee to the Jordan to John, to be baptised in his turn. And so Jesus was immersed and the holy spirit entered through his veins into him. After, Joseph said, "Thou art my beloved son; with thee I am well pleased." And Jesus spent forty days and forty nights in the desert with John, who nursed him.

'But now John's fame reached the ears of King Herod. Some said, "John the Baptizer has been raised from the dead; that is why these powers are at work in him." And others said, "It is a prophet, like one of the prophets of old."

'Herod sent and seized John and bound him in prison. He feared his power and wished him dead. So Herod had John beheaded. Herod ordered John's head to be placed in mockery on a grail, and paraded in front of his courtiers to please Herodias, his wife, and her daughter Salome, for now they thought that their line was safe from the threat of the ancient House of David.

'When Joseph heard the news he was dismayed. He withdrew with Jesus into Galilee and dwelt for a while in Capernaum by the sea. There Joseph and Jesus bethought themselves of a family who lived in Bethany who were dear to them. The sisters were called Mary and Martha, the brother Lazarus. It was decided that Lazarus himself should be baptised. And so the bath was prepared, and he underwent immersion. Thus the holy spirit entered into Lazarus' veins and strengthened him.

'Now it was time for Jesus to begin his ministry, to gather his disciples around him and to begin to teach. He showed himself wise and many flocked to him and made him their rabbi. Joseph urged him to use the arcana of the holy spirit to achieve temporal power. But Jesus had greater thoughts. He would use the secret to rid the world of evil. If he could show that he could conquer death, he could found a cult whose beliefs would have the power to sweep away evil and make of this world a peaceful paradise.

'Others have written of Jesus' teaching. Wisdom poured from him as from no man before, yet all his words were touched by humility, and his gentle manner secured the love of all who listened with a pure heart. Great crowds followed him wherever he went and his fame spread throughout the land.

'At last Jesus decided that the power of the holy spirit should be tested, and that the task first set by Joseph for John should be fulfilled by another. So he passed unto Bethany to the house of Mary and Martha. They were fearful for their brother, whom they loved dearly, but Jesus spoke to them, saying, "He will conquer death and be glorified by means of his victory. Everlasting fame will be his."

'Near the house of Mary and Martha was a tomb, which could be closed by a heavy stone. Jesus entered the cave with Lazarus and Judas Iscariot, his trusted disciple. Lazarus was stripped of his robe, and a sharp blade was plunged by Judas into his side so that he fell down dead and a pale liquid flowed forth. They anointed his wounds and, binding him with strips of cloth, laid him gently down. They left the tomb and placed the stone across the entrance.

'Jesus went back to his teaching. On the fourth day he returned to Bethany and ordered that the stone should be moved away. But Martha, the sister of the dead man, weeping, said to him, "Lord, by this time there will be an odour, for he has been dead four days." But Jesus said to her, "Did I not tell you that if you would believe you would see the glory of the holy spirit?" And so they took away the stone, and Jesus cried in a loud voice, "Lazarus come out". And the dead man came out, his hands and feet and side bound with bandages. Jesus said to them, "Unbind him, and let him go."'

'Judas Iscariot, who looked after the money box and used to take from it what was put in, was angry. "These spices, this secret, we should sell for many denarii." But Jesus said, "Let it alone, it must be kept for the day of my burial.'

'As well as gathering together a great following, now Jesus had made many enemies, for his teaching threatened the Pharisees and the established order and gave hope to the poor and the weak. The Passover was approaching, and he knew the time had come to enter into Jerusalem and to confront his foes, so that his plan could be fulfilled.

'On the next day a great crowd heard that Jesus was coming to Jerusalem. They cut the branches of palm trees and ran out to greet him, laying the boughs before him as he rode on a young ass. Others laid out their cloaks and garments in his path. They cried "Hosanna to the Son of David, blessed is he who comes in the name of the Lord, even the King of Israel." And so the words of the prophet were fulfilled, as it is written, "Fear not, daughter of Zion, behold your king is coming, sitting on an ass's colt."

'Jesus entered the Temple of God. He flung over the tables of the money-lenders, and the stools of the pigeon-sellers, and drove out all who bought and sold in the Temple, saying "It is written that this shall be a house of peaceful prayer but you have turned it into a den of thieves."

'Then Jesus taught the people gathered in the Temple and told them many wise stories. The Pharisees demanded by what right he taught in the Temple, and to test him they asked "What is the greatest commandment in the law?" And Jesus replied, "You shall love the Lord your God with all your heart, all your soul and all your mind. And a second is of the same importance, that you shall love your neighbour as yourself." And the priests saw how the crowd hung on his words, and the sway he held over them, and they feared him. They dared not seize him before the crowd. And when Jesus saw how he had stirred the priests, he returned to Bethany, pausing on the way to teach another crowd on the Mount of Olives.

'Now the feast of the Unleavened Bread, the Passover, drew near. Jesus sent two of his disciples, Peter and John, saying, "Go and prepare the Passover feast for us, that we may eat it." And they asked him, "Where will you have us prepare it?" He said to them, "Behold, when you enter the city, a man will meet you carrying an alabaster jar containing all that I will need. Follow him into the house that he enters, where he will show you a large upper room; leave the jar there and make everything ready."

'And he sent another of the twelve, Judas Iscariot, to the high priests, in order to betray him to them in the absence of the crowd. "Tell them that they will find me in the Garden of Gethsemane in the hours of darkness after our Passover feast." And the priests were glad, and engaged to give Judas money.

'Peter and John prepared the Passover feast as their Lord had said, and when the time came he sat at the table, and his apostles with him. And they ate, dipping their bread into the dish that had been prepared for them. Jesus said, "All is ready. The betrayal has been prepared by he who dips his bread into the dish at the same time as me." And that one was Judas.

'And then he came out, and went, as was his custom, to the Mount of Olives, and his disciples followed him. He withdrew from them about a stone's throw, for he would be alone in his torment, and he knelt and prayed. "Oh my poor dead father, if only there were a way to achieve our plans without going through this suffering." And his sweat became like great drops of blood falling down upon the ground.

'And then he gathered his strength and rose, returning to the disciples, and found them sleeping. He said to them, "Why do you sleep? Be ready. Rise."

'While he was still speaking, there came a crowd with

swords and clubs from the chief priests and the scribes and the elders, and Judas was leading them. Now the betrayer had given them a sign, saying "The one I shall kiss is the man; seize him and lead him away safely." And when he came, he went up to him at once, and said, "Master!" And he kissed him. And they laid hands on him. But one of those who stood by drew his sword and struck off the ear of the slave of the high priest. Turning to his follower, Jesus said, "Put your sword back into its place; for all who take the sword will perish by the sword. Do you not remember my teachings?"'

'And Jesus said to them, "Have you come out to me as against a robber, with swords and clubs to capture me? Day after day I was with you in the Temple teaching and you did not seize me."

'Then they led him away, bringing him to the high priest's house. When day came, the assembly of the elders gathered together, chief priests and scribes; and they bound Jesus and brought him before Pilate. And Pilate asked him, "Are you the King of the Jews?" And he answered him, "That is what my father would have had me say, and you have said it." And the chief priests accused him of many things. And Pilate asked him again, "Have you no answer to make? See how many charges they bring against you." But Jesus made no further answer, so Pilate wondered whether he wished for his own death.

'Now at the feast he used to release for them any one prisoner whom they asked. And among the rebels in prison, who had committed murder in the insurrection, there was a man called Barabbas. And the crowd came up and began to ask Pilate to do as he was wont to do for them. And he answered them, "Do you want me to release the King of the Jews?" For Pilate perceived that it was out of envy that the chief priests had delivered him up. But the chief priests stirred up the crowd to have him release Barabbas instead. And Pilate again said to them, "Then what shall I do with the man whom you call the King of the Jews?" And they cried out again, "Crucify him. Crucify him." So Pilate, wishing to satisfy the crowd, released for them Barabbas, and having scourged Jesus, he delivered him to be crucified.

'And the soldiers led him away inside the palace. And they clothed him in a purple cloak, and plaited a crown of thorns which they placed on his head. And then they began to salute him, "Hail, King of the Jews." And they struck his head with a reed, and spat upon him, and they knelt down in homage to him. And when they had finished mocking him, they stripped him of the purple cloak and put his own clothes back on him. And then they led him away to be crucified.

'And they compelled a passer-by, Simon of Cyrene, who was coming in from the country, to carry his cross. And they brought him to Golgotha, which means the place of the skull. Now the centurion in charge of the escort was named Longinus, and he was a disciple of Jesus. And he offered Jesus wine mixed with myrrh and other spices, and he took it. And then, at the third hour, they crucified him, and divided his garments among them, casting lots for them, to decide what each should take. And the inscription of the charge against him read "The King of the Jews."

'And with him they crucified two robbers, one on his right and one on his left. And when the sixth hour had come, there was darkness over the whole land until the ninth hour. And at the ninth hour, Jesus cried out with a loud voice, "Eli, Eli, lama sabachthani," which was a sign. And the centurion ran, filling a sponge full of wine, spices and myrrh, put it on a reed and gave it to him to drink. And when Jesus had received the drink, he said in a loud voice "It is finished" and he bowed his head.

'Since it was the day of Preparation, in order to prevent the bodies from remaining on the cross on the Sabbath, the Jews asked Pilate that their legs might be broken, and that they might be taken away. So the soldiers came and broke the legs of the first, and of the other who had been crucified with him, but when they came to Jesus the faithful centurion ordered them not to break his legs. Instead, he pierced his side with his lance, and at once a clear liquid flowed forth. I who have seen it have borne witness and I know that I tell the truth. And so the scripture was fulfilled, which says, "Not a bone of his body shall be broken," and again, "They shall look upon him whom they have pierced."

'After this, Joseph of Arimathea, who was a friend and secret disciple of Jesus, asked Pilate if he might take away the body, and Pilate gave him leave. And Nicodemus also came, bringing the alabaster jar of spices and myrrh. And they took the body of Jesus and bound its wounds in linen cloths with the spices. And they took him and laid him in a tomb nearby, whose entrance they closed with a rock.

'Now Judas Iscariot's greed drove him again to the chief

priests and scribes. He told them of Jesus' plan to rise from his tomb, and how once he had conquered death, his power would be great. He told them too that like John the Baptizer, his life could be ended only by striking his head from his body. And for his pains, the chief priests took the traitor and hanged him.

'Next day, that is, after the day of Preparation, the chief priests and the Pharisees gathered before Pilate and said, "Sir, we have uncovered the impostor's plot to rise from the dead in three days time. Therefore order the sepulchre to be made secure until the third day, lest his disciples go and steal him away, and tell the people, 'He has risen from the dead'." Pilate said to them, "You have a guard of soldiers, go, make it as secure as you can." So they went and made the sepulchre secure by sealing the stone and setting a guard.

'So his disciples were unable to roll away the stone at the appointed hour and they despaired. Jesus woke in the tomb, and finding it still closed, he knew that he had been betrayed. Now this cave tomb had been chosen because a hidden passageway led from it. Jesus stripped from himself the bandages and made his way out through the passageway.

'Now after the Sabbath, toward the dawn of the first day of the week, the chief priests became impatient and they ordered the stone to be rolled away. And so, with a noise like thunder, this was done. But the guards trembled and became like dead men, for they found the tomb empty, save for the linen clothes in which his wounds had been bound.

'Mary Magdalene was also watching, and saw that the

stone had been taken away from the tomb. So she ran, and went to Simon Peter and another disciple whom she loved well, and said to them, "They have taken the Lord out of the tomb, and we do not know where they have laid him." Peter then came out with the other disciple and they both ran to the tomb. At first they could not go in because of the guards, and they hid. But when the guards left they were able to go in. They saw the empty tomb and the bandages and returned to their homes.

'Mary remained weeping near the tomb. She turned round and saw Jesus standing there, but she did not know that it was Jesus for he was dressed like the gardener, wrapt in a brown mantle. Then he said to her, "Mary, it is I." And she said to him, "Rabboni!" (which means teacher). And he said to her, "Do not be dismayed. Go, tell the disciples and Peter that I will go secretly before them into Galilee, and that they will see me there.

'While they were going, behold, some of the guard went into the city and told the chief priests all that had taken place. And when they had assembled with the elders and taken counsel, they gave a sum of money to the soldiers and said, "Tell people, 'His disciples came by night and stole him away while we were asleep.' And if this comes to the governor's ears, we will satisfy him." So they took the money and did as they were directed, and this story has been spread among the Jews to this day.

'Now the eleven remaining disciples went to Galilee to the secret place to which Jesus had directed them. Because of his betrayal by the twelfth he could not show himself openly. He was seen by two friends on the way to Emmaus, but thereafter he took more care.

'And then Jesus went back into the rocky desert and we saw him no more.'

✳

"We've already had the Gospel of Lazarus in full in *'The Waste Land'*" the Master grumbled. He was feeling better, in spite of the harrowing experience of the Oxford Detective's funeral. He was also comforted by the redoubled security around the College. Now that it had been handed over to his former agency – justified by the attempt on his own life – he was sure that no strangers could get in to threaten them.

"Do you really think it is acceptable to repeat it verbatim here? Won't people who have read the first book be bored with it again?"

The Best-Selling Author scratched his head. "I can't see any alternative. Some readers may pick up *'The Flowers of Evil'* without realising it is a sequel. It won't make much sense to them unless the Gospel is there to explain what's what."

"It won't make much sense to them even if it is," muttered the Computer Sciences Tutor, not quite audibly. As a new boy in the SCR he was still deeply in awe of the Master, but he viewed the fanciful plot of the new book with derision.

"And even if it is the only part of the book not rendered in my own limpid prose," the Best-Selling Author went on, "It is not a bad bit of writing, not a bad bit of writing at all. A lot of inherent interest, I would say. Most of the people who have read *'The Waste Land'* probably won't remember it very well. And those who do can always skip the gospel bit if they want to. Trust me on this."

The Master shrugged crossly.

❉

Chapter Eleven

AUTUMN SONG

Courte tache! La tombe attend; elle est avide!
Ah! Laissez-moi, mon front posé sur vos genoux,
Gôuter, en regrettant l'été blanc et torride,
De l'arrière-saison le rayon jaune et douce!

✳

I looked up from reading these final words and wondered if I saw tears brimming in my listener's eyes. I could not be sure because he stood up quickly and left the cave. I thought for a moment that I had heard him murmur "Poor old Lazarus" or something similar. But I could not be sure. I followed him outside. When I found him he was smiling again.

"Well, it is certainly an interesting story," he said. "You must copy it out properly. The monks give me writing materials when I wish them. I still have a few sheets of parchment and a little ink with me. When you have used that up I'll pay them another visit."

We found a flat stone to do service as a crude table and he set me to work. He allowed me time to walk in the hills when he judged I had sat still for too long. Sometimes he accompanied me; sometimes he just stayed quietly near the cave in contemplation. When my ink or my parchment ran out, or my quill broke and was too short to sharpen, he would set off to collect more supplies from the monks. On occasion he came back drained and exhausted and I knew that he had used his powers to heal some sick brother in the community. Then he would throw himself down and sleep, sometimes even for days on end.

By the time my task was finished, and my scrolls were stored away, the days were short and the weather was cold. One morning I woke to find that the world outside the cave was white, covered deeply in snow.

"Well, Hugh, what do you say? Should we move and find shelter further south, lower down and warmer? There is no point suffering unnecessary hardship even if it can do us no real harm. I know a place close to the sea, still isolated, with a fine view. We can settle down there until spring and you can pass the time by telling me your story."

And so the seasons passed. My own story was told, and then written, or some of it at least, as you can see. When my friend judged that the older monks at Saint Katherine's had seen too much of him for too long and that the rumours were getting too loud, we moved away to shelter elsewhere. When he first met them they had been the younger monks. But always we stayed well away from places of habitation, and away from what was going on in the world. Occasionally we heard news from the nomads upon whom we chanced in the desert, and if they had sick we would heal them. Always after these encounters we would move on, so that none might quite know for sure whether we were real or wraiths.

Try as I might, I could not get my companion to repay me in coin of my own kind. He would not tell me his story.

"You know it as well as I do," he might say in excuse. Or "My memories have faded with time, and many things happened so long ago. I can no longer be certain what is what and who is who. Would you have me mislead you? You see, Hugh, I lacked a friend to make me write it all down, as I have made you. You should be grateful to me."

And he would melt me with his smile.

"If you will not tell me your story, Master," I would then say, "at least teach me how I should lead my life."

When I closed him into this corner, he would tell me stories, parables in the old style. He always laughed if I later recorded them, content perhaps to divert me further. I was satisfied, because I loved his tales.

"There was a city which lay on the sea. It so happened that all the rats in the city came up out of their holes and began to die. The cats went too, and then the plague came. The governor of the city was told by his overlord to close the city to prevent the spread of the disease beyond its bounds; not a soul was to be allowed out. Reluctantly he agreed; he had no choice. The busy port was closed. Waiting ships were turned away. The walls and the gates were manned by soldiers with orders to kill any who attempted to pass. It was as if the tightest siege were in place although no army lay outside the walls.

"There, Hugh, you can see this is a story for you, for you understand about sieges!

"A good doctor lived in the city. His wife was ailing and needed the cool air of the hills beyond. He sent her away just before the city was closed. He was pleased that she was safe, but also sad that she was gone. He was now left alone with his old mother, for he and his wife were childless. He threw himself into tending the sick.

"The doctor soon found that he could do nothing for the victims of the pestilence, nothing at all. With whatever care, howsoever he tended them, they died. Then their families died, and then their neighbours, and their neighbours' families. So the governor decided that at the first sign of plague in a household, everyone else who lived there should be taken to the amphitheatre and enclosed there away from the healthy.

"The bishop of the town demanded a week of fasting and prayer. At the end of the week of penance, he preached in the cathedral to a great crowd. He told the crowd that the plague was a punishment from God and that it was richly deserved for their evil ways. He preached that they should accept their punishment willingly, and that then they would find God.

"Some accepted the bishop's message. Others resolved instead to resist. One, a trader from far away, had come to the town shortly before the gates were closed. He paid a smuggler – a petty criminal whose suicide the good doctor had once prevented – to help him escape so that he could see his wife again, for he loved her.

"Spring moved into summer and the heat in the city became intense. It was nearly as hot as it is here, Hugh. The number of dead and dying rose and the graveyards began to overflow.

"Still the plague worsened. One young wanderer, a guest at the town's largest inn, came to offer the doctor his help tending the sick and separating their relatives.

"It happened that the trader was lodging in the same inn as the young wanderer, and he came to offer his help also, for the smuggler – who had refused to help the doctor in spite of his debt to him – had not yet been able to arrange his escape from the city. The doctor was not angry with the smuggler for this but accepted him for what he was.

"These three – the doctor, the wanderer and the trader – were joined by an old clerk. The old clerk was tired of copying out the same manuscripts again and again, changing a word here and there. Together these four battled the plague tirelessly but still had time to become friends. The wanderer also became familiar with the smuggler, who seemed to enjoy the terror of the plague. When at last the smuggler offered the trader his escape, the trader declined and decided to stay in the city.

"Clouds of dust blew into the streets from the desert. The smell of salt and seaweed filled the air. The city groaned with the howl of the wind, like an island of the damned. In places fires were set by men maddened by fear and grief, and they blazed uncontrollably, adding their smoke to the vile air. Many tried to escape but died on the swords of the guards stationed at the gates. Looters roamed the streets.

"Now the magistrate who enforced the governor's will had a young son, who caught the plague. According to the laws for which he himself had responsibility, he was obliged to go to the amphitheatre to be isolated with the other families that had come into contact with the plague. This he did, leaving his son in the doctor's care. The boy died slowly and in awful agony. The governor lived, and was allowed to leave the amphitheatre once it was certain that he had not caught the plague. However, he decided to stay there to help the inmates. Later, he succumbed to the plague and died.

"The bishop who had preached that the plague was God's punishment on the town had watched the governor's son die in agony, for he too helped to tend the sick. He and the doctor argued about the reasons for such suffering. When next the bishop preached, he insisted that the plague was a sign of God's love, incomprehensible perhaps to man, but, he said, either one had to believe all or nothing. Two days later, the surgeon was summoned, and he found the bishop dying, a crucifix gripped in his hands."

"Like Bishop Adhemar in Antioch," I murmured into the pause.

"The young wanderer battled the plague indefatigably, perhaps hardest of all. He explained to the doctor that his father had been a judge who condemned men to death. This, he told the doctor, was murder, and all who allowed it to happen were murderers too. Death was his enemy and he would fight it by every means at his disposal.

"The weather came to his aid. The heat of summer gave way to winter and the plague began to falter. The rats returned and were welcomed for the first time. Now the old clerk fell ill, and the doctor despaired for his life. The old clerk ordered the doctor to burn all his manuscripts, everything he had written out so painstakingly, and in the morning he was better. The doctor began to take hope.

"The only man who was disappointed by the retreat of the pestilence was the smuggler. He would disappear for days on end and then emerge, bad-tempered and crazy.

"Then, the young wanderer, the one who had fought death harder than all the rest, and whom the doctor loved, fell victim to the disease. The young man struggled hard, but in the end he lost the battle. The doctor watched as the plague delivered him to his enemy, death.

"The good doctor realised that he had lost the best friend he had ever had. The next morning he received news that his wife had died in the hills from her illness.

"In the following days the authorities decided that the pestilence had been defeated and opened the gates of the city. The citizens rejoiced. The smuggler whom the doctor had saved from suicide was the only one who regretted this and he provoked a fight with the militia, who killed him.

"The good doctor himself knew that the plague never went away. It might return at any time."

He remained looking out into the distance over the plain, and then turned to me, his enigmatic face empty of any expression.

"Yes, I see," I said slowly.

"I am glad of that," he said, and laughed softly.

I do not know how long we spent our life together in this way, wandering from place to lonely place in the desert. But at last we returned to Sinai, to the place where we had first met. My master judged that we had been away for long enough for the monks' memory of him to have faded. I think he loved this place above all others.

"When I first came here, Hugh, Saint Katherine's Monastery was not even built."

I looked at him with surprise, expectant.

"The Emperor Justinian came here with an army. Monks

came too, and they sought for hermits who lived in these hills. When they asked for the place where the bush had burned for Moses this spot was pointed out to them. After all, they needed a site with water nearby, and this is the best spring in these parts!"

His smile was mischievous, even slightly sheepish.

"Some of the soldiers stayed and hewed rock for the monks. The defensive walls went up first – I suppose that was soldiers' work – but they helped to build the church as well. I liked to see those violent hands wielding tools of peace.

"Later an Arab army came from the south, led by their new prophet. The monks were afraid, or most of them anyway, at the thought that the end of their life on this earth had come. Some – the older ones, I suppose – might have welcomed a new beginning. But I disappointed them."

The confusion in my face begged an explanation.

"It was simple. I urged them to throw open the gates, to show their visitors hospitality. I welcomed their prophet and brought him up here."

My eyes widened.

"Come, Hugh, surely you are not jealous! You cannot have thought that you were my first guest! We talked for a long time. I liked him. He was a wise man, tolerant of others' beliefs, happy to leave them in peace if they so left him and his followers."

He sighed, and looked at me more sharply, as if wanting me to note carefully what he said.

"Why are the disciples always more fanatical than those that they follow? Why does their belief have to be more certain than their teachers'? Why do they not understand that what is right for one may not be right for another? Why should one man's right be another's wrong? If that prophet, and all the prophets before him, had known what would be wrought by their followers, would they have taught them as they did?"

And then he sat in silence, looking out over the desert's

folds of burnt ochre. Beside him I sat and watched them redden in the sunset, silver under the moon, and then blue as dawn came. Then the sun poured its heat back over the earth once more.

He turned to me.

"Do you love me, Hugh?" Sorrow and anger seared me that he had to ask that question. He saw my hurt.

"It is all right, Hugh, I am sorry. I know you love me. I am tired, so tired. But can you love me enough to do what I will ask of you?"

My chin lifted as I put my answer silently into the set of my face.

"I have lived long enough, Hugh. I am too tired to go on. I want you to finish it for me. With that sword of yours. I want to sleep! To sleep instead of to live! You know what has to be done."

I was dazed. I heard the sound of his words but at first I could not grasp their meaning. He hung his head as I had never seen him do before.

"I am sorry, Hugh. I have no right to ask such a thing of you. But I have nowhere else to turn."

I froze in horror as it dawned on me what he meant. Aping the sunrise I had just watched, the blue cold inside me turned to a burning heat as I understood what he asked. Without realising, I found myself standing up, my arms outstretched in a gesture of helplessness. I could not speak, and ran from him.

I came back hours later. He was sitting unmoved where I had left him.

"Why, Master? Why? I cannot refuse you yet how can I do what you ask? Why? Explain to me."

"When you have lived as long as I have you will understand."

"Then that is when I will do what you want." For the first time I spoke to him in anger, but my rage melted away as he turned towards me, his face infinitely sad but with the ghost of a smile flickering deep down in his eyes.

"Hugh, Hugh. I cannot wait until then. I cannot bear it. I am so tired," he repeated. "I have been here so long. And not one of those countless days passes without me asking myself how I might have done things differently. Think how that must feel – spending cruel lifetimes in an agony of self-doubt. Was I right to turn my back on the world, to live here as a hermit? Could I have made a difference in the world if I had preached tolerance and respect for others? Or would it have just made things worse, and created yet another set of fanatics to fight the rest? Should I have been out there, healing as many as I could? I could not have helped everyone. How would I have chosen who to save? I do not know, Hugh. And it is now too late. I am beginning to feel my age, Hugh. You are still young. You can do what I did not. You can go back to the world as a knight, not some strange prophet whom all would view with suspicion. By your example perhaps you can lead other men, mould others in your own likeness, and work for a world of peace and tolerance. At least you have time to try. I have left it too late."

Tears rolled down my face. I could make no answer.

Days passed. I could no longer look my companion in the eyes. Instead I cast sidelong looks at him, trying to determine what he really wanted, hoping that I could see that his wishes had changed. From time to time I felt his gaze on me, perhaps trying to assess my intent. The air between us was thick like before a storm, where once it had been limpid, perfectly clear. Most days he left me alone and climbed by himself to the top of the mountain. The view from where I sat had lost its majesty and was now just bleak and barren.

At last the day came when I could stand it no more and I dragged my long neglected weapon from its bundle. For hours I sat unseeing above the view, cradling across my knees the scabbard of whose Venetian embroidery I had once been so proud. At last I gathered enough strength to draw out the blade and give my master the reply he wanted – unspoken but sounded plaintively by my small whetstone scratching away on the edge. As if summoned, he returned from the top of the mountain. I shivered at his eager smile, thrust the sword back into its sheath, and hurried it away to its bundle. More days passed before I could bring myself to take it out again, and work away at it with the whetstone, determined that it should be perfect for its task.

At length I knew that it could be no sharper. I had no further excuse for delay. I could not find the words, but my master knew. He gripped my shoulder.

"So, Hugh, my friend, you are ready."

My eyes flooded, and I could not speak. I nodded my head and he tried to make a joke out of it.

"So, is that yes, or no? Are you an Arab today, or a Frank?"

I burst into sobs and flung my arms around his neck. He hugged me back and kissed me on both cheeks.

"I hope I am not betraying you," he smiled, as if his gesture awoke a distant memory. "Know that you are being as faithful to me as any friend has ever been."

He looked once more at the view he had loved, and knelt with his head over a rock.

And I swung my sword, and it was done.

I carried his body into the grave cave and laid him down gently on his back. He weighed much less than I had thought. Then, shaking and shuddering, scarcely able to look, I collected the other part and laid it where it belonged at the end of the body. I brought out my possessions and summoned the courage for one last look. The sun was now low in the sky, blood red, and shone deep into the cave. Then the rays passed on but the body there seemed to glow back with a strange luminosity. I thought that perhaps I had done right. Then night fell and I sat on guard through the hours of darkness.

At first light I began to fill the neck of the cave with stones, building an impenetrable barrier. None would ever roll these rocks away. When the task was done, I buckled on my cruel sword. Unworn for so long it felt strange at my side and cumbered me as I walked slowly down the mountainside.

All that I can recall of my journey back north was that the black irises were in bloom in the desert. I have no memory of returning to the monastery. I had no horse, no camel, so I just walked. I did not have much to carry – only my old mail coat, the quiver-shaped case that contained the tightly rolled scrolls of my story and his, a few simple household items, and my memories. These last were perhaps the heaviest burden of all.

❋

SAINT LAZARUS' COLLEGE

"Where on earth is he?"

"It is unlike Mark to be late for dinner."

The Master had a sinking feeling. He reached for the telephone and rang through to the security men in the Porter's Lodge.

"Have you seen the History Don? He could not have left the College? No. Good. And no strangers have come in. Right. Well make sure you keep checking."

The Senior Common Room was absolutely silent. The anxious faces relaxed a little as they listened to the course of the Master's conversation. He put the telephone down.

"Mark, of all people, must be safe. There aren't any horses in the College after all. But we had better delay dinner and send out search parties."

He rang the bell for the Head Scout who arrived looking flustered.

"The History Don has disappeared. We are going to have to delay dinner while we look for him. It's roast lamb tonight, isn't it? Well ask Cook to keep it warm as best he can. And gather together as many of the College servants as possible. We'll scour the place systematically."

The dons and their servants fanned out in pairs through the College. The Master, with the Best-Selling Author as his companion, used the privilege of his position to start in the Senior Common Room itself, and then to go through the Master's Lodge, where the Best-Selling Author was also staying.

Before long they heard shouts from the other side of the quad, and they broke off their search to hurry in that direction. They were greeted by the Head Scout emerging from the door that led through to the kitchens.

"We've found him, Sir. It's all right, he's alive. A bit shaken and bruised. His left arm might be fractured. I'll call the doctor."

"Where is he, for Heaven's sake?"

"This way, Sir. Follow me."

The Master hurried behind the Head Scout down a corridor near the kitchens towards a room that he had never visited, indeed of whose existence he was scarcely aware.

He hurried down the flight of four steep steps into the College laundry, stumbled and might have fallen if the Best-Selling Author behind him had not caught his arm and steadied him. The Computer Sciences Tutor and the Geography Fellow were comforting a dazed History Don, whom they had propped up on a wooden chair.

"Mark, are you all right? What on earth happened?"

The History Don sighed weakly. "I did not have any clean shirts. I had sent some to be washed yesterday, and I thought I would come down here to see if they were ready and pick one up. I was in a hurry because it was nearly time for dinner. So I suppose I was just a bit careless. Anyway, those steps did for me. They are lethal; I've nearly fallen down them before. This time I went completely head over heels and crashed into the clothes horse." He gestured to the shattered frame of the offending item which now lay in the middle of the room covered by a few damp tea towels.

"I think I must have knocked myself out. When I came to I found myself completely tangled up in the thing and my arm was hurting so much that I could not get myself out of it until you all appeared to help. Thank you."

The Best-Selling Author gave up his attempts to keep a straight face and guffawed loudly, earning a scathing look from his host.

"Are you sure nobody pushed you? I know those steps are dangerous; I nearly fell down them myself just then. But to end up in the middle of the room. You must have had a lot of momentum."

The History Don looked puzzled and made a visible effort to gather his thoughts.

"Well, now you mention it… It's strange. At the time I did wonder whether I had tripped over something at the top of the steps, and in the split second when I was flying through the air it occurred to me that I had felt a shove in my back. But maybe not. I just can't be sure. It all happened too quickly."

❋

CHAPTER TWELVE

MOESTA ET ERRABUNDA

Comme vous êtes loin, paradis parfumé,
Où sous un clair azur tout n'est qu'amour et joie,
Où tout ce que l'on aime est digne d'être aimé.

✳

Something drew me inexorably towards Jerusalem. I suppose
that I must have followed the main road north, ignoring the
by-ways which I had become accustomed to follow with my
master. Any number of days and nights might have passed
when I was woken from my reverie by cries and the clashing
sound of weapons.

I had crested the brow of a hill and found myself looking
down a gentle slope into a wide wadi. In the hollow below
nine horsemen wheeled about a group of travellers. Two had
backed against a large boulder and were offering stout
resistance. Others cowered on the ground, pleading for mercy.
The prayers of three or four more had been ignored – or
perhaps they had fought and died – for they lay motionless,
dark blood patches seeping into the sand around them.

The harsh clash of steel on steel and the shouts of
aggression and defiance woke something inside me that had
been long asleep. I felt the sudden rush brought by fear and

excitement. Before I knew it, my sword was in my hand and my legs were running me down the hill. I came in silence for I knew no longer what war cry to make, and it was good that I did so, for I took two of the assailants by surprise, striking them down before they could turn and defend themselves. One toppled forward over his horse's neck and slid to the ground; the other, not quite dead, lost his saddle but kept one foot in its stirrup, and was dragged screaming by his terrified horse until his bouncing body struck a rock and went limp and silent. His noise turned his three nearest comrades towards me.

I registered with relief that they were lightly armed with scimitars, not lances. At the last moment I sidestepped the first charging horse and with both hands thrust the point of my sword upwards beneath its rider's ribs. His raised blade slipped from his lifeless fingers. As his body fell from the horse, my sword, stuck deep in his chest, jerked me forward, under the second horseman's blow. I felt the wind of the flashing scimitar on my cheek as the horse charged past, and then a stinging pain as the tip of the blade tore the flesh down the back of my upper arm. I tugged my blade out of my opponent's body so hard that I span round with such momentum that I caught the third horse a blow in the neck, bringing it to its knees, and throwing its rider over its head. He lay dazed and winded from his fall. Before he could move I pierced him through to the ground. Now the second rider turned back at me, but when he saw his two comrades dead he thought better of the odds and pulled his horse's head round, shouting "Away, away!" at the top of his voice.

It seemed that this coward was their leader, for the remaining horsemen broke off their attack at his order and galloped away in his dust. The two fighting travellers leaned on their weapons, breathing heavily. Both were unhurt; they had chosen their position well, backed against the rock, for their assailants had been unable to press home their numerical advantage from the back of their horses.

"Well fought, sirs!" I spoke first, for they were struggling to catch their breath. "You were lucky that those bandits did not have the foresight to dismount."

"God smiled on us when he sent you this way, sir," said the senior of the two, grim-faced in spite of our small victory. "We could not have held them off for much longer. And I have to say doubly well fought to you. You accounted for four of them. I can see that you are a veteran of many battles. That is more than I can say for most of our companions who are pilgrims, men of peace. The three others who dared to offer resistance were cut down before they could make the shelter of these rocks. God rest their souls. They were good men. Curse those heathen bastards – but also those fools at Montréal who told us that this way was safe. Perhaps with the King's death these bandits saw their chance for some plunder without the fear of retribution. They'll soon learn that the second Baldwin will be just as strong as the first."

"The second Baldwin?" I could not keep the surprise out of my voice. "When did the first Baldwin die?"

"Where have you been, my friend?" For all his courtesy, my interlocutor's voice contained as much surprise as my own. "King Baldwin the First passed on last year, God rest his noble soul. Surely you heard of the hot debate about offering the crown to his elder brother Eustace, keeping it in the Boulogne family? There was talk of nothing else in Jerusalem for weeks. Eustace was sent for but then Baldwin of le Bourg came down to the royal funeral. He made such an impression that it was decided to give it to him instead. So for the second time he has followed his namesake and taken the crown of Jerusalem where before he had taken the county of Edessa. Count Eustace had already reached Apulia when he received the news that he had travelled too slowly and that the kingdom that might have been his was another's."

For a moment I wondered if I could have dreamt all that had happened since my encounter with Baldwin. Then it dawned on me that the only explanation could be that my lance blow had not been fatal. I scarcely knew whether to laugh or cry. In my confusion I forgot myself. I had liked Eustace and smiled at the memory of his plump courtesy.

"I cannot imagine that Eustace was very sorry. Godfrey always used to tease him about his attachment to the life of comfort on his estates in green Normandy. He always said that as soon as Jerusalem had fallen, Eustace would be straight back home, never to return. But he did fight bravely for Jerusalem."

Confusion, then suspicion, marked the grim face of the knight.

"How did you know the Boulogne brothers? Where have you come from? Duke Godfrey has been dead these last nineteen years, and Count Eustace was in Europe all that time. You look far too young to have fought at their side."

"Yes, of course," I said hurriedly, trying to smile. "But their fame spreads wide and I have heard many tales of their exploits."

The knight relaxed. "But, come, I am sorry, I forget myself. We have time later for reminiscences. You are hurt. Let's get you bound up. One of these pilgrims has some surgical skills. Come."

I protested that it was nothing, a mere scratch, and that it would soon heal. Of that much I knew I could be sure. But I could not deny the blood staining the left side of my cloak, and I submitted to the deferential care of the good pilgrim. He fished some sweet-smelling salve from his baggage and lifted my robe gently over my head. I stood there in my loose cotton britches, naked to the waist, and sensed his curiosity at the scars which marked my body – the jagged line of the javelin blow I had taken at Antioch, and the deeper, neater puncture left by Hasan's lance.

"You are a survivor, I can see." Then I winced at the sting of his ointment on my wound, and the pressure of the bandage as he pulled it tight.

182

"Now you need some fresh garments."

"No, I have some – in my pack. I dropped it at the top of the slope up there." I found I could not easily raise my left arm, so twisted round awkwardly to point with my right. My doctor gestured to the young fellow who had been watching with interest as I was patched up. The lad scampered off up the slope and ran back carrying my things.

With a feeling of reluctance, partly for the weight and the heat, but partly for what it would make me, I pulled out my mail coat. It was dull but had not rusted. I had kept it dry and greased it from time to time. The air of the desert had done the rest. I made to drop it over my head but could not raise my wounded arm far enough, so the boy came to my aid. I smiled my thanks and managed to perform by myself the task of pulling on the white surcoat. Its red cross marked my chest accusingly.

I was buckling back my sword when the knight came over.

"Ha – that is the emblem we should adopt. The old signs are always the best." The solemn grimace he made as he pointed at my chest seemed to be the closest to a smile that he could manage. He had pulled his mail cowl back so that it hung down his back – like mine – but where I wore my brown hair long, he revealed a closely shaved skull shaped curiously like the pointed end of a gull's egg. He bent it forward stiffly as if showing it to me and said, "Sir Hugh de Payns, in your debt and at your service."

I smiled and bowed.

"A good omen. We share our given names. I am Sir Hugh de Verdon. Also at your service and doubtless soon in your debt."

"My friend, I wish I could offer you a rest after your exertions. But I fear we must move on in case our attackers return with reinforcements. Accept this horse in gratitude for what you have done."

The sergeant who had fought at the knight's side led

forward a fine bay stallion that I recognised as the mount of the first bandit I had killed. He shied slightly and whinnied at my approach, but seemed to bear me no ill will for my dispatch of his former master. He was a fine beast, with a small head proudly poised at the end of a strong neck, and moist eyes that looked at me with intelligence. I took the reins greedily and stroked his nose in introduction, before placing my foot in the stirrup and raising myself, heavy in my mail, into the saddle.

De Payns commanded respect among the other travellers. I soon saw that he knew what he was about. Two of the best-mounted pilgrims were sent forward to alert us to any ambushes ahead, and our small column moved off in careful order. At Sir Hugh's request, I took the rear, so had no more opportunity to talk to him until we stopped to camp after an uneventful day in the saddle.

The day's dull ride had afforded each of us the opportunity to stoke our curiosity and to prepare questions and answers for each other. When the camp was established in a gully which would conceal our fire and protect us from attack except from the front, my namesake and I settled down as befitted our status whilst the others waited on us. The fare – some thin wine watered with brackish water, and a haunch of gazelle whose flavour betrayed that it had been hunted some days before – scarcely deserved the respect with which it was offered, but it was more than I was accustomed to.

For a while we chewed the stringy flesh in silence, neither of us wishing to be the first to show unseemly curiosity. Then we burst into speech simultaneously, and stopped, embarrassed. I laughed, but Sir Hugh's face kept its habitual solemn expression, finding no humour in the event.

"Please…" I invited his question. I had had time to prepare my story.

"God brought you to our rescue this morning, of that there is no doubt. But how did you come to be alone in this desert?"

"Three years ago I came south this way on a pilgrimage to Saint Katherine's Monastery at Sinai. There I fell in with a hermit, a holy man, and I went to live with him to learn what I could. He was old, and became frail, but would not return to the monastery walls. So I stayed with him – I had grown fond of him – he was almost a father to me – until he died. I hope that I eased his passage into the next world. So now I travel back to Jerusalem."

"And before?" A tone of suspicion remained in Sir Hugh's voice, which I might not have detected if we had not been speaking together in our common vernacular.

"Before?" I paused and sighed. "My father was a knight. Like me, his eldest son, he was named Sir Hugh. He held land near Verdun from the Duke of Lower Lorraine. So it was no surprise when he answered the call of the Cross, and followed Duke Godfrey here to Outremer. Of course, I only remember this from my mother. I was too young – scarcely four years old when my father left.

"Ah – so you now have lived for twenty-three or twenty-four summers?"

"Now almost twenty-five, I believe. And my father – he never returned. Later came word from one of Count Eustace's returning retinue that he had fallen at the siege of Jerusalem. They said he had scaled the wall bravely alongside the Count and the Duke – that he was one of the first to storm the ramparts – but then was never seen again. At least he fulfilled his Crusader oath and now sits with Our Lord and His Angels in Heaven. And that is how I know of the exploits of the noble Boulogne brothers."

I had told myself that my story would be the more convincing, the closer I stayed to the truth, even if much of what I attributed to my father I had in fact done myself. It had also given me the chance to cover up my earlier indiscretion.

"My mother died. I always wanted to do what my father

had done. I was unmarried. I had nothing to keep me. So I handed my land to my brother for safe-keeping and made the great pilgrimage east. I had always been a good fighter, and in this troubled land I have had opportunity to hone my skills, but had it not been for that I might have taken orders or entered a cloister."

Sir Hugh de Payns appeared to approve of these sentiments. All suspicion faded from his manner and he warmed to me as much as his grim earnest would allow.

"Well, well, you certainly sound a man after my own heart. I came to this land about the same time as you, in the company of my liege lord, Count of Champagne. He is another Hugh."

I bit my tongue before I made an ill-judged joke to this humourless man about the trinity of Hughs.

"What a holy man he is! He has given many generous endowments to our Holy Mother Church. Two years hence, he gave a fine tract of land in the Valley of Wormwood to the white monks of Cîteaux to build a new foundation there. Bernard, who will be Abbot, has renamed it Clairvaux, the Valley of Light, and indeed it will become a beacon casting illumination on the true teaching of our Lord Jesus Christ.

"But in this land here the task of the soldier of Christ cannot be limited to peaceful prayer. You have seen today yourself how honest pilgrims are hunted and slaughtered by infidel brigands. For the last four years I have ridden with these poor travellers, lending my sword and shield as protection to those who carry only a purse and staff. I have seen enough. Now, with my Lord Hugh's blessing, I will set up an order of knights. We will take vows of poverty, chastity and obedience, and live according to the monastic code, save that we will share no cloister. Instead we will live in the world and devote our lives to protecting honest travellers in this Holy Land that Our Lord God has returned to our care. Our pilgrims must not suffer the intolerance of those whose do not believe. In Jerusalem I have five fine fellows waiting who will join me. I travelled to the new stronghold at Montréal to find others, and there I have added two more to our number, who will follow me to Jerusalem. Now divine Providence has thrown you into my path. Will you join me? Will you become the ninth Poor Fellow Soldier of Jesus Christ?"

Behind his grim aspect a passion burned which could not but impress me.

"To protect innocent pilgrims, yes, that is a worthy cause. But to attack adherents of Islam just because their beliefs differ from ours...of that I am less sure."

Sir Hugh looked at me hard.

"In the desert, you see, I have had time for thought. My hermit was a man of peace. He preached tolerance. If I were to join you, I would want to know that we would never act as the aggressor, that we would fight only in self-defence and in defence of those in our charge."

"Yes, yes, that is just what holy Bernard preaches at Clairvaux, my friend. He condemns homicide – the killing of man – but condones malecide – the killing of evil. Our Lord Jesus Christ was a man of peace. So shall we be, insofar as this world allows."

"Then I will join you with pleasure."

We grasped each other's hands warmly. Then he drew back.

"I'm sorry – did I hurt you? How is your wound?"

"It's fine. Almost healed."

"How can that be? The pilgrim's salve must have magic powers. From the way it bled it looked to me a deep cut."

I tried to shrug off his puzzlement by saying that it had been no more than a scratch, but surprise tinged with suspicion crept back into his face.

"Nevertheless I am tired. I think I'll turn in," I said.

I know now that I should have thought longer before I spoke my fateful words of acceptance. At the time I sank quickly into a peaceful sleep, warmed by my dreams of the comrades of similar mind that I would find in Jerusalem.

These pleasant thoughts sustained me for the rest of our uneventful journey. My new friend Sir Hugh had little purpose for small talk, no humour, but I told myself that his fine, firm, upstanding character was what mattered. My excitement rose as the familiar walls of the holy city came into sight, even though we approached from the south, through the Sion Gate, which had been the sector taken by Raymond of Toulouse and his band of Provençals in that famous summer of 1099, and not the northern wall which had been my station with Godfrey.

The streets inside the city were strangely empty. Many houses appeared to be unoccupied, as if inhabitants driven away or killed in the siege had never been replaced, even after all this time. Later I learned that there were simply not enough Christians in Outremer to fill the city, and that Moslems and Jews could not feel welcome there.

First we went to the palace occupied by the Count of Champagne. De Payns presented me proudly to his Lord and distant cousin, a thin, courtly gentleman whose sorrow at the disgrace of being cuckolded was written in the lines of his face and made him seem older still than his forty-five years. De Payns had confided in me that the Count believed that his purported son and heir had been fathered by another, and that I should avoid talking overmuch of my own paternity. The Count planned, de Payns said, to return to France as soon as he could, to disinherit the bastard and replace him with a cousin, and then would come back to Outremer to take his vows as a member of our order.

For the time being he provided shelter to the other five knights recruited by Sir Hugh – his special friend Godfrey de Saint Omer, young Archambaud de Saint Aignan, Payen de Montdidier, burly Geoffrey Bissot and Roland de Broussillon – some of the finest flowers that French chivalry had to offer, I am sure. But when I was introduced to them

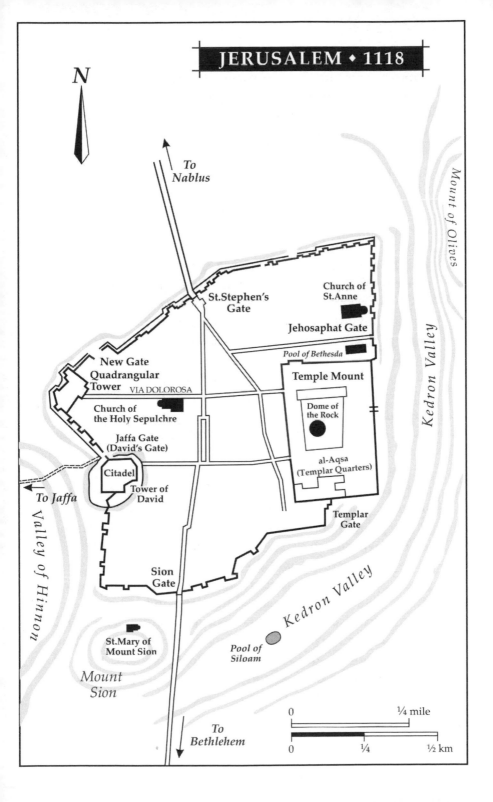

JERUSALEM ◆ 1118

N

To
Nablus

St.Stephen's
Gate

Church of
St.Anne

Jehosaphat Gate

Pool of Bethesda

Temple Mount

New Gate
Quadrangular
Tower   VIA DOLOROSA

Dome of
the Rock

Church of
the Holy Sepulchre

Jaffa Gate
(David's Gate)

al-Aqsa
(Templar Quarters)

Citadel

To Jaffa

Tower of
David

Templar
Gate

Valley of Hinnon

Mount of Olives

Kedron Valley

Sion
Gate

Kedron Valley

St.Mary of
Mount Sion

Pool of
Siloam

Mount
Sion

To
Bethlehem

0   ¼ mile

0   ¼   ½ km

I was disappointed. I suppose that I had hoped for a warm, comradely greeting or some friendly jokes. These five knights made their taciturn leader seem positively loquacious. They competed with each other to show their solemn piety, speaking only when directly addressed, and then replying in as few words as they could.

While waiting for our two remaining colleagues to arrive from Montréal, and for the date to be fixed for our vows and our presentation to the King, I did all the normal things expected of a devout traveller to Jerusalem. First I steeled myself to attend Mass at the Church of the Holy Sepulchre, and tried to drive from my mind all memories of a lonely mountainside in the desert. I contemplated the holiest place in Christendom with a heavy heart and was relieved to find little to impress me in the newly repaired tomb gleaming in false gaudiness beneath its modest naveless rotunda. I had seen finer mosaics in many other places – Constantinople, of course, but also Aleppo and Damascus. And here the rotunda had the appearance of being unfinished, being of wooden beams in the centre, which did not even close it fully to the sky. Then I went to marvel at the Temple Mount, and the great Dome of the Rock. The splendour of its bronze gilded dome and the harmony of its design took my breath away and I was pleased that its new Christian owners had done nothing to spoil the genius of its Moslem architect.

I kept my personal pilgrimage until last, and found a moment when I was able to wander alone beyond the northern end of the Temple Mount. In the little maze of streets there I rediscovered the square that hid the Church of Saint Anne. With trepidation I approached the door, and I almost leapt back in alarm when the postern swung silently open at my touch, just as it had nineteen years earlier. I both hoped to find, and hoped not to find, the old leprous monk who had greeted me before and entombed me by his trickery in the hidden sacristy crypt down in the bowels of the ancient building. But the church was empty, deserted except for a clutch of doves that startled me as they scattered noisily at my entrance and clattered though the broken glass of a high window. Damp stains on the wall showed that the old building was no longer weatherproof, and heaps of broken plaster scarred the floor. The altar furnishings and other decoration had been long since pilfered.

I picked my way down the dark aisle to the altar. There, to its left, the worn steps curved down and stopped at a solid blank wall. Any visitor would have assumed some mistake, some second thought by the mason. I knew – unless I was mad – that there was a secret door in that wall, and that behind it lay the room where I had discovered the Gospel of Lazarus, but try as I might I could not discover its outline, nor any mechanism for operating it. Thwarted, but not wholly unwillingly, I made my way back into the crisp autumn sunlight outside. It was better, perhaps, for my memories to remain bricked up in that hidden chamber.

The last two knights joined us from Montréal, and the seven became the nine. These last two – Gregorias and Grinomalant – had a different cast about them to the others. They were deeply tanned from their station in the desert, while the pallor of the five Jerusalem knights suggested more service before the altar than in the open air. They moved faster, like the young men they were, not at the measured monkish pace of the others. Gregorias's sharp nose lent his face the appearance of perpetual enquiry, and Grinomalant was oval faced, handsome, in a slightly girlish way. Their eyes burned with a bright light of humour rather than the dim glow of sanctimony. And from time to time I heard the corridors of the Count's sombre palace echoing with their laughter, although in the presence of the others their demeanour was always restrained and proper. These perhaps could be the comrades for whom I had hoped. But I had no opportunity to get to know them any better; away from communal gatherings and mealtimes, which were silent in the monastic style, they kept to themselves. Still, I told myself, there was plenty of time to befriend them after we had taken our vows and our Order had been formalised.

It had been decided that we would swear our oaths in the Church of the Holy Sepulchre on the Feast of the Nativity in front of King Baldwin. That to me would once have been a cause for excitement, but my comrades seemed to treat it as no more than their due – except perhaps for Gregorias and Grinomalant, under whose measured exteriors I thought I detected some normal enthusiasm. For my part, I just began to feel nervous. It was inconceivable, I kept telling myself, that King Baldwin could remember my face from the fleeting glimpse he had had of me in Turbessel over sixteen years before. After all, it was not as if I had an unusual face, or any striking characteristics which might set me apart from others. Shorn of my hair – for Sir Hugh had insisted that we all adopt the same style to demonstrate our lack of personal vanity – I would be even less recognisable. Nevertheless, as the great day approached, I could not shake off my unease. As the burden of prayer laid upon us by our leader increased, I had more time than I would have wished to contemplate it.

⁂

SAINT LAZARUS' COLLEGE

The Master was now almost certain that one of the members of the College was responsible for the attacks. The question was, which one? Could it be an undergraduate? The thought of bringing in the Police again to interview all the students was simply too awful to contemplate. A scandal of that sort could put paid to his ambitions. The attack on the platform at Green Park had given them a bit of a fillip. It had been hushed up, of course, the station platform CCTV cameras inexplicably empty once again. But for a few very senior people in the know it had provided a timely reminder of the services he had rendered the nation. And having his own life put at risk could do no harm. He really did not want to spoil the positive effect.

It would be best of course if the sequence of accidents turned out to be that and nothing more. Next best would be to identify the perpetrator or perpetrators himself. If they really were some sort of latter day Templars then they would not want any publicity either. Perhaps, now that the Gospel of Lazarus had been published, they could just be persuaded to back off. After all, what could they possibly have to gain?

He looked pensively out of the window. The Geography Fellow and the Computer Sciences Tutor chose that moment to emerge from the staircase on the opposite side of the Quad. The Master stared at them. They looked shifty somehow, furtive. If one were critical, one might say that the Geography Tutor's sharp nose and dark, pointed features gave him a rather untrustworthy cast. The Computer Science Professor's round bland face was also rather unsavoury. Were they up to something?

From where the Master sat he was unable to see the fond squeeze that his newest recruits gave to each other's hand as they parted to walk in opposite directions round the quad.

Chapter Thirteen

THE BAD MONK

Mon âme est un tombeau que, mauvais cénobite,
Depuis l'éternité je parcours et j'habite.

✳

In the week before the Nativity the first snow fell and the cold
in Jerusalem became bitter. Inside, though, when we left our
lodging on the feast day to process the short distance to the
Church of the Holy Sepulchre, I was warmed by the reception
given to us by the crowds. The powers that be had lost no
opportunity to spread the word in the city about the new order
of monastic knights – or soldier monks – established to protect
pilgrims. I felt vindicated in my decision to join them by the
enthusiasm of the ordinary people. I strutted proudly with the
others in my polished mail under my new white cloak
emblazoned with the red cross – for Sir Hugh had stuck with
the intent he had expressed to me of appropriating that old
Crusader symbol.

In the holiest shrine of Christendom we took our places
under the rotunda, facing the gaudy new structure which was
said to mark the tomb where Jesus had once briefly lain. Hugh
de Payns stood at the centre of our line, flanked on either side
by four of us. As the newest recruit, I took my place humbly

at the left hand end of the row, and bowed my head like the others with outward piety. A blast of trumpets announced the arrival of King Baldwin and Warmund, the Patriarch of Jerusalem. As the King took his position in front of us I started, for in spite of the passage of time I knew him well. His blue eyes passed up and down our row, and to my relief their friendly, encouraging expression changed not at all when they reached me. A warm smile played under the beard which had been pure blond when I had seen it last, but was now flecked with grey. Then he took his place in a great armchair set to the side. The Patriarch, a small man almost swallowed up by his large mitre, took his place and addressed us in Latin.

"It has been deemed fit that as comrades you should recite in unison the vows of poverty, chastity and obedience."

In response, our vows rang out around the rotunda in an emphatic echo.

Then the King rose and joined the Archbishop, dwarfing the little man who scarcely reached the level of Baldwin's beard. He smiled warmly. "I would extend the name of your new order, my friends. You shall come to lodge with me in the palace I have made of the Al-Aqsa Mosque on Temple Mount, and henceforth you shall be known as the Poor Fellow-Soldiers of Jesus Christ and of the Temple of Solomon."

'That'll make a catchy battle cry,' I thought irreverently, but the others were plainly of a different mind and a ripple of excitement passed down the line at such a sign of royal favour. I though felt uneasy at the prospect of being so close beneath the King's eye.

The service over, we processed proudly back to our lodgings, where we gathered up our few belongings to carry them over to Baldwin's palace. It was clear from the quantity of our possessions – our weapons, equipment and a few spare clothes – that we were all in compliance with the vow of poverty we had just taken. My own small bundle was one of the larger, containing as it did the tube that held my scrolls, and which I had passed off as my precious writing materials.

I had to admit that the quarters given us by the King were splendid, not so much for their size or comfort, for they were no more than cells perhaps occupied before by the imams who had staffed the mosque, but for their position on the plateau which dominated the city. Here we were well above the smell of the narrow streets in the lower neighbourhoods, and as the weather warmed into spring I came to appreciate the winds which refreshed the air around the Temple. It was a practical location too, for we were able to keep our horses in Solomon's underground stables once we had dug out the ordure that had accumulated in the corner of the vast complex allocated for our use. We had plenty of room for training and honing our fighting skills away from prying eyes. And because no group of pilgrims would ever leave Jerusalem without visiting the Temple Mount once at least, de Payns thought it would be easy for them to find the escorts that they needed when we were ready to offer our protection to those travelling to and from the coast.

Of course, there was a limit to what the nine of us could do in the face of the many brigand bands that preyed on the travellers along the pilgrim routes. De Payns divided us into three groups of three, and Baldwin agreed to spare each group half a score men-at-arms. I made sure that I was teamed with the two young knights from Montréal and I found myself looking forward to our first escort mission, and the opportunity to get to know my comrades better away from the solemn atmosphere that prevailed under our dour leader.

Our first journey with a body of three score pilgrims down to the port of Jaffa passed peacefully. No bandits threatened us. They doubtless preferred to concentrate on easier prey. My colleagues Gregorias and Grinomalant were pleasant enough, but to my disappointment I was unable to break through the bonds that tied them tightly together. Perhaps they saw in me the same grim piety that I saw in the others, and were cautious about opening up lest they showed excessive warmth or levity which I might think sat awkwardly with our stern purpose. My approaches toward Gregorias were met with a pointed look of enquiring suspicion; Grinomalant responded with a bland expression on his neat oval face. Rebuffed, I observed their intimacy with some jealousy, but told myself that there would be many more journeys like this one when I would be able to win their trust and break down barriers.

How wrong I was! We had shepherded a flock of pilgrims safely back to Jerusalem. I felt tired but satisfied with this first success as I pressed my steed up the ramp to the south of the Temple Mount that led into our subterranean stable. As soon as we had dismounted, three more of my fellow knights appeared, grimmer-faced than ever. They spoke quietly to Gregorias and Grinomalant, who, like me, were busy tying up their horses in preparation for brushing them down. They in turn glanced over at me in surprise. Then all five came over to me.

"We have orders to make a prisoner of you and lead you before the Grand Master," growled Geoffrey Bissot sternly, an expression of distaste on his face so strong that it bordered on hatred. I knew then that only one thing could have happened and I cursed my imprudence.

They surrounded me. Gregorias and Grinomalant roughly grasped each of my arms and marched me to the plain room that served as our refectory. There sat Hugh de Payns behind the table from which we were accustomed to feed, and the two remaining knights – Godfrey de St Omer and Payn de Montdidier, if I remember correctly – stood behind him. On the table in front of de Payns lay my scrolls. Three pairs of eyes blazed their horror at me, whilst the loathing of my five guards pressed almost palpably into me from behind.

Slowly de Payns rose to his feet, his gaze not leaving mine for a moment. Then he walked round the table to stand in front of me. Without warning he spat in my face, and then jarred my head sideways with a heavy blow from the back of his hand. Spittle flew from his lips as he spluttered at me in outrage.

"You filthy heretic. You heathen blasphemer. You have tricked us all and so nearly brought disgrace upon our heads."

Another blow knocked me sideways. Only the tight grip of Gregorias and Grinomalant kept me from spinning around and falling to the floor.

"King Baldwin asked me what I knew of your origins. He could not be quite sure, he said, but he thought that you bore an uncanny resemblance to someone who had once tried to murder him. I took advantage of your absence to go through your things, and we found this…this…this evil filth."

For a moment de Payns was at a loss for words and he covered the silence by striking me again. "These vile heresies…some false gospel making out that Our Lord Jesus Christ is not the true Son of God, that He did not die on the Cross, but is the member of some sacrilegious cult which claims to have the secret of eternal life, in a ceremony involving some sort of grail." He shook his pointed head in a gesture that was more eloquent of his shock than his words. "What do you have to say for yourself? No, save your breath. I don't want to hear. I want two volunteers to take this dog far outside the wall of this holy city and to kill him, kill him by striking the head from his body, just to make sure, and then to burn him to leave no trace, with these…these…"

He could not find words strong enough to express his disgust. Instead he swung round to the table and swept the manuscripts to the floor.

"The shame of it, the disgrace. You might have strangled our order at birth. Praise God that I uncovered you so soon. Praise God that Sir Payn has enough learning to make out Greek. Volunteers…?" His voice rose in a crescendo and his rage now seemed to encompass all the other knights. Hurriedly Gregorias spoke up.

"Sir, please give me and Sir Grinomalant the honour of disposing of this traitor and all the manifestations of his sins. After all, his crime touches us most closely of all – we were his nearest comrades."

"Very well, I grant your wish. Not a single soul outside this room must know of these events. Not a single soul, do you hear? I will tell the King that his suspicions were correct and that we have dealt with the renegade, but even the King must not know the full nature of his crimes. When you have done your deed, ride on, and rejoin the others on the Acre road. There is another group of pilgrims ready to travel. Go on, get on with it."

A set of heavy iron fetters was waiting in the corner of the room, and Bissot dragged them over. In disgust Sir Hugh ripped off my red-crossed surcoat. My feet were shackled; my hands were manacled behind my back, and the two chained together so that I could scarcely shuffle forward, let alone hope to escape.

They dumped me in a corner, dealing me the occasional kick whenever they passed my way. I resigned myself to my fate. I supposed that it all had to end at some stage. Once night had fallen Gregorias and Grinomalant came to me and yanked me to my feet. They seemed to have retrieved my manuscripts, for Gregorias had slung the quiver which had sheltered them over his shoulder. Impatient with the pace at which I could walk, they half dragged, half carried me back down to the stables. They pulled a hooded cloak over me so that my identity was hidden and slung me face down over the back of my horse. With ropes they secured my hands and feet to the stirrups on either side. I could see little of my upside down world under my mount's belly, but I heard a cruel laugh, presumably at my expense, and the sound of knights getting into the saddle. Then they clattered down the steps, leading me behind them.

The fame and mystery of our order had already spread, so

even though it was well after sunset, my captors had no problem at the double gate at the foot of the Temple Mount.

"They are the Knights of the Temple," I heard one guard say to the other in a voice touched with awe. His comrade replied in a similar tone. "Templars with a prisoner. I'd not want to be in his shoes. We must let them through. Come, help me here." The gate groaned open a horse's width, and when we had passed, banged ominously shut once more.

I judged that we swung to the left, to ride north down the Vale of Kedron beneath the walls of the city. To the east I could picture the Mount of Olives, and I thought to myself bitterly that we must be close to the spot where I had emerged from the catacomb of Saint Anne with the Gospel of Lazarus. Under my breath I cursed all the trouble that the book had brought me.

Gregorias and Grinomalant must have had orders to take me far from the city walls before finishing me off. Then I realised of course that they needed to find a place where there was enough fuel for my pyre. I remembered from our siege of Jerusalem all those years before that there had been no wood to find for miles around. So we rode for hours through the night, hours stretched for me by the sickening discomfort of my position over the saddle. Somehow I managed to avoid vomiting. I determined to preserve as much dignity as I could in the face of my fate.

At last we came to a halt. I did not know whether to be happy or sad. I tried to tell myself that what was about to be done to me was as much an act of mercy as I had done on the slope of Mount Sinai. But in my heart I knew that I was not ready yet.

I heard a snide chuckle from one of the knights as they untied me and pulled me down from the horse. How stupid I had been to want them as my friends. They were no better than the others. Hands pulled my hood back. The night was clear, cloudless, and the moonlight shimmered over the rocky landscape. They had chosen a small wadi for their act, and I could smell water. 'It is still only spring,' I thought, and filled with an all-pervading sadness.

One of them pushed me onto my knees, and I flinched with pain as my joints jarred down onto the sharp rock. I heard the rasp of a sword being drawn from its scabbard and obeyed the gruff instruction to stretch forward my neck. 'I might as well do all I can to make sure it is a clean blow,' I thought.

The blade whistled through the air and in the fraction of time before it landed my shoulders hunched and I asked myself, 'I wonder what it will be like?' Then the force of the blow knocked me forward. My face landed in the dirt but, surely, was still attached to my body. Dazed by the force of the blow, I heard wild laughter and my anger rose as they dragged me back up. 'The bastards are playing with me,' I thought. I raised my eyes and saw Grinomalant hopping around convulsed with laughter. It had been Gregorias who had struck me with the flat of his sword, and he too was beside himself.

"Did you really think we would kill the milk cow?" he spluttered. "You are the one who can lead us to the man with the recipe for eternal life. I think we might be able to persuade him to give us the same treatment in return for handing you over, don't you? And as for burning your precious Gospel! That would be criminal; it is a gold-mine. The Church will pay us fortune upon fortune to suppress a document that would do them such damage. We are not like the others, you see."

That much, at least, I had got right.

"We could not care less about protecting a few sweaty pilgrims. We joined old de Payns because of the opportunity for fame and riches. And we could not believe our luck when you turned out to be a bit of a surprise! We'll have your treasure and turn it to our advantage. De Payns and the others – they'll soon get themselves piously killed, and we will make the order our own great empire. With your secret we will still be at its head a thousand years from now!"

"Come on," said Grinomalant. "I am knackered. Let's spend the rest of the night here."

From the eager look that passed between the two tormentors I realised that there was more to their friendship than I had at first thought. I began to understand why I had not been admitted inside its bonds. I lay awake in discomfort on the rough ground, tortured by the unnatural position forced on me by my manacles, but also by the grunts and giggles from the acts being perpetrated a few yards from where I lay. To the breach of their vow of obedience, they added the rupture of their vow of chastity. Eventually they had sated their lust for each other and their animal noises stopped, but even so I could not sleep.

In the morning I asked for some water. Grinomalant indifferently pointed to the trickle of water at the bottom of the wadi. "Help yourself," he shrugged. How could I ever have thought him handsome? The pleasure he took in his cruelty scarcely registered on the blank oval of his face as he watched me struggling to raise myself to my feet. I could get no further than my knees; the chain between the shackles was too short. Nor, with my hands manacled behind my back, could I crawl down to the stream. Determined not to give in, I wriggled on my belly like a snake over the rock, while the two Templars roared with laughter. Almost as soon as I had reached the edge and started lapping at the sandy water they pulled me away.

"We know that you do not need water and food to survive," Gregorias sneered.

"But I can feel thirst and hunger as much as any other man."

"What is that to us?" Grinomalant chimed in. "We'll enjoy watching you suffer. After all, you must atone for your sins. Then, when we have no more use for you and we do finish you off, maybe you will end up in the right place. You see, we are doing you a favour."

I tried to ignore their sniggers and wearily submitted to

being heaved like a sack of grain over my horse's back, and tied on either side once more.

I have undergone some uncomfortable journeys in my time, but none were as bad as this trek north towards Alamut. My physical pain was made worse by my mental torment because, try as I might, I could devise no scheme which might lead to my escape. My shackles were too secure. Even if I could find some way to get the key from Gregorias or Grinomalant – I assumed that one or other of them carried it – I would not be able to fit it into the locks on my hands without help. I had no friends towards whom I could guide my captors. I just had to hope that we might encounter some Moslem soldiers, and that they would overcome the Templars and free me, taking me for an enemy of their enemies. But even before we crossed out of Christian territory, Grinomalant and Gregorias travelled very cautiously. I surmised that they did not want to meet anyone who might carry a report back to Jerusalem of Templar Knights travelling with a prisoner in a direction that they had no honest cause to take. I feared that as we travelled north away from Outremer, and deeper into Moslem territory, they would become more careful still, but I kept my hopes alive by telling myself that there was more chance of an encounter which might lead to my escape.

Gregorias and Grinomalant were also very distrustful of my directions. For this I suppose I cannot blame them. From my journal, over which they would pore with excitement when they stopped to rest, they could form a general view of the direction of Alamut. They resisted my efforts to lead them across the River Jordan and out into the desert, which I insisted would be the most direct route, but which they saw correctly as the most dangerous. Instead they required me to take the road past Damascus and on to Aleppo that I had followed in reverse on my last journey from the Assassins' stronghold.

It was only north of the Sea of Galilee that I was able to

lead them across the river. It was still fat with melting snow from the mountains so when we forded it the water reached our horse's chests. Tied face down over the saddle, as I was, my head was submerged and I suffered the agonies of a death by drowning, giving great amusement to my captors when we reached the far bank and I struggled, gasping and choking, to draw air back into my lungs.

"Now perhaps you will stop complaining that we have not given you enough to drink," sneered Gregorias, producing gales of laughter from his friend.

Beyond the Jordan, Gregorias and Grinomalant planned to skirt Damascus safely to the north, sticking discreetly to the foothills, as I had done when I had ridden towards Homs in my failed attempt to thwart the assassination of its emir many years before. They had finished their provisions, and now began to grumble that they needed to find a village where they could replenish their supplies, bickering with each other like the twisted lovers they were.

"You should have been better prepared when we left Jerusalem."

"Don't blame me. De Payns gave us no time to prepare. Anyway, he'd have been suspicious if we had taken more than we needed for a couple of days, wouldn't he?"

"Well, we need to find some food somewhere. It is all right for him, but I cannot survive on an empty stomach."

They rode on in a sulky silence, but a little further on Grinomalant piped up again.

"Look, up there, there are some buildings. And that must be a church on the rock. See the crosses on its domes. It must be a Christian village out here. So we'll be safe if we go and ask for some supplies. If they won't sell to us, we'll just take what we want. And we are far enough from Jerusalem. De Payns will never hear of us passing up here."

Gregorias agreed. I tried to twist my head to see where we were going, but gave up. The hammering in my temples from my position over the horse's back was agonising and turning sideways just made it worse.

A little further on, some small houses came into sight. We stopped. One of the Templars dismounted. I could not see which. I heard him hammering on a door which then creaked open.

"We want bread," I heard Gregorias growl. "And wine. And any other food you have – meat, fruit? Do you hear?"

A woman's voice came in response. I recognised the Greek tongue. She sounded scared but was trying to project as friendly a tone as possible. "Sirs, what can we give you? Have you come for food, or do you wish to collect some of the holy oil from the *Shagoura*? In the church we have some bottles prepared already."

"Damn it. I cannot understand a word she is saying."

"Get Hugh to translate, you fool. He is meant to be able to speak these people's language."

Gregorias came round and I felt the ropes around my hands and feet being loosed. Then he pushed me forward so that I slid head first over my horse's saddle, somersaulted and ended up flat on my back in the dust. He pulled me roughly to my feet, where I struggled to overcome my dizziness and stay upright. He slapped me on both cheeks.

"You dirty heretic," he spat, "wake up and tell me what this peasant is saying. And tell her we want the best food and wine in this stinking village."

Seeing the way they treated me made the poor woman look even more frightened. Nevertheless she stepped forward into the street. She was stout, motherly, but handsome, and wore her dark hair pulled tightly back. Through her fear I could see sympathy for my plight. I smiled as reassuringly as I could and spoke in Greek.

"These men want meat and drink. It would be wise to bring the best you have, for otherwise they will just take it."

Then I stopped. Over her shoulder I saw a man emerging from the house, her husband perhaps. His beard was grey, and he was a little stooped. But I could not mistake those close set desert eyes. His identity as Samir, Assassin and former caravan master, was confirmed by the astonishment that spread over his face when he stopped and looked at me. I tried to show no sign of recognition and rushed on.

"They are in a hurry so may not harm you if you give them no offence and provide what they want."

"So they have not come for the holy oil?" She looked confused. "I have no meat to give them. Here in Seydnaya we have eaten no meat since the Emperor's vision."

I looked at her in enquiry. "Vision?"

"It was here that the Emperor Justinian came hunting. But when he was about to loose his arrow at the deer, she turned into an icon of the Virgin Mary. So he built this church to mark the spot and to house the icon, the *Shagoura*, the Famous One. She cries oily tears which are treasured."

Grinomalant was losing patience. "What is she saying, damn it? Get on with it or I will slay her in front of you."

I repeated her words to him, adding, "She says that the oil is very precious and that just a few drops of it will fetch a very high price."

Now the man whom I supposed to be Samir took charge. He pushed past his wife and addressed the two knights in something that passed as Latin, interspersed with the occasional Arab word where his vocabulary failed him.

"Please, Sirs. Your prisoner I know. He my enemy. So you my friend. He try kill me."

He took a step towards me, and slapped me twice across the face before Grinomalant pushed him back roughly.

"What is this? Do you know this man?"

Wearily I answered, "I do know him – from years back. He was one of the Assassins. I fought him, and could have killed him, but I spared his life."

The ingratiating smile that Samir turned on the Templars sat incongruously on his desert face.

"Now I Christian. I marry woman years ago and come Christian. Lodge here tonight? *Shagoura* cry most at night. In morning more oil. More very precious oil. Is late. We feed horses. Woman get food for you."

Grinomalant looked across at Gregorias.

"We need to spend the night somewhere, I suppose."

The sun had disappeared behind the mountains and it was getting dark.

"Many pilgrims they come. We make welcome. Make meal – no meat but bread, good cheese, much wine. Stables here behind."

Gregorias was still suspicious. "Are you really a Christian?"

"Christian. Yes Christian." Samir seemed to have shed enough of the Arab and become enough of a Greek to remember to nod his head, not shake it. He pointed at the cross emblazoned on the Templars' surcoats, and bobbed obsequiously. "Good, very good. See on wall inside."

"Come on Gregorias, we'll be fine here. We can feed the horses properly, eat – even drink, for God's sake. Tomorrow we'll take as much of this precious oil as we can carry. Why not take our chance? We can take it in turns to watch. If they try any tricks we will just kill them. Or we will kill them anyway."

The deadly sins of gluttony and avarice caused Gregorias to acquiesce with his lover. My heart sank further still. I now had to contend with another enemy. For all I knew, Samir might plan to murder me in the night to settle his old score. I knew that I should not have let him live.

"Bring prisoner," Samir said. "Safe in here."

He led the way into a storeroom, one side of which was lined with large barrels. Gregorias shoved me hard in the small of my back so that I measured my length on the floor. The door slammed shut behind me and some sort of bolt grated into place. I struggled round in the dark into a sitting position facing the door and tried to make myself as comfortable as

I could. In my despair I could not even be bothered to test the door; I just resigned myself to my fate.

Later on, through the door, I heard laughter and some snatches of song. I guessed that Samir was fulfilling his promise to provide the knights with their fill of wine. They were providing their own song, and from what I knew would need no women. I smiled bitterly. Then I must have dozed off, for everything was silent when I heard the bolt sliding slowly back. I detected the outline of Samir's head. My fear that he had wanted to get me into his power had been correct. I steeled myself to resist his attack as best I could. Perhaps if I made enough noise I could attract the Templars' attention and they might come to my help, for they would not want me dead so soon. As if reading my mind, Samir clamped his hand over my mouth.

"Quiet." He now spoke in his native Arab tongue instead of the Latin that he had mangled for the benefit of the knights. "You have my wife to thank for this. She is soft and kind. Anyone in distress, especially a prisoner, she must help. I benefited years ago when you spared my life. I crawled into this village. She took pity on me, bound my wounds, gave me shelter, and later we married. When she heard that you were the man who brought me to her, she insisted that I come and release you. Soft and gentle she may be, but she is also strong, and when she swore that she would throw me out if I did not do what she asked, I knew that she was speaking the truth."

Having imparted the news that he was helping me, he removed his hand from my mouth. I was choked with hope and excitement and could not speak for a moment.

"But the knights?" I asked.

"I slipped a little something into their last flagon of wine," he said. "They'll sleep soundly till morning. She won't let me do anything to harm them either. Nor must you – or my life won't be worth living."

"But if they suspect you have helped me…"

"I'll loosen some planks in the roof so that it will look as if you have escaped by yourself. Make yourself scarce. I could not get the key for your shackles – they are sleeping with their bags as pillows."

"And my scrolls? I must have my manuscripts."

"Be grateful that you have your freedom. Go, quickly and quietly."

He pushed me out through the door.

"I won't be able to get far shackled like this. I'll have to hide close by until they are gone, and then come back to find a blacksmith."

"Just make sure they have gone."

"Thank you. Say thank you to your wife."

Samir grunted. I staggered down the hill away from the village. A safe distance away I turned off the path and hid deep in the trees to wait for daybreak. When it was light I made my way back to a point where I could watch the track unobserved.

Perhaps two hours later I heard the drumming of hooves. Up the track a cloud of dust appeared, thrown up by three horses – the Templars' and mine, bearing Samir. He looked grim and his hands were tied, but, I thought, at least he was alive.

When they had passed safely out of sight I climbed as fast as my shackles would allow down to the track and back up into the village in search of a blacksmith.

I planned to stop at Samir's house when I was free of my chains in order to express my gratitude to his wife and to promise that I would do whatever I could to free him in his turn. But as I passed, the sound of sobbing stopped me in my tracks and I entered through the open door.

Samir's wife lay on her back on the floor. She was ashen-faced. The sobbing came from a girl, eight or nine years old, kneeling by her side. Two women, neighbours maybe, tended her, one cradling her head and dabbing at her brow with a damp cloth, the other trying to staunch the flow of blood from a vicious sword wound in her side.

I fell to my knees at her side. "What happened?" I had to lean forward to catch her words.

"They were angry, raging, when they woke and found you gone. The sharp-nosed one stabbed me in a fury. They were about to kill Samir, when one of them – the pretty one – said that he was an Assassin and could show them the way to Alamut. He said they did not need you – said they had your writing and that was enough. Then they took Samir. Thank God and the Blessed Virgin that I made the little one stay out of the way in the upper room, otherwise they might have killed her too."

This provoked increased wailing from the girl, who had her mother's soft dark features and had been spared Samir's close set eyes.

"I may be able to help," I said hesitantly. "But I must get my manacles off. Take me quickly to the blacksmith."

I could see that there was no time to lose. The woman's life was ebbing away. "Quickly, please, then I can help your mother."

The little girl did not want to leave her mother's side. Instead, the matron holding her head relinquished her position and sternly led me to the village smithy. Before she could take charge I ordered the blacksmith to strike through the chains that held my hands behind my back.

"That's all I need for now. I'll come back for the rest later."

Back in the sorrowing house I motioned the other nurse away. With reluctance she made room for me to kneel down at the woman's side. I shut my eyes for a moment and summoned all my strength. I did not know if my healing power would have any effect on a wound like this. Disease and illness I had cured in the desert, but I feared that a mortal wound might be beyond me.

Gently I removed the towel pressed against her side to

staunch the flow of blood. Both women watching pressed their lips together tightly with disapproval, and one made as if to stop me.

"Let him!" the little girl shrieked, and then started to sob more loudly when she saw the horrible extent of the wound.

I placed my hands over the gaping mouth left by the Templar sword. The woman moaned as I pushed the edges of the wound together. I felt her blood dribbling through my fingers, but also power draining from me into her. My hands became hot, and the woman relaxed underneath my touch and became still, so still that I feared she was dead.

I kept my eyes shut. I did not dare to look. I tried hard not to pray, even from habit, lest my hypocrisy thwart me. The body beneath my hands did not feel dead. I could not contain myself any longer and I opened my eyes a crack. The flow of blood seemed to have stopped, but I knew that happened in death. Did her face have a little more colour about it? The watchers all looked serious, anxious, but not as if her end had come. I closed my eyes once more, and entered into some sort of trance.

❋

SAINT LAZARUS' COLLEGE

"1118," said the History Don in excitement. Under his sling his left arm was in a heavy plaster cast, but otherwise he seemed none the worse for his accident.

"Without a doubt. That answers one question about the Templars. Previously it was unclear whether they were founded in 1118 or 1119. William of Tyre, the closest we have to a contemporary source, indicates one date in one place and another in another. But we know for sure that King Baldwin the First died in 1118 and here there is confirmation that the Templars were sworn in at Christmas in the same year. To be frank, I had always thought 1118 was most likely. Baldwin the Second was travelling a lot in 1119 – he had to contend with the aftermath of the defeat of Roger of Antioch at the Field of Blood, for one thing. I doubt he would have had much time to approve the establishment of the Templars. He had too much else on his mind. And there is a record of him celebrating the Feast of the Nativity in 1119 in Bethlehem with his wife Morphia. He could hardly have been swearing in the Templars at the same time, in another place, could he?"

The History Don looked round the Senior Common Room in triumph. "And it also means that we can pinpoint precisely Hugh's dates in the desert. He was there for fifteen years."

"Not just the usual forty days and forty nights, then." The Geography Fellow's pointed nose twitched. He had taken on the late Chaplain's sarcastic mantle, even if his approach to matters biblical was somewhat less pious than the late churchman's.

The Master sighed. His pleasure in the long-awaited arrival of the Templars in the plot was somewhat diminished by his fear that their secretive successors were on his tail and out for revenge. His attention was drawn back by the History Don, who was in full flow.

"And one of the mysteries about the Templars is that there were nine founder knights but we only know six of their names for sure : Hugh de Payns himself, Godfrey de Saint Omer, Archambaud de Saint Aignan, Payen de Montdidier, Geoffrey Bissot, and a character called Rossal or Roland something or other."

"As in the Chanson de Roland, you mean?" suggested the Computer Sciences Tutor, receiving a withering look for his pains from the History Don.

"The other three seem to have been written out of history. I'd suggest that their names were none other than Gregorias, Grinomalant and Hugh de Verdon. Three renegades – or two and a half perhaps." This last revision was made in response to an angry glare from the Best-Selling Author, who had become rather fond of his anti-hero.

"And here in Hugh's story we have the germs of all those myths which later built up about the Templars. You know – all that populist stuff about digging in the Stables of Solomon and finding some sort of treasure. Well, obviously the treasure was Hugh's gospel, and the only digging they did was to shovel out the old horse shit. But then when Philip the Fair set about destroying the order two centuries later they were accused of homosexuality and blasphemy, of worshipping a severed head, the so-called cult of Baphomet. It looks to me as if those two gay knights started those rumours, or maybe began traditions that were just carried on."

Anyone watching the Geography Fellow and the Computer Sciences Tutor might have said that the two of them looked rather uncomfortable.

✳

Chapter Fourteen

TO A MADONNA

Je te ferai de mon Respect de beaux Souliers
De satin, par tes pieds divins humiliés

✳

When I came to, I found myself flat on my back on the earthen floor of the room. My question was answered before I had asked it, by the girl's expression. She looked happy. Her dark eyes danced, like a child's should.

I felt myself smiling back at her, and I raised myself on one elbow, before sinking back in utter exhaustion.

"Where…?" I could not find the strength for any other words. One of the matrons came forward, bobbing with fear and awe.

"Master, we carried her upstairs to her bed. She sleeps too. Almost all…almost all sign of the wound has gone. It is a miracle."

My eyes closed in relief and I could not stop myself from sinking back into the depths of sleep.

I was woken by the sun on my face, pouring in through the small window. Too hot in its rays, uncomfortable in spite of the pillow that had been pushed under my head, I staggered to my feet. At least my hands were no longer chained to my ankles. I felt nervous, full of foreboding. Another day must have passed. The Templars would be far ahead of me.

I shouted for attention. The girl clattered lightly down the stairs.

"Where is your mother? I must get these chains off quickly and then follow them."

"She is upstairs. Sleeping. Peacefully."

Her smile of soft trust and respect melted me, and I found myself responding with a smile of my own.

"Begin to wake her gently. I must go after the others as soon as I can. I must rescue your father."

Her earnest eyes widened in concern.

"But first I must get off the remains of these shackles, so you have a little time to stir your mother."

I plodded back to the forge at the edge of the village. It seemed that my fame had spread rapidly, for the blacksmith bustled forward with quick respect in his leather apron to file the shackles off my feet. He showed reluctance to let me do the same myself for the manacles which, separated, still pressed around my wrists.

"Master, allow me to perform that service for you."

"No, I am in a hurry. Do my feet and I will do the wrists."

More practised at this work than me, and far stronger, with arm muscles like small hams, he had both shackles off my ankles by the time that I had done one wrist, and then he took over the job from me. I breathed a sigh of relief when the last fetter fell away, clanking to the floor. I stroked ruefully the painful sores where my skin had been rubbed away, but knew that they would heal quickly. I could already feel them itching.

I thanked the smith; I had no payment to offer him but knew anyway that it would have been refused.

"Give me a blessing. Please."

With a heart heavy with hypocrisy I made the Sign of the Cross in his direction. "May good health and good luck be

215

with you and your family, *in saecula saeculorum*, for ever and ever," I muttered, and hurried off.

Back in Samir's house, the woman was up, preparing provisions for my journey. When I entered she threw herself to her knees at my feet and took my hands.

"Thank you, Master. Thank you. You have saved my life."

"It was I who brought all this trouble upon you. It was the least I could do. And now they have taken your husband. I must do whatever I can to get him back for you."

"Had it not been for your mercy he would never have come here at all. He is not a bad man – he gave me my jewel, my flower – but… . Why not let him be? When he has shown those men what they want perhaps he will come back. What is fated, is fated. Perhaps… . Stay here yourself. Our village could do with a man like you to protect us."

Did I detect a trace of coquettishness in her expression? Her daughter jumped with excitement and clapped her hands together. "Yes stay, do stay."

"I have to go," I said, in a sterner tone than I meant. "I am now in Samir's debt and I would not let him down. And those knights have some documents that I must take back. Don't worry about food – but I need a mount, and any weapon that you can find."

I thought with regret of my sword, given to me by Godfrey, which had hung at my side for so long that I missed it like a limb, and my anger began to rise at the Templars who had robbed it from me.

"Please be quick. The sooner I leave, the better my chance of catching up with them."

When I saw the best animal that the village could provide for me, it shattered my hopes of catching my quarry before they reached Alamut. I have hated mules ever since. This one was an ugly, stubborn brute with wild wall eyes and long yellow age-gapped teeth which it bared at the slightest provocation. Its head, with great drooping ears, sat oversized at the end of a spindly neck. I tried not to seem an ingrate – the village was poor – and so concealed my dismay. Nor was my weapon much better – a long dagger that Samir might have used in the days before his respectability but had neglected so that it was blunt and pitted with rust. Nevertheless I strapped it to my side. My mail rattled against it in reproach.

A blanket served as saddle on the mule's bony back. I climbed on and the animal shifted edgily. I took the woman's bundle of food with as much grace as I could muster and now I was sure that I saw regret in her expression.

"Goodbye," I said. "Thank you. I will get him back for you."

Of that at least they seemed to have no doubt. They seemed to think that I could do anything and with sudden gloom I knew how my own master must have felt.

Before I could kick my heels into the mule's flanks, the girl reached something up to me.

"Here," she said. "It's my lucky stone. I want you to have it. My daddy used to say that it could open the way into paradise. Go on, take it." And she pressed into my hand a smooth black oval pebble the size of a small pigeon's egg. "It'll bring you luck."

I smiled goodbye. The mule lurched reluctantly forward and I stifled my curses.

As I descended the foothills I worried about the route I should follow. I remembered Samir saying that he had never been to Alamut. It was that statement that had stayed my hand and caused me to spare him all those years ago, for it had told me that he at least could have played no part in Blanche's dishonour. But presumably he must know the direction to Hasan-i Sabbah's stronghold; presumably too he would be able to persuade his fellow Assassins to grant him access once he was there. After all, they would not know how he had embraced the Christian faith and lived as a recidivist for so many years. I thought it most likely that Samir would take the route he had known intimately as a caravan master between

Damascus and Aleppo, and would turn eastwards onto less familiar ways only once he had reached the northern city. I resolved to travel the same way, hoping to take advantage of any delays that might befall them, and perhaps to pick up their sign along the way. As I rode – if that is a fair description of the poor progress I made on my mule's back – I puzzled about how my adventure might end. Somehow it was right that it should play out at Alamut, the castle which housed the golden grail, the ominous castle of life and death. How did the Templars plan to persuade Hasan to tell them Medea's secret? What could they offer him in return? How could I gain access into the eagle's eyrie? Once I was there, how could I hope to escape again with my documents and with Samir?

Some call memory a fickle mistress. But they do her an injustice. To me, she is a faithful wife who does not like to stir far from home. She stays close to the places that she knows. That is how it seemed when she embraced me on my journey back towards Alamut. Returning through the places I had passed years before, I remembered with shocking clarity the events that had taken place there. Worse by far, I was seared again by the emotions those events had stirred in me. So south of Aleppo, I was burned again by my guilt at the awful death I had brought on my friend Mohammed. I could not rid myself of the vision of the Goldsmith's podgy hand forcing his delicate blade between the white bones of Mohammed's gashed neck. I took a little solace again from the soothing memory of Samir's kindness – false kindness as I later found out – but at least on that journey from Aleppo the man had been a friend to me. Fate had described for me a large circle in now sending me back to rescue that same man, albeit for the sake of his wife and daughter.

Beyond Aleppo, I remembered my excited satisfaction at my success in duping the master of Alamut. How I had laughed when he had thought me a good Moslem, when he had released me to go to murder Baldwin, the only man I hated almost as much as him. Then, of course, that smugness was proven to be false vanity, and I had nearly killed the wrong man. And later, when given the chance to face the right Baldwin, I had failed.

Beyond the Euphrates and the Tigris and the ancient Mesopotamian fertility enclosed by those two great rivers, the landscape became bleak and mountainous. I knew that I was nearing Alamut once more. My memories now rekindled my hatred for Hasan-i Sabbah, fanning embers that I had long thought cold, blowing off the white ash and making their hearts glow red hot once more. The ferocity of my hatred for Hasan eclipsed even the loathing I felt towards the two Templars. I wanted my documents back, the documents which gave private purpose to my existence. I wanted to satisfy my debt to Samir and to restore him to his family. Then – a flood of exhaustion washed my hatred down again and I felt ineffably tired – then I would go, leave Outremer, perhaps return to the land of my fathers and try to make some sort of life for myself.

I soon found that I was closer behind my quarry than I had feared, for near one of my paths I found traces of a camp, and of a fire that from the state of the ashes could not have been more than a day or two old. Perhaps the way that I had learnt from Mohammed was a short cut unknown to Samir.

My mule refused to accommodate any change of speed. Nevertheless, I drove him a couple of hours longer every day, and I fancied that the campfires now regularly by the wayside were a little warmer each time that I found them. But before I could come up with my quarry I found myself at the entrance to Alamut's baleful valley. I would have to go the rest of the way on foot. That delay was frustrating but it was still with pleasure and relief that I loosed my mule. From the way he pulled back his lips and showed me his gapped, ill-meeting teeth one last time when I slapped his rump to send him away I don't think he was any sorrier to part than I was.

For days I had wrestled with the problem of how to get

into Alamut. It would be impossible to near the gate of the castle without being detected. Even after dark the sleepiest sentry would spot any man or beast wending its way up the steep narrow switchback that gave the only route up from the valley. As a last resort, I had even thought of presenting myself at the gate and allowing myself to be taken inside as a prisoner. But once more my memory acted the faithful wife and stirred a strange faint image. When, at Hasan's behest, I had thrown myself off his battlements to prove my loyalty and obedience, I remembered that I had landed in some sort of garden at the base of the walls. For all that I had passed in and out of consciousness from the pain in my shattered body, I was almost certain that I had not been carried back into the castle by the main gate. I thought that I remembered a tunnel, almost a canal of rebirth, and some sort of strange rising motion carrying me through it. Could this memory be telling me there was another entrance into Alamut from this secret garden? Anyway, I had nothing to lose. I determined after dark to hunt for the garden. If it existed outside my imagination I would gain access to it and search for a hidden passage into the castle. If I found nothing I would return the next morning to give myself up at the main gate.

I pressed myself into a fold in the rock near where I had parted from my mule. There, hot with impatient discomfort, I watched as the sun climbed slowly through the sky. At long last it began to dip towards the western peaks. As it touched them it flushed red, gashed by their jagged edges, and poured its blood into the valley. I shuddered in this sanguinary twilight, suddenly cold. Perhaps too hastily, before it was quite dark, I moved from my hiding place and flitted towards the base of the crag from whose peak Alamut scowled.

By the time I reached my goal, night had fallen solidly. The moon, waning towards her monthly nadir, threw a faint, ghostly light which seemed all the colder for the contrast with her diurnal brother. High to my left I could just make out the path that looped up to the castle's main gate. I went the other way, to the right, edging along a slope which became steadily more precipitous. Soon I was struggling sideways on all fours like a crab, and wishing that my hands were pincers which might give me better purchase than my broken nails and fingers, bloodied by scrabbling for a hold on the rock. I paused to draw breath and looked up at the castle. The moonlight silvered the walls above, and showed me the battlements from which I had thrown myself at Hasan's command. I could now see that falling from there I would have landed beyond the ridge at whose base I now perched. Encouraged, I pressed on round what was fast turning from a slope into a vertical cliff face.

No sane man would have risked his life on that climb. Two things made me able to drive myself upwards. I knew that if I slipped my life would not be forfeit, for I had fallen before and survived. And the moonlight was merciful enough not to reveal the precipice, leaving the depth of my folly shrouded in shadow. So I inched round and upwards, feeling out the rocks for ledges and cracks that I could not see and forcing my fingers and toes into them. The sinews in my arms stretched almost beyond endurance. Once the fragment of rock that I had made my footing sheared off, and as I flailed desperately to find another hold I had to listen to the clattering stones measuring the awful depths below me. Then, little by little, the slope bent forward again. Panting, streaming with sweat in spite of the cool night air, I pulled myself over the lip and looked down.

I had found Hasan's false paradise. Nothing else could explain the trees below. They rustled their leaves to waft up to me the honeyed scent of jasmine. I lay still, sucking in the sweetness, until the sweat dried cold on my brow and my clothes were clammy. I made out the reflection of the stars and of the moon's narrow crescent on pools of water beneath me. I heard streams tinkling, or fountains, and then, in

221

extraordinary invention, the exquisite trill of a nightingale. This was Eden, unspoilt by Adam, yet created not by a god but by a man for his own purposes of evil.

High above in the cragged castle, candlelight, or firelight perhaps, glimmered from double arched windows that could only belong to Hasan's library. Someone there was awake. Above them jagged the battlements from which I had dived. Somewhere the garden beneath me must hide the passageway up which I had been carried, broken from my fall.

My heartbeats were now pumped by excitement, no longer by fear. Careful to make no noise – the shy nightingale told me that for the time being this Eden was untroubled by Man, but I could not be sure – I scrambled down the incline into the bowl below. Here the smells were still more intense; I stood on carpets of aromatic herbs, my feet crushing the scent from camomile and thyme. Against the midnight sky, whenever they crossed the stars or the moon, I saw bats darting, turning in wild zigzags through the dark. If only I could see like them.

A rill of water trickled gently in a straight channel down the middle of the paradise garden before disappearing somewhere underground. On either side lay a smooth path of white marble. I kept well back in the trees behind and stepped silently towards the castle.

At the base of the cliff a stone doorway was clear to see. In place of any handle it had a small round hole, and I slipped my finger inside to pull it open. It would not budge. I tried again, and felt carefully around inside for some secret catch, some trigger. I found nothing.

Frustrated, furious that my perilous climb had been wasted, thwarted by this door, I leant against the wall. I tried to sooth my spirit with the sounds and smells of the garden. But in vain. Something hard in the bag of belongings that I carried slung across my shoulders pressed painfully into the small of my back. Annoyed, I lifted the strap over my head and reached inside. I found myself laughing softly. I pulled my hand out, and unclenched it to find myself looking at the stone egg given me by the girl. I could not stop myself laughing under my breath.

"My lucky stone," I murmured to myself. "Daddy says that it can open the door to paradise. Does he indeed!"

Still chuckling, I turned to find that the bulb of the egg fitted snugly through the keyhole. I pushed it in, and heard it tumbling down against some hidden mechanism. With a click the door opened. In the silence the sound was so loud that I jumped and looked around nervously.

I left that garden with regret. It was a strange oasis of peace in a brutal world. I fingered a salute at the bats. Were they feeding, dodging around like that, or chasing each other for fun? Was the one in front a female, teasing her lover, by staying just out of reach? Whatever they were doing, their quick freedom was something I could never know. Sombre now, suddenly almost angry with them, I turned back through the doorway.

What a fool I was! Would I never learn? In the Church of Saint Anne in Jerusalem my enthusiasm for the end of my quest made me forget the leper monk, allowing him to seal me into the library that nearly became my tomb. Now, a breath of wind pushed the door to and closed out what little light the moon had spared. It clicked again, sounding even louder inside, and so final that I scarcely bothered to test if the door was firmly shut. I was in the pitch dark again. I cursed the craftsmen whose skill had balanced the hinge so cunningly and then cursed them again. Frightened, and angry more with myself than with them, I felt forward blindly into the blackness.

I stubbed my foot and from stone I stepped up onto wood. I knew it was wood because it echoed slightly hollow. I tried to walk forward but came against a stone wall. I moved right and came against another wall. I felt something else, like a tentacle. Scared, I pulled away. Cautiously I put my hand out again. There was a rope hanging down in that corner. I moved the other way, and found the same; a wall, a corner, a rope. I seemed to be in a dead end. I turned round and inched back the way I had come, my arms wide out now so that I could touch the walls on each side. On the left I found another rope, no two, and then a third; on the right just one more.

I investigated further. The four furthest ropes were taut, almost hard to the touch. The two on my left dangled loose, wait, no, they were joined in a loop. Suddenly I thought of the bell tower at Cluny, where sometimes as a novice it had been my duty to join in feast day pealing. Could I be in some sort of bell tower? If I pulled on the ropes would I sound an alarm? I did not have to think long in that dark. Whatever happened, my position could not be worse. So which rope should I pull? As there was no give at all in the four furthest ropes, I turned my attention to the loop on my left. I pulled, bracing myself for a peal of bells to hammer my ears as it echoed around the small chamber. Instead I felt a lurch beneath my feet, as if the floor were moving. I pulled again. Again no noise, but now I was sure that the floor was rising beneath my feet. With growing excitement I pulled again, and again. I was standing on a strange mechanism that lifted the floor, and lifted me with it. This must have been the sensation that I remembered in my semi-consciousness after my dive from the ramparts. After all I had succeeded. I had found the secret passage that led from Hasan's paradise garden.

The craftsmen who had built this lifting device were perhaps the same who had made the door, for the skill in its manufacture was equal. As I pulled it murmured upwards with no more than a faint rumble. Then I stopped. Above my head I had surely heard the sound of voices. I strained my ears but could hear nothing. I pulled the rope again, more gently than before, holding my breath. I could definitely hear voices. As I rose, they became more distinct, until the platform would rise no further and it was as if the voices were in the same room as me. Feeling gently around, I found that the wall on one side was tapestry, or carpet. Through this hanging the voices came, and they were voices that I knew.

They spoke in Latin. One, harsh, strangely accented, belonged to the Master of Alamut. Hearing it once more turned my blood thin. How clearly I could imagine the scene in that great room, the pools of light cast by the lamps on the polished brass tables, the shelves of books reaching far up into the dark shadows beneath the ceiling. Hasan, my nemesis, would be standing there, his back to his arched window, his eyes lurking in the dark pools beneath his brow.

"So you would make an alliance with me? That is all you offer? And in return you want me to perform the ceremony that can grant you eternal life?" An incredulous mirthless laugh cracked round the room. I could picture the doubt, the fear now stealing into the Templars' expressions. In the seconds of silence that followed Hasan's laughter I heard the low sound of groaning somewhere in the room. Perhaps one of them had already been wounded. I took pleasure in that thought; I hoped it was Gregorias – no, Grinomalant. But then I heard both voices tumbling over each other.

"We are already a great force in the land."

"With our secrets we will become greater still, richer and more powerful than kings."

"What have you to lose?"

"We are alike, Assassin and Templar. We are warriors, feared by all."

"As allies we will be the ones to exercise real power in this land."

"No-one, Christian or Moslem, prince or priest, will be beyond our reach, outside our influence."

"We tell you we can lead you to the documents you want."

"We hid them carefully on our way here – the Gospel of Lazarus, and de Verdon's own story which is stranger still."

"In it you can read for yourself what really happened to your son."

"All we ask in return is one copy of Medea's magic recipe. You do not have to perform the rite for us."

Behind my tapestry I imagined the look flashing between the two knights. Of course you do not want him to perform it, I thought, you'd not trust him to treat you like Aeson, not Pelias. Rather take the recipe, and try it out on some innocent before risking yourselves.

"Enough!"

The harsh cry, like an eagle's swooping down towards two lambs, silenced the Templar bleating.

"I will think on it. There may be some sense in what you say. I have no need of another Gospel of Lazarus. De Verdon's tale for Medea's treatise, perhaps. But I could easily torture you for that, of course."

I pictured the two Templars blanching, shifting awkwardly before Hasan's fierce, mocking gaze, wondering if they had made a terrible misjudgement.

"But the alliance you propose. That is not without merit... . And if it were secured by mutual self-interest... . Let me think on it. We'll talk more in the morning. Take them away. Give them comfortable lodgings – but mind they are secured."

I heard the movement of guards, the sound of a door opening, and shutting again. I knew that Hasan was accustomed to be alone in his library, his guards stationed close at hand, ready to answer their Master's secret signal, but outside.

I stepped out from behind the tapestry.

✳

SAINT LAZARUS' COLLEGE

The Best-Selling Author woke in the middle of the night in a cold sweat. He felt for the bedside light. It was not in its normal place. For a moment he panicked. Where on earth was he? He fumbled further, found a switch and snapped it on. He looked round the room and breathed a sigh of relief as the bland decorations announced that he was in the Master's guest bedroom.

What an awful dream! He often had these nightmares when he was getting close to completing a book. He supposed that they must be caused by the strain of pulling all the loose threads of the plot together into a suitable conclusion. It was always the most difficult part, trying to make sense of the ending.

And the dream-broken nights made the job more difficult still, depriving him of sleep. Somehow fantasy and reality were becoming confused, all mixed up. He was no longer sure that he could tell the difference between fact and fiction.

He rolled back the blankets. Trust the Master to have stuck to this old-fashioned bedding. Personally, he would much rather have a duvet. He swung his feet to the floor and walked over to the chest of drawers where he had left a glass of whisky just in case. He downed it in one and noted with embarrassment that it had left a wet ring stain on the polished wood. He'd have some more explaining to do.

❋

Chapter Sixteen

SORROWS OF THE MOON

Ce soir, la lune rêve avec plus de paresse

✳

I stepped straight into my imagination. The room was just as I had pictured it. The pools of light gleaming on burnished copper tables, the books, the shadows were all there as I had remembered.

Hasan stood in his customary position, gazing through his window, turbaned and cloaked in white. I made no sound as I moved from behind the hanging carpet, but the Old Man of the Mountains felt my presence and span around. With satisfaction I saw momentary fear in his aquiline face, before he twisted his sneer back into place.

He made for the bell pull to alert the guards outside but I was there well before him, Samir's old dagger in my hand. Close up I could see I had nothing to fear from him physically. He really was an old man now, lined, frail. By force of will he held his frame erect, but his ascetic life and the passage of the years had reduced him to little more than a cadaver. He was gaunt, the yellowed skin of his face stretched tight over the sharp bones underneath, all straight lines and angles. My hatred began to ebb away and then I saw the flash of his eyes. Those yellow-rimmed irises had lost none of their venom.

A faint moan distracted me. In the darkness behind one of the copper tables lay a body. I ordered Hasan back against the window, a safe distance away from his bell, and hurried to kneel beside the prostrate figure. It was Samir. In the excitement I had forgotten him.

I gagged. He was naked and had been horribly mutilated. His arms were bloody stumps; both hands were missing. His genitals had been hacked off, and his chest was crossed by stripes that made his dark skin light by contrast. They oozed blood. Strips of skin had been flayed from his body. Only by the feeble moan that I had heard could I tell that he was alive.

"Your wife lives; your daughter is safe."

His eyelids flicked open and the pain beneath changed to recognition and calm.

"In the cistern. At the valley's mouth. That's where they left it."

I could not see his lips move, and his words were so soft, little more than a breath, that I was hardly sure I had heard them. Then a trembling sound came from the back of his throat, his eyes went glassy, and I knew he was at peace.

I sprang back to my feet. In the few moments that had passed Hasan had edged forward towards his bell pull. I blocked his way again and confronted him. Hate must now have burned bright in my eyes to provoke the uncertainty and concern I saw in his.

"He was a traitor. He turned. He showed his fellow infidels the way to our valley."

This poor justification incensed me more and my lips curled in an involuntary snarl as I moved towards him, Samir's old dagger held in front of me. Hasan backed away, and there was now no mistaking his terror.

"So for all your beliefs, you still fear death, old man? So you should, for you will burn forever."

229

"If you kill me, you will never escape from here."

I laughed. "Fool. You forget that I know your back door. I will just return the way I came, and nobody will be the wiser. It will be a mystery. Perhaps they will come to say that you have been struck down for your sins by some angel of god."

Hasan had now backed as far as he could go against his great window. I was close enough to strike. I drew back my arm, savouring the moment.

"She still lives, you know. Blanche still lives."

My hand stopped. My heart stopped. Everything stood still.

"No. It cannot be." I grabbed his beard and dragged his face to mine, pressing the point of my dagger to his throat. "How can that be?"

The malice and amusement that came to his expression maddened me. My arm began to shake as my emotions told me to thrust the blade up into his brain, and my reason fought to hold it back.

"How can that be?" he mimicked. "I told you she was dead, with her child. Part was true. The child died. She lived. As you know, we are not unskilled in medicine here. She was useful to me, if you remember."

My hand pricked the dagger into the skin under his beard and a red trickle ran through his scraggy hair down the blade. He winced and tried to hold back his head.

"We still hold her here."

"And me? Did you tell her that I was dead too? What did you tell her?"

"I just told her that you did not bother to come back. Call it part of my revenge on you if you like. It gave me satisfaction to keep her, saddened, withering. And I thought perhaps this day might come when I could show her to you, show you what you had done."

Now triumph joined the malice in his eyes. I could not bear to hold their gaze any longer, and feared what I might do if I did. I released his beard, seized the scruff of his neck, and pulled him round, setting the dagger lengthways under his chin. My mouth was so dry that I could scarcely get out my words, and when they came they croaked like some foreign voice.

"Take me to her. Take me to her, damn you. If you, or your men, play me any tricks, remember that you will die before I do."

As roughly as I could, I half pushed, half carried him forward towards the narrow passageway that led from the great library like the birth canal from a womb.

"Open the door. Are there guards outside? Always before there were two. Tell them to drop their weapons and call them in – otherwise – you know what will happen."

The door swung inwards. Hasan spoke the words I had ordered. However surprised the guards might have been, Assassin discipline allowed no questions. I butchered them both viciously, slashing open their throats, taking out on them my all-consuming hate for their master. The passage filled with blood more innocent than his. Hasan's white cloak was soaked red, and from the way he sagged against my grip I sensed that my wild ferocity had intimidated him further.

Carefully I peered round the door into the corridor. Save for the guards' white-shafted lances, leaning obediently against the wall, it was empty. I forced Hasan forward.

I remembered the eerie emptiness of this part of the castle of death, when I had been led as a prisoner through its dark passageways to Hasan's lair. Opposite one of the oil lamps that vainly fought with the shadows, we turned into an opening from which a narrow spiral stairway twisted upwards.

Now I was almost carrying Hasan, for his old legs could not manage the steep steps. By the time I had reached the door at the top I was myself breathing hard from the effort. Enough light had followed us up from the corridor below to show that it was bolted top and bottom.

"Open them," I croaked.

Hasan's thin hands were shaking. But the bolts slid back easily, as if they saw regular use.

"And now the door."

My voice now shook as much as the old man's hands. He turned the metal ring and the door swung inwards.

I pushed Hasan forward into the room. A little moonlight ghosted through a narrow window, enough to show a bed, and a figure stirring on it in surprise.

"Blanche? Blanche, is that you?"

"Hugh? Hugh, can it be?"

Before I knew it we were in each other's arms. Our embrace closed out the world, until the sound of the door slamming brought it back to me. Released, ignored, forgotten, Hasan had slipped away. I leapt towards the door, only to hear the sound of sliding bolts, followed by a laugh of wicked satisfaction, a crash, a fading scream, and silence.

"The old man must have missed his footing and fallen down the stairs. From the silence he is unconscious at least, maybe even dead. We will have a little time before the alarm is raised."

We were back in each other's arms, sobbing with laughter and tears.

"Just a little time after so long," she murmured in the voice that I remembered. But the Blanche beneath my hands was not the one I recalled. Her breasts, once pert, now sagged heavy beneath her gown. Her belly, once flat and firm, pressed loose against my side. Her back bore flaps of skin where none had been before. And when I covered her cheeks in kisses, I found them hollow as if there were no teeth behind them. She pulled away.

"Let me look at you." Our voices spoke in unison, and tentatively we turned our faces so that the moonlight could catch them.

She lifted her hand to my face, and I felt her fingers on my cheek, knobbled and twisted, an old woman's.

232

"How can it be," she asked in wonder, "time has not changed you at all?"

"I have changed inside," I murmured, struggling to hold back the sobs that threatened to erupt as I stroked her ruined, wrinkled face, "where I sense you have not changed at all.

"I did come back for you, you know. To find the book he wanted I fought in a great battle at Antioch. But the book was no longer there and I had to follow its trail to Cluny and back to Jerusalem again. We took Jerusalem after a brutal siege and I found the book. I found out too what Hasan's grail rite had done to me. His ancient magic stops my body from aging. I recover from mortal wounds like others do from scratches. I can go without food or drink. And later I found that I have the power to heal others."

She smiled at me softly as if I were a boy.

"And I came back for you. But Hasan told me you were dead, that you had betrayed me with other men and died bearing a child. My faith was too weak." I dropped my gaze. "I went mad for a while, mad from rage and grief. But later I found a way to escape from here, and many strange adventures have brought me back once again."

She sighed.

"He tortured me by saying that you had just decided not to come back. And sometimes, well, I confess that I did wonder. But with the other men – I just had no choice. The child – the child was not yours at least. It was better that way, I think. He was born dead. And I think I did nearly die. Afterwards I could no longer conceive, which was a blessing of sorts. Eventually, as I aged, they left me alone and I was grateful for that too. Instead, I had to tend the other poor girls he brought to fill his *da'is'* paradise.

"But enough of memories. You must escape while there is still time. Inside my mattress I have a rope – it took me years to make – from scraps of cloth torn from clothes and bedding – so that by the time it was ready it was too late, and I had no reason to escape. But now my work will not have been in vain."

Her gentle smile buried her eyes deep in wrinkles and brought me back to the present. I leapt to my feet.

"Yes, quickly, we must go before the alarm is raised. Come, stand, dress."

"Not we, my darling, you. I cannot climb down a rope. Look, my hands and limbs are far too weak."

From the way that she was struggling to rise to her feet from the bed, I saw that she was right.

"I will tie you to my back and carry you down."

"No. The rope will scarcely bear the weight of one, let alone two."

Again, as she pulled the string of plaited rags from her mattress, I saw that she was right.

"I will not go and leave you here again."

"Don't be so silly. If I came with you, what would you do with me, a sick old woman, old enough to be your mother? Besides, I know that I do not have long to live. Something hard is growing in my belly where our babies should have been. I can hardly keep down my food any longer."

I looked at her in horror, unable to stop the tears pouring down my cheeks.

"Do not cry. I will die happy, knowing that you did come back, knowing that you did still love me. And in time perhaps we will meet on the other side."

I thought of Sinai and was glad that I had not told her that part of my story.

"Come, quickly, pull the bed towards the window. Tie the rope around it. You will be able to squeeze through. Quickly."

Her voice became more urgent, because in the distance, through the door, we could hear shouts. They must have found Hasan.

"Come on, do what I say."

In a daze I bent and pulled the bed across the small room.

She thrust the rope at me and I looped it round the foot of the bed, knotted it and threw the other end through the window.

"Come with me," I faltered.

"No. Go. Just go," she said fiercely, and then smiled. She made an imperious gesture towards the window which reminded me of when she had been young. I stepped towards her and took her in my arms. My emotion made me careless of her frailty and I felt her wince. Surely the rope would bear our weight?

As if she could read my thoughts, she said, "No. It is too weak. I am too weak. With me you will not get away. I do not want to die knowing that they caught you because of me. I want to be able to imagine you safe. And I want you to remember me as I used to be."

She was now trying to push me away, but she was far to weak to break my grip. My tears started again. She stopped wriggling.

"Sssh. Don't be silly. You know I am right. Kiss me and go."

I next remember my legs hanging through the window, trying to find some purchase on the rag rope while I pushed the rest of my body through. Then I was out, gripping with my hands and using my feet to fend my body off the wall. I looked up at her as she leant through the window, the lines fading from her face, and her hair shining in the moon so that it might not have been grey, but blonde, as it had been before. Then I found a firm rock slope beneath my feet. Moments later, a pale hand waved from the window, and the rope fell snaking down towards me. Had she untied it, I wondered, or like one of the Fates had she cut it through? And was it her thread that had been severed, or mine? Almost unconsciously I gathered up the rope. Later I thought I had kept it perhaps as a last memento of Blanche, or perhaps just to leave no indication of how I had made my escape.

Up there, I thought I heard a commotion and angry shouts.

A faint scream rang out and stopped abruptly. Helpless, I turned and ran as fast as I could towards the mouth of the valley. If only for Blanche's sake, I was determined to make good my escape.

As I ran, I thought. For the moment, the advantage was mine. Hasan's accident would cause confusion. If he were dead, nobody would know that I had been in the castle. His followers would be most likely to suspect the Templars. If Hasan lived, but was unconscious, or dazed, I might still have a good head start. I could imagine the confused looks of the *da'is* as he spoke of an intruder who had appeared in his room. How many of them knew of the secret entrance from the paradise garden? It was perhaps only shared with a small number of senior lieutenants. In the worst case, it would take time to summon them, explain what had happened, ready some horses and prepare the pursuit.

My second advantage was geographical. Blanche's window gave out on the side of the castle away from the paradise garden. I had been dropped down to a level well below the gate and the twisting track that led from it. Even if they set out after me sooner than I expected, they would have to descend the path, which was too steep and too windy to take at anything faster than a walk. I should be able to reach the cistern where the Templars had hidden my documents, retrieve them, and conceal myself in the wilderness. Then…well, I would have time to decide what to do next.

I reached the cistern before first light. In fact, it had become darker than ever, in the hour when the moon sulked before being driven from the sky by her brighter brother. The cistern had been constructed to trap rainwater and melt water from the slopes above so that it could be used to irrigate the valley during the fierce summer months. Now, in the autumn, it was exhausted, dry and empty. I thanked the instinct that had made me bring Blanche's rope with me, for the great rock-hewn tank was far too deep for me to climb out of without assistance.

What a fool I would have looked if I had clambered down to fetch my precious possessions, only to be trapped there like a netted fish. I found a boulder nearby, secured the rope around it, and cautiously lowered myself into the opening. Inside it was too dark to see. I scrabbled around in the dark, my hands extended in front of me, and breathed a deep sigh of relief when I touched my wooden quiver rolled into one corner. In the blackness I could not hope to make out whether its contents were all safe, so I slung it around my neck and struggled back up the rope, half expecting to be greeted by the leering faces of the Templars, but knowing there was no way by which they could have reached their hiding place so fast.

I climbed high into the hills, going where nobody could follow on horseback, careful wherever possible to step from stone to stone to make sure that I left no footsteps to mark my way. With daybreak I rested, opened my quiver and carefully pulled out the documents. My own story was there, safe, but I found that the Templars had taken with them the copy of the Gospel of Lazarus. I cursed, not for my own loss, as I had transcribed it word for word into my own text, but because I knew the value that it would have to them. Still, there was nothing to be done. I could scarcely fight two mounted Templar knights with poor Samir's dagger, and they might well be reinforced by their new Assassin allies. And although I longed to see their expressions when they came to their hiding place and found their treasure missing, I knew that to creep back and watch them would put everything in jeopardy. Instead I climbed deeper into the mountain wilderness and hid.

❉

SAINT LAZARUS' COLLEGE

"So did Hasan-i Sabbah survive his fall?"

The History Don took a deep pleasurable breath before answering the Computer Sciences Tutor's question.

"Without a shadow of doubt. His death is clearly documented in Ismaili writings that were preserved away from Alamut. It definitely took place in 1124, five years after Hugh's third visit to Alamut. In fact – you are not going to like this, Justin – Hugh may have unwittingly helped his hated enemy. One of the interesting things about Hasan-i Sabbah, setting him apart from so many sectarian leaders of his ilk, was how well he prepared for his succession, even though he was childless. Well before he died he chose Buzurgumid, one of his long-standing lieutenants, who for twenty years had been commandant of another Assassin stronghold, Lammasar. My guess is that Hasan's fall did him enough physical damage to remind him of his mortality and prompted him to put the succession plans in place to make the Assassins a lasting force. I doubt that was what Hugh intended!"

The Best-Selling Author was feeling too exhausted from another restless, dream-filled night, to protest. Why did the real facts matter anyway? It was all just a story.

✳

CHAPTER SEVENTEEN

THE INVITATION TO THE VOYAGE

Mon enfant, ma soeur,
Songe à la douceur
D'aller là-bas vivre ensemble

✻

I travelled for two days, stopping only when the night became too dark to see. Sometimes I was able to walk on tracks made by the animals that live in those mountains, but often I had to scramble, or climb. Then I found for myself a shelter of sorts under an overhanging rock. It was not a proper cave but it was better than nothing. I had no way of lighting a fire, even if I had dared to risk giving myself away with its smoke, and it was bitterly cold. Knowing that even the most wintry weather could do me no lasting harm, I just settled there and steeled myself against the discomfort.

Strangely, I began to feel at peace. Before, Blanche had lived, but she had been dead to me; now, when she was as good as dead, she lived for me once more. Before, my memories had been putrefied by her imagined betrayal; now they were restored by the certainty that inside she had been utterly faithful. I was cleansed by a sense of relief too, for now any doubts that might have troubled her about my own behaviour had been wiped away. She had died, or would soon die, knowing for sure that I had after all returned as I promised, not just telling herself that I must have tried to be true.

At first I questioned whether I had been right to obey her instructions to leave her. But she had always been far wiser than I. When my reason had conquered my emotion, I knew that she had been right to make me go, right to refuse any effort to escape. If I could have devised a way to rescue her, all that I would have achieved was to take her from a physical prison into a spiritual one. As it was, we had given each other the most valuable gift of all – the real freedom and sense of self worth given by the absolute certainty of another being's unconditional love.

The snows came, and then I knew that I was safe. The thick white blanket that would wrap nature until spring would protect me too. Now no-one could follow me.

I set off towards the west. My desire to distance myself from my enemies was matched by some instinctive wish to return to my place of birth, to soft green fields and trees, and gentle streams and rivers. I took my time, for I had no reason to hurry, avoiding mountain passes, hugging the peaks, like some creature of the snow. I left my anger and my hatred behind and took with me my love. For the first time I truly understood the lessons I had been taught at Sinai. Hate, I knew, was just a drunkard in the depths of a tavern.

The snows began to melt before I had left the highlands. Nature's rebirth filled me with exhilaration. I paused in the foothills, just dawdling through days listening to birds singing as they prepared their nests, watching the trees push forth their leaves, and the earth thrust out new growth.

I no longer know how much time that journey took me, nor even the way I followed. I do know that at some point I came to Constantinople, for near its eastern shore I sold my mail coat. A plump Byzantine merchant gave me in return a long tunic, some suspicious looks and a few small coins. Once

I would have taken offence at the merchant's supercilious manner, perhaps habitual, perhaps prompted by my ragged appearance. Now I watched with amusement the struggle between greed and distrust, knowing that in spite of his suspicion his human nature would be unable to resist the unfair profit in the bargain he struck. I would have happily given the armour away; I was glad to shed the last vestige of my knighthood. But my rags needed replacing and I wanted money to pay for my transport across the strait. Once more I found myself regretting that I could not swim, and thinking that perhaps I would be able to learn when I reached home.

So I found myself being drawn steadily back towards the place I had come from – the borderland where the Holy Roman Empire rubs uneasily against the territories of the King of France. I had left there well over thirty years before. In spite – or perhaps because – of having no family left there it seemed to draw me back.

It was autumn again when I reached the place I had been born. I am sure I did find the house, or what remained of it. At first I was confused, because it all seemed smaller than I had remembered. But I was able to distinguish the pattern I remembered in the broken walls. The hall was there, and the chamber leading off it that been my mother's. The outline of the buildings that we had used as stables clustered around where the yard had been.

Judging by the hold taken on the ruins by the undergrowth, the fire that had destroyed the place had taken place years before. Many of the stones had been removed, doubtless to be reused in other building projects. But under the old man's beard, now covered in its white seed heads, and beneath the thickets of stinging nettle, some of the remaining stones were scorched and blackened. Here and there lay a few splintered beams, their ends still charred, despite the many seasons of rain that had washed them.

There was no way to know whether the fire that had

destroyed this place had happened by accident, or had been set deliberately. Perhaps a band of brigands like the one that had slaughtered my father and brothers had set on the next family to which the Duke of Lorraine had granted this demesne. Perhaps the grantor had been my old patron Godfrey. Perhaps, even, the new tenant had left for the Crusade with us, and the damage had been done while he was away. It did not matter.

I camped in the poor shelter of one corner that still stood higher than the rest, and moved on the next day. I had no regrets. If the house had still been there I could not have returned to it. I could not feel that it was mine in any sense, and I wondered why I had been drawn to it at all. Perhaps I just needed to prove to myself that I had no connections left to the person that I had once been.

I wanted to find a wild place where I could live like a hermit, but close enough to a monastery where I could obtain the materials I needed to finish my story. Why shouldn't the model that had worked for my friend in Sinai work for me? After a while, like him, I would have to move on, before rumours of my existence became strange enough to disrupt my peace. But I would be able to stay for a number of years and had no need to worry now about what might happen later.

As I walked a little further west into thicker wood and steeper hills I found the perfect place. In this remote spot, at the base of a deep west-facing valley, I stumbled on a new monastery, peopled by a new type of monk. They wore white habits, not brown or black. I knew from the relief I felt when I saw them from afar how much I had wanted not to go back near Cluny, or any other Benedictine foundation. From the vigour with which these white monks went about their work I judged that they were mostly young.

Without showing myself, I wandered the woods until I found a small cave which I could make my shelter. It did not enjoy the spectacular views that we had had in Sinai, but it was set well up a slope which was so steep that it was nearly a cliff. At its base a stream ran merrily, and the beech trees which made up most of the forest had a grandeur about them even without their leaves. I would enjoy waiting for them to burst into leaf, and could already imagine the vibrant green.

I bent double under the low roof and swept the floor of my new home with an improvised besom. I noted with satisfaction that the ground was dry. I made journey after journey up the steep slope with armfuls of the rich brown beech leaves which carpeted the forest and spread them on the floor. When I had made my nest I laid in it my few belongings – little other than the quiver that held my documents – and covered them with another layer of leaves. Then, with a certain trepidation, I set off towards the monastery.

My ragged appearance was not in my favour, but the first white monks I approached showed no surprise, only solemn courtesy. I asked in the Latin tongue if I could be directed towards their prior. One of the young novices politely replied that they had no prior yet, but that he could take me to Father Bernard, their abbot. He laid down his mattock to lead me to him.

I looked around with interest. This was a very different place to Cluny. The base of the valley had been cleared between two steep wooded slopes. The stream that ran down the valley had been cleverly channelled to form a moat around the site. Further on two large fishponds had been dug, fed by the same stream. Some of the felled trees had been used to construct a stockade, and to erect other simple wooden framed dwellings covered in wattle and daub. Piles of spare timber still remained, neatly stacked to dry under low shelters. In the middle gleamed a new stone church, plain but of harmonious proportions. Monks and masons laboured to raise other stone buildings. Work was underway on a cloister, and in places the wooden stockade was being renewed in rock. Neat enclosures held

243

chickens and perhaps other livestock, but I could hear only the contented clucking of hens. Orderly strips of cultivated ground still held some winter crops. I recognised kale and turnips.

A Cluniac would have laughed, or sneered, at such simplicity, and more so at the rustic earth-floored chapter house in which we found the Abbot, deep in discussion with some masons. We waited respectfully until he had finished. I observed a man of perhaps thirty years, tall and very thin, as if he ate just enough to keep himself alive and no more. His tonsure was so wide that the remaining wisps of sandy hair around his head looked like a halo. When he was finished giving instructions to his builders, he turned towards me. His eyes burned deep in dark-smudged sockets. Once I would have quailed before his ascetic gaze.

"Father," I said with steady disingenuousness, "I have just returned from a pilgrimage to the Holy Land. It has inspired me to a life of solitary contemplation and prayer. I have found a place, a cave, to make my home, a few miles upstream from here. Is there work I can do to earn some provisions? I also want to study, to copy some sacred texts, and would welcome a few sheets of parchment and material for ink."

"Work we have a-plenty. We Cistercians believe that hard work, the toil of our own hands, is the best way to praise the Lord our God." He crossed himself fervently and his sharp Adam's apple vibrated in his thin neck. "This is our seventh year here in Clairvaux, and we have much still to do to make it a place worthy of the glory of God."

"The Vale of Light," I smiled. Now I remembered Hugh de Payns telling me about this man.

"The Vale of Light indeed," he returned solemnly, "which was named before the Valley of Wormwood. We would accept you as a lay brother or," he sharpened his gaze, "were you once in Holy Orders? It seems to me your Latin has a monastic ring to it."

"I learnt my Latin from Benedictines. And no, thank you, I have resolved to live in isolation for a while. Perhaps later, if your generous offer remains open and you still have a need... ."

He inclined his head in apparent approval.

"Far be it from me to interfere with another's calling. But I will be happy to give you work. Do you have any special skills?"

I smiled again, pleased to know that I would achieve what I wanted. My satisfaction lowered my guard too far.

"I can turn my hand to most things. I have built, I have farmed, I can copy, and I have some skill in healing."

Abbot Bernard looked at me sharply again. "Healing? Is that so?"

I kicked myself and tried to repair the damage.

"Some modest knowledge of medicinal herbs picked up on my travels, that is all."

"There is a young boy, very sick, in the infirmary. His father is a distant cousin of mine and carried him here all the way from Troyes, at least forty leagues. We rewarded such faith by taking in the boy but he has just weakened and I fear he will die. He suffers from some ailment none of us have seen before. He coughs blood, and has a scarlet rash over his body, and a high fever. Perhaps you have seen this illness on your travels. Come, see what you can do."

I had no alternative but to follow the good abbot to the low wooden-built infirmary. The door opened to show one long room and a row of simple beds, all empty save one. The wooden shutters on three wooden windows were folded back, letting in light and the crisp autumn air. The boy, perhaps six or seven years old, tossed and turned. He had thrown off his plain wool blanket and poured with sweat. His father knelt in prayer beside the bed. Tentatively I reached out my hand to the boy's forehead and found him burning.

I rested my hand there for a moment or two and he sighed

and lay still. I took my hand away again and looked across with regret at the boy's father. I straightened up and addressed the Abbot.

"None of the remedies that I know could reduce such a fever."

The boy had started to toss and turn again, moaning softly, his hands plucking restlessly at the blanket.

"Your touch gave him some comfort. Lay your hand on his head again."

I could not disobey although I feared the consequences. In disquiet, I put my hand back on the poor child's forehead. Again, the boy sighed and lay still. Without moving my hand, I shifted down onto my knees beside the bed, closed my eyes and felt the power draining out of me into my patient. I was no longer conscious of the Abbot, or of my surroundings.

I emerged from my trance into a state of utter exhaustion. I was almost too tired to take in the Abbot's astonished expression.

"I must rest. I will lie here." I stretched out on the neighbouring bed and was instantly asleep.

When I woke I found that someone had covered me with a blanket, and closed the wooden shutters. The bed beside me was empty. A white-habited monk rose from a stool in the corner when I sat up and swung my feet to the floor.

"Are you all right, Brother?" he asked anxiously. "The Abbot told me to bring you to him as soon as you woke. Please follow me."

We found the Abbot directing the work on the cloister. This time he dropped what he was doing as soon as we appeared. He indicated that I should follow him and that my guide should stay behind.

The Abbot's chamber contained a desk and a few stools. The only other furniture was a prie-dieu, set with a volume of the Holy Scriptures. If the Abbot slept here, he slept on the floor. He pointed me to a stool, and took one himself, and then contemplated me in silence across his desk. I looked back at him, refusing to be intimidated, holding his unblinking gaze without wavering. Satisfied that he could detect no shame or fear in my expression, he spoke.

"Some modest knowledge of medicinal herbs? None of the remedies that I know could reduce such a fever? Tell me how you worked such a miracle. Some might call it black magic or witchcraft but miracle is what it seemed to me."

I sighed.

"In Outremer I stayed with a holy hermit in the desert. He possessed this power of healing, and I found that I shared it too. I lay my hands on the sick and I feel a force flowing from me. It cures ailments, wounds even, but leaves me drained and days pass before I can do it again."

"Why do you travel in rags like a beggar? Why not offer your power to noblemen and kings? They would reward you well, even vie with each other for your services. With you in their train an army could ride fearless into battle."

I shook my head.

"No, with me in their train an army would be divided. Wounded friends, and their followers, would be at each others' throats like dogs fighting over a bone. I cannot heal them all, only one at a time. So one might live, and the others would die in jealousy and bitterness. It is not for me to decide who should live and who should die. I have no interest in wealth or possessions. If I entered the service of some prince I might myself become the cause of war and death, as others tried to wrest control of me. My gift comes from God. He guides my travels and takes me where He wants me to go. He brought me here. So please let me shelter in your Valley of Light. Please do not let the presence of a healer here become known. From time to time, when you judge it right, perhaps I can be of service to you and heal an innocent whose proper time has not come."

The Abbot contemplated me in silence for a while, our eyes

once again locked together. Then abruptly he stood, and then threw himself onto his knees on his prie-dieu, clasping his hands together and raising his face ecstatically towards where he believed Heaven to be. His lips moved in murmured prayer. Eventually he rose from his knees and sat again at his desk.

"You must be right that the Lord our God guided you here to our holy vale. You may stay, and I will see that tales of your miracles do not spread. And yes, from time to time I will call upon you."

And so I returned to my cave with the supply of parchment and ink that I had sought. They also gave me a handful of goose quills and a plank of wood to serve me as a desk. A day or two later I saw the boy, and his father, walking up the valley towards my shelter.

"You left before we could thank you," the man said. The boy stood clutching his father's hand, shyly half-hiding from me. He was a handsome little fellow, his brown hair cut in a fringe across his brow, long at the back and curling slightly. His dark eyes contemplated me solemnly, and then smiled when he had decided that there was nothing to fear from me. He dropped his father's hand and stepped forward.

"Here." He held out a loaf of the monks' bread, and a bowl of honey gathered from the forest. "Thank you for saving my life."

"And we brought you a blanket," said the father. "I know that you holy men scorn any comforts, but winter is coming… ."

I smiled. "Thank you. I will welcome the blanket."

After that, the boy would visit me from time to time, always bringing some small present. I learned that his name was Chrétien. He was interested in what I was writing, and as we got to know each other better, I found myself telling him some parts of my own story.

I had hidden at Clairvaux for three or four years, I suppose, when Chrétien came to me in great excitement. I had become very fond of him and found myself looking forward to his visits more than anything else in my simple life. He was about the age I had been when my father and brothers had been killed, and when my mother had placed me at Cluny. He was the sort of boy that I hoped I had been.

"There is going to be a great council in Troyes, Brother Hugh. People are coming from everywhere. There will be knights, bishops, and a great fair. Come with us. Remind yourself what the rest of the world is like. Come on. It will be fun."

I smiled and refused, of course. But he came again the week after, and asked me again, and again the time after that.

"The town is filling with people. The Abbot has gone already. Do come and see."

I wanted to please him. I also thought that it would do no harm to remind myself what the world was like outside my little valley.

"Very well then. I'll come." His face lit up with eager pleasure and I thought that I had made the right decision.

Chrétien now had a horse of his own, and I climbed up behind him. I found myself sharing his rising excitement as we approached the town. We passed other travellers, like us converging on Troyes for this great event.

The council, Chrétien told me with the proud knowledge of a native of the town, was taking place in the bishop's palace beside the cathedral. The narrow streets leading to the square in front of the west door became fuller. I said to Chrétien that we should dismount, but he was proud of his horse and wanted to show it off. So he pressed right into the square, which was choked with people. I began to feel uncomfortable in the crowd. Then a hush fell.

"Look, the Templars!" said Chrétien, quietly to me.

"Templars?" I echoed in horror.

"Yes, the knights. Part of the council's business is to give approval to their order."

In front, over the crowd, I could see the familiar figures

riding proudly in their white red-crossed cloaks. They wore no helmets and I recognised the knight in front by the unmistakable egg point of his head. It was Hugh de Payns.

Before I could slip off the horse and hide, some wag, perhaps irritated that Chrétien had ridden into the crowd, shouted at the top of his voice, "Look, two to a horse, they think they are Templars too! Get down from there!"

This caught de Payns' attention. Maybe he thought that the rude shout was directed at him. He checked his steed for a moment and looked towards us. Then, to my horror, he pointed at me and lent towards the knight at his side. A second familiar face, of Godfrey de Saint Omer, turned to me.

Too late, I slipped from the horse, muttering an apology to Chrétien. "I'm sorry, I can't stand the crowd."

I pushed my way back through and hurried on foot in the direction I had come. I walked the rest of the day and through the night back to my cave, retrieved my belongings, and moved on, thinking to go north, perhaps to cross the sea.

I knew that, wherever I went, they would come looking for me. I knew that I would just have to keep moving on.

✳

SAINT LAZARUS' COLLEGE

The Best-Selling Author tossed and turned. His sheets were soaked with sweat. The heat was overwhelming. He must have forgotten to open the window, and the central heating must still be on.

No, the window was open, for sure. Because a hand was reaching through and pulling the curtain back. Now a leg was hooked over the sill. Now two grey figures stood in his room. He could not see them clearly. It was too dark. He tried to move but couldn't. Something, some great weight held him down. What did they have in their hands?

Oh God, no. One held a scourge, the other a sword. Both glowed luminously. They were moving towards the bed. If only he could wake up.

Now there was a third figure. Now there could be no escape. This one had a sword too. Wait, it was turning on the others. Shadows chasing shadows. The first two were turning, running down a long dark tunnel which seemed to open up before them.

But now the third one was coming back, floating towards the bed again. He was leaning forward. His face was indistinct, unclear. What was he saying?

The Best-Selling Author heard his own scream, over and over again. The light in his room came on and the Master rushed in.

"Justin, for Heaven's sake, what is it? You are wailing like a banshee. You must have had a nightmare. Calm down now. Calm down, for Heaven's sake."

The window was banging to and fro. In his old-fashioned striped nightshirt the Master went over to shut it.

"Terrible thunderstorm. I was awake or I probably would not have heard you. I thought you were being murdered."

The Best-Selling Author shuddered. "I thought I was too.

251

I think I would have been, if, if he hadn't come to my rescue. It's funny, I got a good look at his face but it was really hard to describe, almost as if it changed as soon as you had seen it. For a moment I thought he looked young, and then a moment later he was old. I could not even tell you the colour of his hair. His face shimmered and moved – as if it was there but not there if you see what I mean, almost translucent. He said something too. I couldn't quite make it out, but it sounded something like 'My friend Godfrey. You remind me of Godfrey.'

"God, I need a drink. May I help myself to some of your whisky downstairs?"

✳

BIBLIOGRAPHY

Ashbridge, Thomas, *The First Crusade, A New History*, London 2003

Augustine, *Confessions*, Translated by Albert Cook Outler, 2002

Augustine, *Concerning the City of God against the Pagans*, Translated by Henry Bettenson, 1972

Barber, Richard, *The Holy Grail, The History of a Legend*, London 2004

Barnes, Jonathan, *Aristotle, A Very Short Introduction*, Oxford 2000

Baudelaire, Charles, *Les Fleurs du Mal*, 1857

Billings, Malcom, *The Cross and the Crescent, A History of the Crusades*, 1987

Boas, Adrian, *Jerusalem in the Time of the Crusades*, 2001

De Boron, Robert, *Merlin and the Grail*, Translated by Nigel Bryant, Cambridge 2001

Camus, Albert, *La Peste*, 1947

Caner, Ergun Mehmet and Emir Fethi, *Christian Jihad*, 2004

253

Chadwick, Henry, *Augustine, a Very Short Introduction,* 1986

Cobb, Paul, *Usama ibn Munqidh, Warrior Poet of the Age of the Crusades,* 2005

Comnena, Anna, *The Alexiad,* Translated by E.R.A. Sewter, London 1969

Constable, Giles, *Cluny from the Tenth to the Twelth Centuries,* Princeton 1999

Daftary, Farhad, *The Assassin Legends, Myths of the Mohammedis,* 1995

Eliot, TS, *The Waste Land,* 1922

Frazer, Sir James, *The Golden Bough,* London 1922

Gabrieli, Francesco, *Arab Historians of the Crusades,* Rome 1957

Haleem, M A S Abdel, *A New Translation of the Qur'an,* Oxford 2005

Harris, Jonathan, *Byzantium and the Crusades,* 2003

Hill, Rosalind (Ed), *Gesta Francorum, The Deeds of the Franks and the other Pilgrims to Jerusalem,* 1962

Hope, Anthony, *Rupert of Hentzau,* 1898

Hoyt, Robert, *Life and Thought in the Middle Ages,* Minneapolis 1967

Hughes, Ted, *Tales from Ovid,* 1997

Hunt, Noreen, *Cluny under Saint Hugh 1049-1109*, Indiana 1966

Konstam, Angus, *Historical Atlas of the Crusades*, 2004

Krey, August C, *The First Crusade: The Accounts of Eyewitnesses and Participants*, Princeton 1921

Lacey, Robert, and Danziger, Danny, *The Year 1000*, London 1999

Lewis, Bernard, *The Assassins, a Radical Sect in Islam*, Princeton 1967

Ibn-Munqidh, Usamah, *An Arab-Syrian Gentleman and Warrior in the Period of the Crusades*, Translated by Philip Hitti, 2000

De Nerval, Gerard, *Les Chimeres*, 1854

Nicolle, David, *Crusader Warfare Volume 1, Byzantium, Europe and the Struggle for the Holy Land 1050-1300 AD*, 2007

Ovid, *Metamorphoses*, Translated by A. D. Melville, Oxford 1986

Peters, Edward, (Ed.) *The First Crusade, The Chronicle of Fulcher of Chartres and Other Source Materials*, 1971

Python, Monty, *Monty Python and the Holy Grail*

Ralph of Caen, *Gesta Tancredi, A History of the Normans on the First Crusade*, Translated by Bernard S Bachrach and David S. Bachrach, 2005

Ralls, Karen, *The Templars and the Grail - The Knights of the Quest*, 2003

Rider Haggard, Henry, *King Solomon's Mines*

Riley-Smith, Jonathan, *The First Crusade and the Idea of Crusading*, 1993

Robert the Monk, *Historia Hierosolimitana*, Translated by Carol Sweetenham, 2005

Runciman, Steven, *A History of the Crusades*, Cambridge 1951

Scott, Sir Walter, *Ivanhoe*, 1814

Stark, Freya, *The Valleys of the Assassins*, London 1934

de Troyes, Chrétien, *Le Roman de Perceval ou Le Conte du Graal*, c 1180

de Troyes, Chrétien, *Perceval, The Story of the Grail*, Translated by Burton Raffel, Yale 1999

Tyerman, Christopher, *God's War, A New History of the Crusades*, London 2006

Virgil, *The Aeneid*, Translated by C Day Lewis, Oxford 1952

Weston, Jessie, *From Ritual to Romance*, Paris 1919